THE BILLIONAIRE'S CONSPIRACY

MJ JAVANI

Published by:

UNIT 81 PUBLISHING

United States of America

E-book ISBN: 978-1-7330093-4-8
Print book ISBN: 978-1-7330093-5-5
Learn more about the author at www.mjjavani.com

"In the tradition of Robert Ludlum and Vince Flynn, Javani has created a compelling hero in Soltani. The various plotline intertwine in a frequently compelling read..."

—*Kirkus Reviews*

"The Billionaire's Conspiracy is a thrilling read with a captivating plot. I would recommend this book to those who enjoy a thrilling conspiracy theory. Filled with espionage and assassination plans, the suspense will keep readers on edge as they follow this part of the story to the exhilarating conclusion"

— *Literary Titan*

To the towering giants of the Enlightenment, may the flame you lit in service to truth and reason continue to burn through the coming Dark Age

CONTENTS

1. FT. BELVOIR, VIRGINIA

We'll finally have enough weapons to bring down the entire government, Destruction thought while waiting for the steel doors to open. The rain fell in buckets onto his head and bony face as he stood motionless. Water rolled down his cheeks like endless tears pouring out of his eyes. Each dangling drop was a reminder this shit was taking too long. They should have been out of here by now. He had to say something.

"Hey, arse-wipe, you think you can hurry it up?" Destruction yelled.

"You want to do this, be my guest," Lutz replied.

"No, I don't want to do it. That's why I recruited ya. Just tell me if you want us to get caught?"

Lutz ignored the comment.

"Not sure what's going on. I think they changed the combination," Lutz said after unsuccessfully punching in a set of numbers.

"That was obvious five minutes ago. What ya gonna do about it?" Destruction said.

"Plan B. Did you bring it?" Lutz said.

"Hazard, you got the drills?" Destruction growled.

"Ready when you are," Hazard replied.

Destruction stepped out of the way as the third man in the group inched forward. He pointed the drill toward the vault, waiting for Lutz to move.

"Wait, how much noise is that thing going to make?" Lutz said.

"Unless you have a better idea, I suggest you step out of my way. Don't worry, the storm will drown out the sound of the drill," Hazard said.

Lutz hesitated before making room. Seconds later, the sound of the drill echoed through the air. Destruction counted off as Lutz tapped his boot on the wet asphalt.

"Hey, is everything all right here?" an unfamiliar voice growled from behind. They were not expecting visitors.

"Fine, Specialist Evans. Just going over safety procedures with these inspectors from Fort Dix," Lutz replied.

Lutz, Destruction, and Hazard all wore military fatigues.

"No one informed me about this, Sergeant. I'll have to call it in," Evans said.

"That won't be necessary, Specialist. Everything is under control," Lutz declared.

"Sir, why is this man holding a drill?" Evans said as he walked closer to the trio.

It was the last straw. When Kurt Lutz had first walked into their meeting over a year ago, Destruction was skeptical. Lutz's short blond hair and muscular build was a dead giveaway for his military affiliation. Destruction was inclined to ask Lutz to leave, but then thought better of it.

The organization needed access to weapons, and Lutz was their ticket. He had a top secret clearance and an exemplary service record, having been awarded a Purple Heart for wounds sustained during combat in Iraq. More importantly, Lutz was sympathetic to the cause and willing to help. Destruction reluctantly approved his membership.

The only problem was that Lutz was careless. Despite his military training, he had a penchant for overlooking details. For instance, he should have known the vault in question would have had its combination changed periodically. He should have also expected the visitor who was now threatening their mission. All that was water under the bridge. The situation called for swift and decisive action.

"Specialist Evans, get back in your vehicle immediately.

That's an order," Lutz barked.

"But, sir," Evans said.

"Son, do ya know who I am?" Destruction blurted out.

"No, sir," Evans said.

"Perhaps ya ought to come closer," Destruction said.

"What are you doing? Let me handle this," Lutz said.

"Shut up. You blew your chance," Destruction replied.

"What's going on here?" Evans said as he looked from one man to the other. Seconds later, Destruction and Evans stared into each other's eyes.

"Recognize me now?" Destruction said.

"Can't say that I do, sir," Evans replied.

"I'm the angel of death. Your time is up, fuck-face!"

Destruction raised his right arm, pointing the M9 Beretta 9mm straight at Evans's head. The specialist had no opportunity to react. *Pow.* Destruction pulled the trigger only once, shooting the Army specialist right in the face. Specialist Evans fell straight back into a pool of water. The blood running down his face was washed away by the rain. The heavy storm muffled the sound of the shot, and there was no one else nearby.

"Why'd you do that? How am I going to explain this?" Lutz cried out.

"He was going to report us," Destruction said.

"No, he wasn't. He would have left if you'd given me a chance to threaten him with insubordination," Lutz said.

"You blew your chance. Now, help me pick him up," Destruction growled as he grabbed the limp Army specialist by the arms.

Lutz and Hazard grabbed the dead man's legs.

"In my truck. We'll dump him in the back. I'll dispose of the body later," Destruction said.

The three men ambled clumsily toward one of two pickup trucks. A pair of headlights appeared on the road ahead of them. They each froze simultaneously as if their movements had been choreographed. Destruction's heart pounded against his chest. The headlights continued down the road without stopping. The torrential downpour had proven to be a blessing once again.

"Toss him right there," Destruction ordered.

"What about the blood? It'll make a big mess in the car," Lutz replied.

"Ya let me worry about that, shit-brain. You and Hazard get back to the lock," Destruction said before straightening out Evans's body. Minutes later, he stood in front of the vault as Lutz and Hazard broke through.

"Jackpot. What'd I tell you?" Lutz said with pride.

"We're ten minutes behind schedule with a dead body on top of it. Don't pat yourself on the back just yet, arse-wipe," Destruction said while stepping inside the vault.

An assortment of weapons had been neatly stacked inside by the Virginia National Guard. Several racks contained M-4 carbines and M-16 rifles. A second compartment was filled with grenades, M-60 belt fed machine guns, along with accompanying 7.62 mm NATO rounds. There were even several boxes of the MK 153 shoulder-launched multipurpose assault weapon (SMAW), and cases of Mk 3 high explosive dual purpose (HEDP) rockets for use against a variety of targets to include bunkers, concrete walls, and light armor.

"This is fucking amazing!" Destruction howled, grinning from ear to ear.

"Told you. These shipments arrived yesterday from Ft. Dix. They were ordered in preparation for possible unrest in DC and attempts to attack the White House," Lutz said rapidly.

"Ironic. We'll put these to good use," Destruction said.

"I knew you'd like them," Lutz replied.

"How long before someone notices them missing?" Destruction said.

"If we could've avoided drilling through the lock, at least till noon tomorrow. Given the size of the hole, I'd say by daybreak."

"That's good enough. Let's start loading these crates. Any chance we'll be stopped on the way out of here?" Destruction said.

"No, they haven't installed an alarm system, yet. That's why I pushed to do the job right away. The storm is an added bonus," Lutz observed.

"All right, let's move," Destruction said.

He sounded like an officer. The very thought of being one of them sent a cold chill down his spine. Destruction and Hazard carried the crates to the trucks as Lutz monitored the radio chatter.

"No one's asked about Evans yet, but that may change," Lutz said.

Lutz grabbed a crate to help load the trucks. There was a mountain of weapons and ammunition to move. Every minute Evans was out of contact meant someone might start looking for him. A crucial factor in their favor was the ability to work under cover of darkness. When they were finally finished loading, Destruction closed the bed of the trucks.

"I'll drive a Humvee and you guys can follow me out the Walker Gate. It's a back way off base. It'll take us out to Mt. Vernon Highway and onto Route 1," Lutz said.

"I thought the other gates were closed after hours?" Hazard said.

"They are, but I'm with the military police, I've got access to all the gates."

"That's good. Why don't ya do a final check of the vault to see if we missed anything," Destruction said.

"I already did. We got everything," Lutz replied.

"Check it again, just to be sure," Destruction said.

"Okay, but we're only wasting time," Lutz said reluctantly.

Destruction was several feet behind him. Lutz opened the door and walked straight in. Destruction waited outside for his return. Moments later, the door swung open again.

"Like I told you, the vault is emp——" *Pow, pow, pow.* Three shots rang out in succession. Lutz dropped backward instantly. As he stood over him, Destruction observed through the green glow of his goggles that Lutz's eyes were wide open with surprise. The idiot Lutz should have seen this coming.

"What the fuck did you do? Now, we'll get caught for sure!" Hazard yelled out.

"He was careless, and he was a liability. We got what we came for. We don't need him anymore."

"How we gonna find this Walker Gate now?"

"We don't need to. We'll just go out Tulley Gate like we planned. I know the way. No one will suspect a thing."

"Won't they wonder why he's dead?" Hazard said.

"You're a bigger shit-brain than he was. We're taking the bodies with us. They'll assume Lutz and Evans ran off together. We can chop them both up before sunrise. Now, pull yourself together and grab his legs."

2. INOVA HOSPITAL, FAIRFAX, VIRGINIA

November 22

The protruding latch was impossible to open. Janusz pushed hesitantly against the weight of the door, not wanting to see what was on the other side. The squealing of the hinge was perhaps a warning to turn around. He stepped inside the room. The shades were open to a view of the treetops across Gallows Road at the old ExxonMobil facility.

The sun was out, but the sky was strangely devoid of light. It was a stark contrast to the blinding artificial light in the room. Yellow roses were perched on an end table beside a computer. The small envelope in between the flowers had the initials "TV" written on the outside. Several other bouquets included red flowers with shades of pink. The blue couch and reclining chair next to the window were empty, adding to the somber aura of the room. The metronomic beeping of the heart monitor machine was similar to an orchestra that included the beats of the blood pressure gauge and the steady *drip...drip* of the IV.

The man lay motionless on the bed, his eyes closed, his head raised by a pillow, a breathing tube inserted in his nose. Janusz approached cautiously, not wanting to disturb the resting patient. He moved one foot in front of the other, afraid the slightest noise might exacerbate the condition of his mentor, the very man who had given him a new purpose in life after the CIA.

The TV on the opposing wall had no sound. Janusz picked up the remote from the empty blue couch to turn off the nonsense that emanated from the screen. It was a story about a local elementary school that had turned a classroom into a safe space. He placed the remote on the window ledge as he approached the bed. His breath quickened, and a sudden shiver shot from his neck to his toes. He rested his hand awkwardly on Tony, not knowing what to say. Tony's chest rose and sank with each breath. The memories roared back.

What was it he had said the first day Janusz walked through the door? Oh, yes, something along the lines of, "You may have left the government, but your service to your country is just beginning."

From there, it was onto an intensive seminar about private equity and international law. Two additional weeks were dedicated to close-quarters combat. Tony had explained the extra training was necessary because the Unit played by a different set of rules. Unit 81 was not restrained by political correctness or diplomatic courtesies. With greater freedom came greater responsibility, and so it was that Janusz had to relearn many of the skills he had acquired at the CIA.

Not comfortable with the mission of the Unit, Janusz had informed Tony of his intention to quit. The director of Unit 81 would have none of it. Tony took a personal interest in Janusz, inviting him to behind closed doors meetings with the Senate Select Committee on Intelligence, known as the SSCI, that enabled him to see how the Unit was making a tangible difference. From the beginning, Janusz had been given more responsibility than other new recruits. He was anointed point-man on the Middle East, his advice on Iran never second guessed. After killing five Iranian trained assassins in Stuttgart, Germany, a red notice for Janusz's arrest had been issued by Interpol, the international police. Years later, Janusz learned that Tony had cashed multiple favors to make the problem go away.

There was a gentle tug on his finger. Janusz wanted to shout for a nurse, but they were all alone.

"Tony, can you hear me?"

His index finger was being squeezed harder now.

"What the hell happened, Tony? Can you talk?"

Tony turned his head.

"Stan," Tony said.

"What?"

"Stan. Where is Stan?"

Janusz searched for the right words, "Stan didn't make it. You're the sole survivor."

"He smashed into me from the back."

"Who? Who smashed into you?"

"Walked right up to the car and started shooting. Wore a black ski mask and a huge gold Breitling," Tony said in a low voice.

Janusz had his ear close to Tony's face, "Who was it? An Iranian? A Russian? What did he want?"

"Happened too fast...too fast. I couldn't—" Tony said before resting his head back into the pillow. A wave of shame washed over Janusz as he observed the pain on Tony's face.

"Get some rest, Tony. You get some rest. I'll take it from here," Janusz said.

He turned to find his wife standing behind him.

"How is he?" Jennifer said.

"Not good. He can't remember much. We have no choice but to reschedule the vacation."

"And do what exactly?"

"That's what I need to find out."

"I knew you'd say that. This morning, we were on the way to a well-deserved vacation. Who knows when—"

"Listen to me."

"Let me finish. Who knows when we'll get another chance to be together like the old days?"

"You mean, back at the Farm? With the Agency?"

"I thought we could choose our own path and still be together. Obviously, that's not gonna work."

"I'm not quite sure I understand where you're going with this nonsense?"

"Uff da, do I have to spell everything out for you?" Jennifer said eagerly. "It's clear to me the only way this marriage will survive is if we work together."

"Let me guess, you wanna join the Unit. You think I'm going to let you join an organization that's being hunted by God knows who?"

"I don't think you understand, I'm not asking for your permission."

"Absolutely not, you must be nuts. It's too dangerous."

"I went into a village full of terrorists all alone to rescue my team."

"I know that, but—"

"Do you really think I'm going to sit around and wait for word on whether you've been killed?"

"But—"

"You can shove your *buts*. We either work together or I'll leave you," Jennifer said in a falsetto voice.

Janusz could do no more but to nod approvingly.

"I knew you'd see things my way. Where do we start?" Jennifer said.

"Can you arrange for a security detail until he's out of the hospital?"

"You betcha."

"Thanks. Don't know how long we have before the people who did this show up to finish the job."

"I'll call my friend Tammy. Her husband runs a VIP protection service. They can send a team by this afternoon."

"Lovely. Keep your day job until I figure some things out."

She nodded.

"Call me if his condition changes," Janusz said.

The problem with chasing a hidden enemy was not knowing where to start.

3. PACIFIC HEIGHTS, SAN FRANCISCO

November 24

Octavio Souza leaned back in his chair, staring at the Palace of Fine Arts in the distance. He had a perfect view from his rooftop retreat. The red towers of the Golden Gate Bridge stood steadfast beyond the dome of the rotunda. He clasped the half-empty glass of watermelon juice in his hand as he waited. His only thought was on lunch.

Wild caught salmon flown fresh from Alaska, served on a bed of brown rice with baby potatoes, carrots, and asparagus. It was a far cry from the *farofa* with rice and beans he ate almost daily as a child in Sao Paulo. It seemed as though it was a million years ago when he first stepped foot in San Francisco after high school, his entire life before him. Having turned eighty merely weeks ago, he was determined to leave his mark on his adopted land before setting off into the sunset.

"*Chefe,* your guest from Washington is downstairs," Placido said from behind.

Placido was his personal assistant, as well as the man in charge of his security detail. Placido had been a commander of an elite unit in Brazil's 1ˢᵗ Special Forces Battalion. He was a tough soldier, hard as nails, with a keen intellect. Standing over six feet two inches tall with brawny shoulders, bushy brows, and a scar above his left eye, Placido was an intimidating figure to say the least.

"Send him up," Octavio replied.

The election of President Donald Patrick called for extreme measures. Octavio had spent his life amassing a fortune estimated at over fifty-three billion dollars. The true number was much higher, as Forbes was not aware of his offshore investments with unsavory regimes. His wealth had accumulated over decades building Souza Enterprises into a private equity giant of massive proportions. A portion of the portfolio held companies such as the popular chain, Ice Cream King, and Burgers R Us. The rest was comprised of the stock and bonds of publicly traded companies in the beverage, software, social media, restaurant, and travel industries, among others.

Several billions were still invested in commercial real estate. Souza Enterprises collected rent on everything from shopping centers to office buildings in the downtown of every major North American city from Toronto to San Francisco. The net revenue from his vast holdings were over a billion dollars per annum. Since Octavio could not possibly spend all that money, he had established a foundation to distribute the dividends to various causes. Currently, he ran the day-to-day affairs of his foundation, Justice for All, while his eldest daughter was in charge of Souza Enterprises.

"Octavio, I came as soon as I could," the man who preferred to be called Destruction said.

He was tall and thin, with a piercing on the side of his lip. His clean-shaven face was long and reminded Octavio of a weasel. His wavy salt-and-pepper colored hair was cut short on one side while it grew long and shaggy on the other. It was similar to a comb over, yet Destruction had plenty of hair. He wore a black dress shirt with black jeans to go with his ebony boots. The frames of his sunglasses were in the shape of a heart. Destruction took off the glasses as he extended his arm for a handshake. Octavio wondered if it was a mistake to rely on this man to bring forth his grand vision.

"How was your flight? Not too tiring I hope?" Octavio said.

"Thanks to you, it was easy. I've never flown a private jet, especially a Gulfstream."

His guest helped himself to a glass of watermelon juice, "Such a marvelous view, Octavio. I can see the Golden Gate

Bridge, which I've yet to visit up close."

"I forgot it's your first trip to the Bay Area. Placido can show you around the sites if you like. Let's get down to it. How close are we to the execution date?"

Destruction took a sip from his glass, allowing the watermelon juice to linger on his taste buds before pushing it down.

"You'll be glad to know we have all the weapons we need," Destruction said.

"That's not what I asked."

Destruction smirked as he said, "we had an unexpected setback along the way. Nothing that can be traced back to us."

"Vel, I know, I just read about your fiasco at Fort Belvoir. I should've known better than to—"

"Just relax. All anyone knows is two soldiers have disappeared with a shit ton of weapons. The soldiers will be the main suspects for a while. We shouldn't have a problem until after we execute. By then, it'll be too late for the capitalist pigs."

"How much longer?"

"The day following inauguration."

"Is the incoming president going to be there?"

"Yes, he's signing an executive order to end sanctuary cities on January 21st."

"Should I send a few of my people to help?"

"The whole point of this operation is to give the appearance of a spontaneous action by oppressed people. Last thing we need are professionals. I'm gathering the last of the recruits," Destruction said while studying Octavio intently, "what about your end of the bargain?"

"You needn't lose sleep over that. I've placed assets inside district attorney offices at the state and local level around the capital. I also control the US attorneys in Virginia, DC, and Maryland."

"The trials will take a while. The incoming Patrick Administration may replace your US attorneys."

"Washington is an insider's town. The bureaucracy is too

vast for any incoming president to navigate on his own. President Patrick will appoint people based on the advice of career politicians and bureaucrats who owe me favors."

"How can ya be so sure?"

"That's not your concern," Octavio said.

"And the media?"

"I disburse hundreds of millions per year to social causes the media champions. Many entertainment executives I count as personal friends," Octavio said.

Staring out at the Golden Gate Bridge, Octavio was losing his patience, "You've yet to tell me what you're planning?"

"It's quite simple really. I'm planting several men inside the Secret Service. During a staged DC Antifa protest in front of the White House, my agents will open fire, massacring a large number of the protestors. The ensuing media fallout will allow your allies in Congress to impeach President Patrick and rewrite the Constitution as soon as a state of emergency has been declared." *Buurp.*

For a second, Octavio thought his ears were playing tricks on him. His guest burped loudly without excusing himself. Octavio pretended not to hear.

"You're going to massacre your own recruits?"

"A revolution never succeeds without bloodshed. Besides, after the attack, we'll attract thousands more."

"Very vel, continue."

"The carnage will catapult me to the status of a national hero. The social justice movement will worship me. In addition to a compliant government, you'll have an army of street soldiers from sea to shining sea."

"I like it. What do you need from me?"

"Just keep the money coming," Destruction paused briefly, "I need to purchase several additional properties around DC."

"Send a list of the locations to Placido. I'll take care of the rest," Octavio said.

The two men sat quietly, enjoying their meal while staring out into the Bay. As soon as the dessert was cleared,

Destruction excused himself to use the restroom.

"Placido, please see to it our guest gets a tour of the city."

"I don't trust that *puta*."

"That's why I want you to be extra nice. Make sure he enjoys himself. Keep your ears open."

"He takes unnecessary risks. The mess on Ft. Belvoir will bring unwanted attention."

"Most of the media are now advocates. Fortunately, they advocate for positions I support. We'll be fine," Octavio said.

"Are you certain you don't want me to dispose of him during the tour?"

"Absolutely not! He serves a purpose. His involvement allows us to keep our distance if things go wrong. Keep your temper in check and turn on the charm," Octavio ordered.

"What next, *Chefe*?"

"I need you to do a job in Virginia."

"With pleasure," Placido said.

Octavio's security chief walked off to take Destruction on a tour of San Francisco. Alone on the rooftop, Octavio gazed at the blue waters of the Golden Gate. Placido had a point. Destruction was too cocky, on top of being a lowlife.

4. MCLEAN, VIRGINIA

November 27

H e ducked below the steering wheel as a pair of headlights approached on the quiet street. *It's got to be him.* Placido wore black fatigues and a matching ski mask, blending into the darkness. He reached for the latch on the glove compartment. With the motion of his fingers, the compartment dropped open. His palm instinctively grasped the handle as his index caressed the trigger.

Clutching the 9mm Glock 19 sent an uneasy jolt to his brain. Placido had forgotten to do something but could not remember what. He loaded the magazine before racking the slide. Placido proceeded to twist the suppressor over the muzzle. What was it that he had forgotten? His head turned toward the sound of skidding wheels in the distance. He then glanced over at his wrist. The thirty-thousand-dollar gold Breitling was a gift from Octavio. It was 10:37 p.m. and the target was still not home. The sound of wheels rolling on asphalt got closer until the bright headlights in the rearview mirror blasted his eyes.

Placido threw his head down once more. Seconds later, he popped back up. The approaching car climbed the ascending driveway toward the front door. Placido rubbed the top of the Glock for good luck before looking through the night vision binoculars. He quickly zeroed in on the plates. His target had arrived.

A man emerged from the vehicle gathering his belongings. His features fit the description provided by Octavio. Bill Turner stepped inside the house seconds later. Placido exited the vehicle before crossing the street. McLean was a safe neighborhood. Perhaps there was an unlocked entryway. Placido checked several windows in the back of the house where the blinds were drawn. Behind a manicured miniature tree, a window was cracked. He entered as gently as he could. Placido stepped onto the wooden floor, emboldened by a distant memory.

He had helped rid the city of so many of them, those pesky teens roaming the streets. The contract had been for twenty-five thousand dollars, a significant sum in Brazil. The terms specified that Copacabana and Ipanema beaches in Rio de Janeiro would have to be *cleansed* of undesirables. The majority of the unwanted were runaway teens who lived on the streets of Brazil's most famous city. The business community was tired of them. Social services did not have the resources to house them properly. They plagued his city like rodents. After all, those so-called teenagers worked for local thugs running drugs. They committed all sorts of crimes.

The wealthy residents claimed they were tired of the impotent judicial system and corrupt judges that did nothing. That was the impetus behind the private teams that cleared the streets of Brazil. The idea emerged in the 1960s and blossomed over the years. Each subsequent decade provided new opportunities for men with the proper skills to help their community.

Placido was reluctant at first. He had joined the Army to protect his country against external enemies and domestic terrorists. Cleansing Rio was the farthest thing from his thoughts when he retired. Every man has a moment of clarity. For Placido, that moment came when his mother was killed on the streets of Rio. That was the moment he entered the world of private security. His first assignment was a resounding success. It was so humid the back of his shirt was completely drenched.

His team of ex-commandos had driven a group of boys captured the night before up the uninhabited mountain. The trench had been prepared by men with no balls. Two of his more enthusiastic teammates had lined the boys and shot them from behind, like cowards. When they reached the end of the line, they ran out of bullets. But there was still one boy left.

Placido had to finish the job so they would get paid. He walked slowly toward the body-filled trench observing the bloodstains under his feet. Placido placed a hand over the remaining boy's shoulder, turning him so they faced each other. The little brat was petrified. For a second, he thought of sparing him, but then remembered the incident with his mother.

These rats had to pay for their crimes, no matter how young they were. Placido placed the knife blade against the boy's neck as the dirty child plead for his life. The next thing he remembered was the aroma of the blood that soiled his shirt and covered his face. Everything after that was easy.

The creaking of the hardwood underneath his feet could not be helped. The lights were off in this room, and he was aided by the night vision goggles over his eyes. Farther ahead, a winding staircase led to the upper floor. He walked gently forward without sensing the obstruction. His right foot was suddenly tangled by a hard object that disturbed his balance. His chest fell forward as he tried to straighten.

Placido's flailing arms lost grip of the Glock without warning. His heart sank. What would happen when the pistol hit the ground? He was paralyzed with anticipation. There was silence. How could that be? He searched the floor for the weapon, but it was not there. What the hell had happened? A loveseat next to the chair that tangled his leg held what he was looking for. The Glock was just sitting there. Fortune might not be on his side again. The sound of bare feet on hardwood came from beyond the stairwell.

Placido made his way methodically. A short hallway beyond the stairs led to another room beaming with lights. He pushed the night vision goggles above his face, waiting several seconds for his vision to adjust. The first thing he saw was granite. Beautiful pink stone shined to perfection. To the side was a cavernous stainless-steel fridge that went halfway to the ceiling.

On the other end of the kitchen, the target sat facing away from him. Bill's head was bent slightly as he enjoyed his dinner. Placido slowly placed one foot in front of the other. When he was twelve feet away, Placido paused to raise his right arm. Bill stopped chewing. His body tensed reflexively.

"This is the end, *Puta*," Placido said calmly.

Bill's eyes widened as he turned to stare into the suppressed end of the Glock. He tried to swallow the food, but he was unable. He spit the rest on the floor so he could speak.

"Who the hell are you?"

"You're in no position to be asking questions, *amigo*. I think you should say a prayer."

"Sit down so we can talk. I have a family," Bill said pointing to a chair.

"I too had a family once. My mother was murdered on the street. I'm afraid you're not getting any sympathy from me," Placido said.

Bill stood face to face with Placido. His visage suddenly turned white, then green, then white again. His pallid complexion was accentuated by the florescent lights of the kitchen. Something must have snapped inside of Bill. His eyes projected rage. He tightened both hands into fists while clenching his jaw. Placido wrapped his index finger around the trigger in expectation of what was to come.

Bill shouted as he charged like an enraged samurai in battle. Placido tried to pull the trigger, once, then twice, and then a third time. Nothing happened. *Oh, fuck. I forgot to clean this fucking thing after practice at the range.* The force of the impact sent both men hurtling toward the ground. The Glock fell several feet away on the kitchen floor.

"Now, I've gotcha," Bill said before punching Placido in the face. The force of his head hitting the floor was worse than the punch. Bill had mounted his pelvis, sliding his arm back in preparation for the next blow. Everything was happening in slow motion now. Placido instinctively grabbed the compact Beretta Bobcat from his pants pocket.

"Oh, no, you don't," Bill said, leaning forward to block Placido's gun-toting wrist. They struggled for what felt like an eternity before the muzzle of the .22 Bobcat was pointed at Placido's face. The Brazilian used all his might to push the gun away as his opponent did the same.

"Stop, you don't have to do this?" Bill said as they continued to struggle.

They pushed and pulled for control of the Bobcat. *Pow!* The blast was music to Placido's ears. Red liquid flowed forth from Bill's forehead as he slumped forward like a helpless child in the *favelas*. Placido pushed Bill off and grabbed the pistol. He stood over the bleeding man. He could not take a chance. *Pow... Pow...Pow.* Close range to the head with the .22. Placido could picture his drill sergeant back in Brazil derisively mocking his oversight to clean his Glock subsequent to each use.

"It's done. Do you want me to take care of the others?" Placido typed on his encrypted phone.

"No, I need you back here," Octavio replied.

"What about the rest of Unit 81?"

"We're handing that portfolio over to DC Antifa."

"You think that *puta* can handle it?"

"Destruction is flush with an arsenal of new weapons, and I no longer want to risk a direct involvement."

"As you wish, *Chefe*."

"Make sure to take the body with you."

"*Certamente*."

5. GEORGETOWN UNIVERSITY, WASHINGTON D.C.

November 29

As soon as she finished writing the sentence, Lesley tossed the chalk on the table. She turned to face the class, "It's obvious our history is replete with lies. Lies about the Native Americans. Lies about slavery. Lies about exporting democracy. Most importantly," she paused for effect, "lies about all men being created equal."

The room was mesmerized. As she stood there observing them, Lesley Gantz could hear a pin drop all the way in the back. They hung on her words as if their lives depended on it. They absorbed every morsel of wisdom as eagerly as baby hawks devour the carcass of a rodent fed to them by their mother. Lesley had given these lectures to American History 101 students for the past four years. She still got the same tingly sensation down her arm on each occasion. It wasn't nervousness, thank God. It was much better.

She shivered with a chill while her nipples grew hard. The muscles all over her body tensed while her pelvis pulsed with a hungry eagerness. The closest sensation she could compare it to, if she was ever forced, was having an orgasm. That's right, molding these malleable young minds to understand the pure evil of the system that governed their country was as good, if not better, than sex.

A wayward hand rose toward the sky.

"Yes, Mr. Malcolm," Lesley said.

"Don't you think you're being a bit harsh, Professor?

America has made tremendous progress towards equality since our founding. Women gained the right to vote a century ago. We elected a black president. The military trains females for combat roles in the air, on land, and in the water. Many of our top generals are women and minorities. The list goes on and on," Malcolm said.

"Sell out," a random voice came from the back.

"You sound just like them," a female student replied to Malcolm.

"Like who?" Malcolm said.

"Like the racist fascists running our government. You sound just like them. I'm sure if another white guy in this room was to rape me, you'd find a way to justify that, too?" she said as her accusation hung in the air.

"Now, now. Let's give Mr. Malcolm the benefit of the doubt. I'm sure he didn't mean to hurt anyone's *feelings*," Lesley said.

Lesley relished moments like this. Dissenting opinions in her classroom always afforded the opportunity to prove her point while maintaining her grace in front of the students. It was also a great way to deflate the most tumescent egos in the room.

"Mr. Malcom, do you remember our readings about Jacobo Arbenz?" Lesley asked.

"Yes."

"What happened?"

"The US Government worked with local rebels to oust the democratically elected president of Guatemala. Despite Arbenz garnering some sixty percent of the vote, the United Fruit Company lobbied Washington to overthrow him."

"Why?"

"Because his land reforms transferred large tracts of uncultivated land from the landowners to poor farmers. The United Fruit Company, an American corporation, was the largest landowner in Guatemala in those days."

"Ha, ha, burn," Fiona thundered from the back.

"Class, keep your comments to yourself. Now, Mr. Malcolm,

please summarize for us the cause of the 2003 US invasion of Iraq?" Lesley said.

She had him right where she wanted him.

Malcolm bit his lip and looked around the room, "The US military invaded Iraq and overthrew the dictator, Saddam Hussein."

"Yes, Mr. Malcolm, but why? Why did we invade Iraq and overthrow the dictator as you say? What reason did we give at the United Nations for this momentous undertaking?"

Malcolm took a few seconds to gather his thoughts. He squirmed in his seat before replying, "weapons of mass destruction."

"What's that? I can't hear you, Mr. Malcolm. Can you speak up and elaborate?"

"We invaded Iraq because we believed they supported Al Qaeda, and they were developing weapons of mass destruction to use against us and our allies," Malcolm said.

"And what did we find when we finally crushed the Iraqi army and killed thousands of innocent civilians?"

"No WMD," Malcolm said.

"Speak up, please. I can't hear you again," Lesley said as her nipples hardened while the blood rushed to her groin.

"There were no weapons of mass destruction."

"How do we know?"

"Because we searched for months and could not find any."

"We didn't just search. We scoured the entire country with our high-tech gadgets, and there was no WMD. Which only leads to one logical conclusion."

She took a minute to examine the room. Not a single person moved while waiting for her to finish.

"We lied. That's right, just like we did in the Arbenz case. Our leaders always lie. They lie to us, they lie to the media, they lie to the world, and they probably lie to themselves so they can sleep better at night," Lesley said.

She looked over at the clock on the wall. It was three minutes before noon. She had to wrap things up.

"I hope you all take an opportunity to reflect on today's discussion. I'd like to thank Mr. Malcolm for illustrating my point about the duplicity of our government and our leaders. Remember, every relationship has an element of exploitation. The quiz next week will be based primarily on this week's reading assignment. Make sure to read this book from cover to cover," Lesley said, pointing at the blackboard.

Lesley had written the words "A People's History of the United States by Howard Zinn" using white chalk.

"Fiona, I need to see you in my office," Lesley said.

She wiped her chalky hands on her pants before dismissing the class. They all had potential but, truth be told, she appreciated Malcolm's presence more than the others. His naive brand of patriotism allowed her to hammer each lesson more effectively.

She leaned back in her ergonomic swivel chair waiting for the screen to update. Lesley straightened the pile of papers on her desk and placed her purse in the bottom drawer. She was proud of her accomplishments, having quickly climbed from assistant to associate professor in one of America's premiere institutions of higher learning. It was not enough.

Sitting in her cramped office in the Edward B. Bunn Intercultural Center, Lesley had her eyes on a much bigger prize. Her constant struggle, speaking truth to power, and her unfailing advocacy on behalf of the oppressed, were worthy of an endowed chair. It could not come fast enough. There was a knock at the door.

"Yes?" Lesley said.

"You wanted to see me, Professor?"

"Fiona, absolutely. Come in...come in."

Fiona had a habit of changing the color of her hair with each day of the week. Today, it was green. Tomorrow was anyone's guess. She had a pretty face with a button nose and green eyes.

Her earlobes were completely pierced along the outer rim. She wore dark lipstick and heavy mascara. A small ring went through the columella of her nose.

"I'd read Zinn's book in high school. The assignment gives me a chance to—"

"Forget about the assignment. I want you to attend a meeting of the group I was telling you about."

"The self-empowerment group?"

"That's the one. Our meetings are in a historic church not too far from here."

"When?"

"I'll text you the details."

"Looking forward to it, Professor," Fiona said on her way out the door.

Before Lesley could gather her thoughts, the cell phone alerted her to a new encrypted message. It was her master.

"I have a new task for you," the master said.

"How may I serve?" Lesley replied.

"You need to make a new friend."

"Another one? Don't you have enough servants as it is?"

"This one's not for me. She used to work for the government."

"What do you want with her?"

"That's not important. What's important is that you do exactly what I say or you'll get the paddle."

"But—"

"Think of her as another recruit."

"These things take focus away from my work. I need to publish or I'll perish."

"I've mentioned your request to our sponsor. You'll get the position you're after."

"As you wish, Master," Lesley replied.

6. WILDWOOD PARK; VIENNA, VIRGINIA

November 30

He walked down the sinuous path checking in between the trees for anything out of the ordinary. The water rolled with a gentle hum in the nearby stream. If not for the chirping of the cardinals, the woods would be deathly silent. Janusz had chosen this location carefully, next to the National Terrorist Screening Center. It was unlikely for anyone to target them here.

Members of the Unit were either getting killed or disappearing rapidly. A sudden burst of activity rustled a patch of leaves to his right. Janusz reached back, pulling out his 9mm Sig Sauer pistol. His finger near the trigger, he was ready to shoot at the slightest provocation. The disappearance of Bill Turner, a skilled operations officer with a military background,was a wakeup call.

There was indication of a struggle at the house, but no sign of Bill. Someone must have kidnapped him. Whoever was behind all this knew a lot about the Unit. Janusz pointed the Sig toward the noise. Two squirrels jumped out of a tree before disappearing into a pile of leaves.

His muscles twitched. After a long exhale, he lowered the weapon. He continued down the path, periodically checking his rear. He finally found what he was looking for. A gazebo hidden among the trees. At first, he couldn't see a thing. Then he spotted him. A man sat by himself inside the wooden structure. When he was within twenty feet, Janusz recognized the face. The man puffed on a cigarette. Jason Osborne froze for a brief second with the cigarette stuck in between his lips.

"I thought you wouldn't show. Did you get lost?" Jason said.

"I'm taking more precautions than usual."

Jason nodded in agreement as he snuffed the cigarette on the bottom of his shoe. He threw the butt into the woods.

"You really should give those up. It's a nasty habit," Janusz observed.

"Whatever you say," Jason said cavalierly as he sat back.

Janusz lunged forward, grabbing the man by the collar, "Stan is dead while Tony is in the hospital hanging on for dear life. And now, Bill just disappeared. You wanna tell me what the hell is going on, motherfucker?"

"Hey...hey...relax, buddy. We're all on the same side."

"That's easy for you to say, no one is trying to kill you," Janusz said before letting go of the man's jacket.

"Didn't mean to sound indifferent. How's Tony?"

"Could go either way. Any word from the intelligence agencies?"

"You guys are off the radar, remember? As far as the intelligence community is concerned, the murders are a local police affair."

"What about the SSCI? I thought we had an arrangement."

"Your biggest advocate is getting ready to enter the White House. Donald Patrick is busy with his transition at the moment. The rest of the committee does not want to get involved. They'll have lots of explaining to do if the Unit's connection with Congress ever saw the light of day," Jason said.

"Lovely. You mean to tell me we're on our own?"

Jason lowered his eyes for a second before looking up, "I wouldn't count on official support for now. The SSCI is happy to bury this relationship. A few staffers like me are all you have left. I'm looking for a new job, but I'll do my best while I still have access."

"What have you gathered so far?"

"I think the Russians are behind this. They're the only ones with the motive and know-how to come after you."

"The Russians? Not you, too. Everyone in DC sees a Russian

wherever they look. This nonsense is starting to piss me off," Janusz said, grinding his teeth.

"Hear me out on this. Who just assassinated the IRGC Qods Force chief across the street from the Kremlin? Don't you think Moscow is embarrassed about the *disappearance* of a visiting general in its backyard."

"They assumed that was the CIA. Do they know about Unit 81?"

"Perhaps."

"What are you reading in the cables and field reports?"

"Nothing. It's the kind of thing President Putin will only discuss at a Russian Security Council meeting with his inner circle. We won't see any of it in the traffic."

"Don't we have a source inside?"

"Not at the moment. Their discussions are beyond our reach. Anyway, the Russians are vindictive by nature, and I don't think Putin is an exception here. After your most recent mission, they'll want revenge."

"How did they figure it out so quickly?" Janusz said.

"Who knows? I'm sure they have their sources in Washington. Sources possibly inside the Unit."

"Or perhaps inside the SSCI? You guys are the only ones in the government who know about the existence of the Unit," Janusz said with an accusatory tone.

"Anything is possible. Given the magnitude of your actions, the Kremlin will stop at nothing to destroy your entire organization. Every last one of you."

Janusz looked away to clear his head. As much as he hated to admit, Jason was right. Janusz walked to the other end of the gazebo. He placed his hand on the wooden railing looking out into the woods. The scent of charcoal was everywhere. Someone nearby had prepared a BBQ.

Janusz turned and walked right back toward Jason, "Let's get on with it. I need names."

"What names?"

"Read through the reports. Who in Russia is ordering this?

Better yet, who in Washington is responsible for carrying it out."

"We don't have anything."

"Find out. Talk to your contacts. Hell, go to the bars in DC. Find me a fucking name. I'm taking this war to their front porch, and I need a place to start. Let's go, let's go!"

"I'll do my best," Jason said.

Janusz patted him on the back and walked away. If the Russians were behind this, they were going to pay.

7. PACIFIC HEIGHTS, SAN FRANCISCO

December 01

Octavio observed the woman with the tight black dress. She helped herself to another serving of Foie Gras, her fourth, popping it in between her teeth. She was quick to grab a glass of Cristal champagne from the very next tray. He knew everyone in this room, but he did not recognize her.

"Placido, who is that woman with her mouth full of goose liver?" Octavio said.

"That's Janet Smears, *Chefe*. She's a reporter working for *Impressionable Magazine*. They cater to the jet set crowd in New York and Los Angeles."

"Interesting, keep an eye on her. I may want to talk to her later."

Octavio mingled with the crowd. It was no easy feat playing host to this group of dilettantes in search of a new cause to save their souls. His mission this evening was to convince them to be more active in his latest endeavor, politics. Flying in from his hideout in Jackson Hole was T.B. Schuster, the founder of America's largest drugstore chain, TBS.

Through TBS, Schuster held a variety of media outlets, including movie studios, TV news, and talk radio. At seventy-two, T.B. enjoyed the life of a playboy. He had recently divorced his third wife. T.B. had a fondness for collectible cars, Gulfstream jets, and young blondes with fake breasts. In an effort to quell bad publicity, he had established a foundation dedicated to medical science while also donating to universities for the purpose of endowing professorial chairs in his name.

Then there was John Millhouse, heir to the second largest fast-food chain in America. Millhouse constantly flew between the British territory of Isle of Man and the Cayman Islands. His last wife had recently passed under mysterious circumstances, leaving him free to travel.

Finally, there was Herb and Gail Bach from the Lake Tahoe region of Nevada. Their wealth was amassed by growing the nation's largest micro-brew into an international beer powerhouse. Everyone assumed Bach was a German brand. It was amusing as the family had changed their name from Baum.

"Ladies and gentlemen, may I have your attention?" Octavio said as he clanked a metal fork against his empty champagne glass.

The room fell silent, all eyes descending on the man about to rewrite history.

"We're gathered here tonight because our country is in a state of crisis. The United States is now full of racists and right-wing extremists. We need to put an end to this dangerous trend by raising money for social justice, so let's get down to it," Octavio said.

"The whole thing is kind of hopeless if you ask me. Year after year, we out raise our opponents nearly two to one yet still suffer at the ballot box. Donald Patrick is no different than his egotistical predecessor, President Adkins. Despite billions spent in advertising and the assistance of our friends in the media, we're still not able to control the rabble," T.B. Schuster said with palpable resignation.

"Come now. No need for hysterics. Our cause has made tremendous strides since the sixties. We've transformed the universities to produce model citizens. Political correctness is pervasive from boardrooms to courtrooms. Everything from feminism to gay marriage is perfectly acceptable in the new America among civilized folks," Harold Matheson declared.

Harold was the president at a prestigious Ivy League university and a former secretary of education. They took a moment to chew on his words, shaking their heads silently in agreement.

Millhouse greedily swallowed another jumbo prawn shrimp. He then devoured his last piece of crab cake, washing it down with a swig of Cristal.

"Y'all are looking at this the wrong way. Forget the political angle. We need to focus on incremental changes from below. The more the American public is focused on social justice, the more likely they'll vote for the candidates we favor," Millhouse said as he moved uneasily in the center of the room.

It appeared as though Millhouse had one too many servings of the Cristal, "The way I see it, we also need to focus our efforts on raising salaries. I'm talking everyone from grocery store clerks to fast food cooks. For another thing, we got to make a bigger push to raise taxes. That's the best way to fund a Universal Basic Income. The top tax rates are way too low—"

Octavio cut him off with a flick of a wrist. Millhouse had a tendency to get carried away. When discussing taxes, there was always the danger he would suggest taxing wealth instead of income. The billionaires in the room had learned long ago to lower their income while increasing their wealth. Nevertheless, discussions of raising taxes, even on income, was something better left for sound bites on TV. Octavio considered anyone discussing the topic of taxation too freely to be a lowlife. Millhouse was getting close to lowlife territory.

"Let's stay focused. Our main objective is to scuttle the administration of President-elect Patrick by impeaching him as soon as possible. We need to be weary of getting sidetracked," Ocatvio said.

"Folks, I have to admit this is all new to me. I mean, it took me a while to get used to raising money from Hollywood moguls and trial lawyers. Cozying up to a room full of billionaires is not something I'm comfortable with. This type of cooperation strikes me as a betrayal of our rank-and-file members. I'm going to think long and hard about NAT's participation with this group," Joel Silver said.

He was the president of the National Association of Teachers, the largest education union in the United States. His cooperation was an essential ingredient to the entire project. Union contributions were still one of the largest sources of money funneled into the social justice agenda. During the past decade, over a billion dollars of union dues had been turned over to social justice organizations, often without approval of individual union members. Most of that money would vanish without NAT. It just so happened Joel's deputy was a former employee of Justice for All, Octavio's foundation. A shift in the leadership of NAT seemed in order.

"This is a battle for the soul of America. Every day, our country resembles the worst excesses of the Pinochet regime. I saw the same thing in my native Brazil during the military dictatorship. We must not allow lowlife nationalists to thrive under Donald Patrick. The community of nations needs free and open borders. The best way to do this is for each philanthropist in this room to commit at least ten million dollars a year to the cause. That's why I'm announcing the creation of the Freedom Coalition here tonight to ensure we get the most bang for the buck."

"What about the press? Won't they label our collaboration as some sort of cabal?" Herb asked.

"You forget that progressivism is now a corporate philosophy, also known as Woke Capital. I doubt we'll get any pushback from a corporate press corps staffed by graduates of politically correct Ivy League universities, such as the one managed by Mr. Matheson. As I understand it, Ms. Smears is here to address this very concern," Octavio said.

"As mentioned earlier this evening, the problem in contemporary America is rightwing extremism, the base of support for our opponents. I'm confident the generous contributions of the men and women in this room will go a long way in combating that. I can assure you that my colleagues in the press corps will be happy to highlight your efforts to save our country. Everyone at our magazine, from the CEO to the senior editors and beat reporters, wants to see President Patrick and his pro-America agenda defeated. As long as these backward enemies of a diverse and cosmopolitan America are in the White House, the press will attack them," Ms. Smears said.

"That's quite reassuring. I've established lines of communications with ground elements that'll defend our agenda on the streets. We can use those folks as allies to push our beliefs on the public. After all, a little intimidation never hurt anyone," Octavio said.

The next phase of the operation was around the corner.

Sitting across from the crackling fireplace in his private library, Octavio flipped a page before taking another sip from his French, handcrafted cognac stemware. Who would've thought a single crystal glass could cost over two thousand dollars? The owners of Baccarat, that's who. As he swirled the rich liquid over his palate, Octavio was pleased with himself. It had been an arduous journey from the *favela* to his current sumptuous surrounding reading William Hazlitt. He was not only a perspicacious businessman but an erudite scholar to boot. The rap on the door broke his train of thought.

"Come in," Octavio said. It was the reporter from *Impressionable Magazine*. Her lubricious melon-shaped breasts, with protruding nipples, awakened his libido.

He took a gulp of cognac to relax, "Ms. Smears, thank you for joining us this evening. It's a bit out of your way in New York City, is it not?"

"Not at all. It's quite an honor to finally meet you."

Octavio was aware of his shifting genitals. He turned sideways to avoid exposing the emerging bulge. He couldn't help but take pride in the fact his body was as responsive to the opposite sex as most men half his age. Something about this reporter reached deep inside his psyche. Perhaps it was her dark hair, her brown eyes, or perhaps it was the ruby red lipstick that adorned her lips. She was tall for a woman, probably around five feet seven inches, but her body was exquisitely toned.

"Tell me a little about yourself, I'm curious."

"There's not much to tell. My father was an executive at IBM, and my mother was a doctor of internal medicine. They're both retired. I grew up in Manhattan, went to prep school at Dalton, got my degree in journalism at Columbia. Nothing out of the ordinary. I've been writing for *Impressionable Magazine* since leaving journalism school a decade ago."

"That's quite interesting. What made you want to write a story about yours truly?"

"I never said—"

"Vel, yes, but I could sense it in your eyes."

She looked at him before replying ever so softly, "I've always been drawn to powerful men who want to make a difference."

"I assure you there's no need for flattery. I do what I do because I believe in it."

"And what is it that you believe in?"

"If we get down to it, the progressive agenda will not prevail without money. We need a steady infusion of cash to inculcate our values as broadly as possible. The Freedom Coalition will go a long way toward meeting that goal by coordinating donations. I want to raise at least five hundred million annually. The money will go to groups that'll transform America into a more enlightened nation."

"Did you ask me to your study just so you can tell me this?"

"Vel, not exactly. I need your help," Octavio said before pausing to take a sip. He motioned for Janet to sit closer to him on the leather sofa and continued, "There are those, let's call them rightwing racists, who'll portray the Freedom Coalition as a cabal. A sort of conspiracy of radical progressives' hell bent on changing America."

"Isn't that the truth?"

"It is, quite right, but you know we can't sell it that way.

That's why I need you to publish a series of articles that'll put a good spin on things. It'll prompt the other media sycophants to follow your lead. As a matter of fact, there's a group I'm working with in Washington. I want you to write a puff piece about them in your magazine."

"I'm terribly sorry. I thought you wanted to offer assistance with my career," she said with an impish smile. Her lips parted ever so subtly as she used her tongue to wipe the side of her mouth.

"That's also something that can be arranged."

Janet inched closer before placing her hand on his thigh. A tingle shot up from where her hand rested all the way up to his crotch.

Placido tucked another layer of plastic under the leather sofa in the library. The fire was still crackling as Octavio read a few passages from Nietzsche's *Beyond Good and Evil*.

"Are you done, Placido?"

"Yes, *Chefe*. I think that'll hold. I'll go bring our friend."

His assistant had covered all the floors and furniture with a plastic cover. This was after the maid had finished wiping the leather sofa to clean the love stain he and Janet Smears had deposited moments earlier. Although usually fastidious, Octavio could not help himself to the opportunity that had presented itself with Janet on the furniture.

Octavio stood before walking over to the paneled bookcase carved into the wall near the fireplace. Upon tilting a lever disguised as a book written by Hazlitt, a section of wood paneled wall opened up to reveal a refrigerator sized steel safe. Octavio entered a numbered combination on the touchscreen to unlock the treasures inside.

Lined up on a rack under the safe's recessed LED light were an assortment of shotguns. They were all double-barreled, both side-by-side and over-under action twelve-gauge beauties. The manufacturer of this collection was the famous Browning brand. Octavio was an avid hunter of birds. Endangered or not, if it had wings and could fly, Octavio enjoyed killing it. He had paid millions for the privilege of shooting at some of the most endangered birds in the world, including the California Condor. In order to sharpen his skills, Octavio shot both skeet and trap clay targets whenever the opportunity arose.

His weapon of choice was the Browning Citori 725 shotgun with the thirty-inch barrel in a black walnut glossy finish. He had scored a perfect one hundred during a recent skeet competition with this over-under masterpiece of craftsmanship. He used a handkerchief to buff the wood before cracking open the weapon to drop two red-jacketed three-inch slugs into the chamber. Octavio proceeded to close the action before placing the Browning on top of his desk and covering it with a soft cloth. Seconds later, he heard the rapping on the door.

"Come in," Octavio bellowed.

"*Chefe. Senhor* Silver is here," Placido said, standing next to the president of the teacher's union.

"That'll be all, Placido. You can leave us," Octavio said before standing to extend his hand. "Joel, thank you for accepting my invitation to meet so late."

"I missed my flight back to DC, but Placido said you'll fly me out on your private jet. It's a fair trade, I suppose."

"Don't worry, my staff will take excellent care of you."

"What's with all the plastic?"

"I'm doing a little interior decorating in the study. The painters will be here early in the morning," Octavio said before moving toward the alcohol cart.

"Can I offer you something to drink? Aged scotch, or maybe some cognac?"

"No thanks. It's late, and I've got a busy schedule tomorrow. I'd like to leave as soon as possible."

"Vel, I'll make it brief, then," Octavio said with the same

smile he offered the world whenever angry.

Joel shuddered.

"What's this I hear about your hesitance to work with us?" Octavio said.

"I said no such thing. I simply stated I'm going to think long and hard about this proposition, and I meant it."

"I know, but Ms. Smears, who was here a little earlier, said she spoke with you during the party, and you were emphatic about keeping union dues away from the Freedom Coalition."

Joel's face turned beet red as he clenched his jaw, "That lousy woman. I spoke with her off-the-record. This is outrageous."

"It's still off-the-record. She just told me, and I'm sure she is not going to write a story about it."

Octavio chuckled on the inside as Joel seemed ready to combust. He loved making his opponents uneasy.

"Fine. It's nothing against you. I was raised in a blue-collar household, and I just don't trust billionaires. I understand we have mutual interests, but I'd rather spend NAT's money on activities I oversee. Now, I'd appreciate it if you could arrange my return back to DC like you promised."

"Not so fast. What would happen if, hypothetically speaking, you resigned your position tomorrow to do something else?"

"Really? You're going to bribe me?" Joel observed with a nervous hand twitch, "let me save you the trouble. I wouldn't give you the pleasure of resigning in exchange for every penny of your fortune or all the gold in Fort Knox. You should save yourself further embarrassment."

"Then humor me for a second. Technically speaking, what would happen?"

Joel took a few seconds to ponder his reply. He appeared uneasy but decided to play along, "I guess my deputy would take over until there'd be a union wide election for my replacement. Look, you're wasting—"

"I can afford to waste whatever I want, my dear Joel. I'm a billionaire, remember?" Octavio said while shuffling over to his desk. He removed the cloth covering before grabbing the Browning by the barrel. He took a handkerchief out of his pants pocket to shine the walnut stock once more.

"Are you a bird hunter, Joel?"

"No, I have no interest in killing animals."

"How about skeet? Have you ever gone skeet shooting?"

Joel laughed at the top of his lungs. It started with a series of short chuckles but quickly devolved into a hearty laugh, prompting him to lean against the plastic covered leather sofa when he was through.

"If this is your childish attempt to intimidate me, then save your breath. I dealt with the mob when I was a community organizer in Chicago and New York. Not just the Italians, but also Russians and the Japanese. There is nothing about your stupid old Brazilian ass that's even the least bit intimidating."

Octavio continued speaking, "I performed flawlessly at a nearby skeet competition not too long ago. My score was better than all the other Silicon Valley oligarchs."

"Good for you."

"Usually, when one goes skeet shooting, one loads his weapon with bird shot. But this fine instrument, with which I rarely miss, is currently loaded with two slugs."

"Okay, asshole. I'm going to arrange my own flight back to DC. Then I'm going to have a little chat with some of the other union heads from around the country. When I'm through, no union will ever contribute a dime to any cause with your name on it."

"Do you know the secret to becoming a billionaire, Joel?"

"That's it, I'm through with this nonsense," Joel said before turning toward the door.

Octavio took aim at the moving target. He pulled the trigger once. A thunderous blast jolted the study.

It took barely a second before Joel let out a deafening cry that could be heard even in a cemetery, "*Aaaahhhh* my arm, you fffffuuuuuucking baaaastaaard. You blew off my arm. *Aaaahhh.*"

Octavio moved closer toward his prey. It was not considered sporting to leave an injured animal to suffer.

"The secret to becoming a billionaire is conquering resistance."

It was difficult to hear himself over Joel's incessant screaming. The head of NAT was crouched against the door, trying to stanch the blood gushing out of his right stump with his left hand. Octavio was impressed with the man's vocal cords and his ability to scream while losing so much vital fluid. Placido had done an excellent job of covering the room with plastic. There would be no need to clean the mess off the furniture when this was over.

"You won't get away with...with this," Joel said, his voice fading.

"Don't worry, Placido has disposed of plenty of bodies before. On the bright side, your name will be synonymous with Jimmy Hoffa. People will be looking for you for years."

Octavio pointed the barrel at the dying man's chest. The idiot raised his remaining hand as if that would make a difference. Octavio took aim at center mass and fired. There was no screaming once the smoke had cleared. He opened the shotgun to eject the empty shells.

"Damn, I shouldn't have stood so close," Octavio said out loud as he removed chunks of Joel's guts from his clothes.

"Placido, get in here!"

8. GEORGETOWN UNIVERSITY, WASHINGTON D.C.

December 03

Te students strolled across the lawn and pathways in front of Healy Hall, oblivious to the dangers that imperiled their future. It was easy for them to forget the oppressive system that ran their lives as they made their way among the impressive Gothic style stone buildings that surrounded them. After all, tuition was not a subject most of these spoiled children of capitalism worried about. Their parents made sure that they did not lack for anything.

Destruction's own parents were affectionately known as yippies in the sixties. They were members of the Youth International Party. They had dropped out of college to fight against the corrupt capitalist system. They also taught Destruction to oppose all illegitimate authority from an early age.

Following high school, Destruction became a community organizer in the suburbs of Washington DC, while also running a pot business with a few friends to make money. There was nothing he hated more than college students who were financed by the Bank of Mommy and Daddy. Perhaps the only thing worse was abstract art.

The one redeeming quality these students had was naivete. They were idealistic, which made them perfect recruits for DC Antifa. Destruction and Hazard stood side by side as a gust caught them from behind. Several of the flyers flew off into the wind, prompting Hazard to chase them in a hurry. Hazard bent over, working furiously to pick up the scattered mess in haste. Destruction couldn't help but laugh at the sight of his lieutenant's deference towards the rules and institutions of the capitalist pigs.

"Leave those be," Destruction cried out over the howling wind.

"They won't let us come back if we litter," Hazard said.

"It's better to pique passer interest this way. Who knows, we may snag a janitor or two a—"

Destruction was not able to finish his sentence. Someone had bumped into his shoulder.

"Hey... hey, shit-brain. Why don't ya pay attention to where you're going?" Destruction shouted. The man walked a few more steps before he finally turned.

"N-n-no, y-y-you're in the way. Y-y-you and your little buddy here should be more careful," the man said with a red face and bulging veins on his forehead.

He was of average height with a goatee. His hair was unusually messy. He had pale skin with blue eyes along with an athletic build. He wore trendy jeans over brown boots and a Georgetown stenciled jacket.

"I happen to be exercising my First Amendment right. What's your problem, arse-wipe?"

"Your face, t-t-that's my problem. Now, g-g-go fuck off," the man said before continuing on his way. Hazard stood with a retarded expression. He probably could not believe how calmly Destruction took all this. But this was not a street altercation. They were here to recruit. The young man's anger was palpable. Something had to be bothering him or he had a huge chip on his shoulder. He was perfect. Destruction tried to catch up.

"Buddy. Hey, buddy. Hey hold up," Destruction said.

The young man turned to peer into his eyes.

"Take it easy, we're out here to help make your life easier when you graduate. I know what it's like. You're either indebted to your parents or to the banks. To top it off, you might not have a job when you graduate. You've got a right to be angry."

The man's scowl melted away. He unclenched his muscles as his body grew more relaxed. It was time to pounce.

"I'm Sean. What's your name?" Destruction said.

"Jake."

"Jake, we could use a guy like ya. You should attend one of our meetings."

"Meetings? About what?"

"Can't tell you here, but it won't hurt for you to find out. If you don't like what you see, you can walk out."

"When?"

"This afternoon. We start at five on the dot."

"Where?"

"St. Joseph's Episcopal Church."

"A church?" Jake repeated incredulously.

"It's not what you think. They let us hold our meetings there after hours. You'd be surprised how progressive churches have become these days," Destruction said with a smile.

"I'll see if I can make it," Jake said as he snatched a flyer out of Destruction's hand before walking off. It was then that Destruction knew.

"Let's go, Hazard."

"But we haven't finished passing out all the flyers."

"We got what we needed today," Destruction said as Hazard stood there staring at him.

They gathered in the cavernous basement of St. Joseph's Episcopal Church in DC. The participants were from all walks of life. They were nurses, architects, nonprofit employees, and university professors. They all had one thing in common. They wanted to bring down the US Government and its evil Constitution. Destruction and Hazard mingled among the crowd. Most of the attendees were regulars. They did not excite Destruction.

He was always searching for new recruits to inject greater enthusiasm in the group. As he prepared to take center stage, he was overtaken with joy. The young man and woman he was expecting walked in together, as if on cue.

"Jake, I'm so glad you could make it. And you must be Fiona," Destruction said as he studied the pair standing near the red exit doors, "please, take a seat anywhere ya like."

The new recruits split up to find seats among the crowd.

"We have a special guest joining our meeting, her name is Janet Smears. You may have read her articles in *Impressionable Magazine*. I'd encourage you to have an open dialogue with her about your reasons for joining our group," Destruction said as he zigzagged among the participants.

"If this is your first visit, welcome. Officially, we're recognized as DC Antifa according to the media. This means we're the chapter of Antifa responsible for combatting fascism and racism around the capital of the United States. Unofficially, we're what we've always been. Proud anarchists on the front line of the battle against America the exploiter," Destruction said. Destruction scanned the room. The ones he cared about most, Jake and Fiona, sat quietly with stone cold interest.

"The origin of our movement is the hardcore punk scene in the eighties. The groups were originally called Anti-Racist Action, a network of like-minded anarchists in various cities across the country," Destruction said as he shifted his weight from side to side.

"But enough about history. What does it mean to be an anarchist? It means we care. It means we want everyone's needs to be met. It means we're all a part of a community. A community of self-sufficient people opposed to big business and the consumer culture. We reject capitalism and the concomitant culture of exploitation it exemplifies. Our enemies are racists, fascists, and capitalist pigs," Destruction said.

He went on in this way for another five hours as their eyes glazed over. Destruction was certain they were past the point of exhaustion. It was the perfect moment to switch things up.

"Why are ya here tonight?" Destruction asked, pointing at Fiona, "go ahead, don't be shy. You're amongst friends."

"I've been lied to my whole life. Everything I was taught about this country and its history is a lie. Our country is a patriarchy run by misogynists," Fiona said.

"You've come to the right place. Anarchism is about combating oppression and helping your neighbors. We stand as equals against the patriarchy, men and women alike. We don't see a difference between men and women or any other gender. We believe sex and gender are categories used by the capitalist pigs to divide us," destruction paused briefly, "anyone else care to share?"

A hand went up. It was Jake, "I've spent the past three years racking up debt. The average house in this city, and many like it around the country, costs over a million dollars. How is anarchism going to solve that?"

"I love your passion. This is exactly the point. What good is a society that burdens its future with debt? What good is a society where the best and the brightest can't afford a roof over their heads? You and thousands like you have been shafted by this society. You've been sold a lie. Democracy and freedom are illusions. Anarchists won't lie to you. We'll invest in your future. We'll empower you to control your own destiny. When we're in charge, there'll be no more banks and no more student debt," Destruction said.

"How?" Jake said.

"By creating an entirely new type of society. By learning to take collective action. By working with the other people in this room to build a community, one that values the individual instead of the corporation. By taking the fight to the doorstep of America the exploiter. Anarchism is about mutual responsibility. We reject hierarchical societies because they lead to exploitation. We want to create a society in which there are no laws besides mutual respect. We believe in a society of voluntary authority between individuals who are free to trade goods and services. Such as society is within reach. The only thing required of you is commitment."

"How do we get there?" Jake asked once more.

"Don't worry about the how. Instead, ask yourself, 'What am I willing to sacrifice to get there?'"

The room fell silent. Jake and Fiona clearly wanted to learn more. It had been six hours since the meeting began. They were probably exhausted and hungry. It was perfect.

"Now, for the best part. Hazard and a few volunteers prepared dinner for everyone upstairs. No need to worry. There's plenty of food to go around. If you haven't visited us before, make sure to introduce yourselves to everyone. And, by that, I mean everyone."

Jake raised his hand again, "A few people in the room called you Destruction. What's the meaning behind that?"

"All shall be explained in due course. For now, ya must decide if you're ready to commit to your future."

Destruction had Jake right where he wanted him.

9. RUSSIA HOUSE RESTAURANT, WASHINGTON D.C.

December 04

He entered the oval-shaped room behind the waiter. Janusz was seated at a small table for two next to a window overlooking Connecticut Avenue. Seeing his contact had not yet arrived, Janusz attempted to settle in by ordering an assortment of house vodkas, considered among the best in DC. There was little traffic on the street, giving him a direct view of the steak house on the other side of the boulevard.

A lot had changed about the city over the years, but the Russia House had a sense of permanence, despite recent renovations. He perused the menu. Out of the past ten occasions he had eaten here, Beef Stroganoff had been the way to go on at least eight of them. Janusz ordered a caviar medley to start things off. An annoying habit the Russians shared with Iranians was a lack of punctuality. In this case, he was more worried the prospect might not show at all.

"Mr. John King," a man said, calling out Janusz's operational name. He was tall with short blond hair, blue eyes, and a small paunch. He approached with an extended arm. The Russian looked to be in his forties, well-built with big hands. More than likely the man had come up through Spetsnaz special forces, which meant he was probably with the military intelligence GRU and not the civilian SVR. If the Russians were behind the attacks on the Unit, they would slip up sooner or later. Janusz intended to catch them in the act when they did.

"Pleasure to meet you, Mr....?" Janusz said.

"You can call me Kalugin," the man replied as he shook Janusz's hand with a vise-like grip.

Janusz did not acknowledge this obvious power play. They both sat facing each other. There was something about this man that made Janusz uneasy. He could not yet place his finger on it.

"I took the liberty of ordering us some vodka and caviar. I hope that's not a problem?"

"Not at all, do you speak any Russian?"

"A few words here and there, short conversations. I don't consider myself fluent," Janusz lied.

"Very well, English it is," Kalugin said.

Despite the uneasy smile on his face, Kalugin's icy blue eyes had an intensity bordering on ferocity. This man had certainly killed before, more than once. Why had the Russians sent an assassin instead of a case officer? The conversation flowed awkwardly until the vodka arrived. After several shots, both men grew more comfortable with each other.

"I'm sure your embassy told you why I'm here," Janusz said.

"They did. Why do you want to work for Russia? You can offer your services to any number of countries with a presence in this town."

"The Agency fucked me out of a pension. They claimed I went rogue in Iraq and Afghanistan. That I was a bit too eager with my trigger finger. Fuck those Jihadis, they deserved what they got. You guys understand that better than anyone," Janusz said.

Kalugin studied Janusz's words as well as his demeanor. The longer Janusz sat across from this man, the more he realized the Russian was more measured than he appeared at first.

"I do, I lost my older brother in Afghanistan. He was killed in 1984, a Mujahadeen ambush in the Panjshir Valley. That's still no excuse for being hot-headed. Why would we want to take someone who does not follow directions?"

Playing mental chess against a Russian was a delicate task.

"A valid observation. What I did on the front lines in service to my country is a lot different than what I will do under your employment. One was to settle a score for the twin towers, this is business. Besides, our country is absolutely paranoid about Russia these days. Most our politicians have worked themselves into a frenzy about Russia, Russia, Russia. This will be my special gift of revenge on behalf of Russia."

The meals arrived faster than expected. Both men dug into their food as Kalugin contemplated what he had heard. The Russian chewed slowly and methodically, similar to the way he seemed to think.

"What if I said no, we don't need you?"

Janusz let the silence linger before responding, "I have a large network of friends and contacts at Langley, some of them in high places. You can use me as a conduit to people with knowledge about operations in Russia and around the world."

"What do you want in return?"

"I want to be your muscle here in the DC area. If someone is giving you problems or not cooperating, I can deal with them personally. I'm not talking about Russian expats. I know you use the mob for that. The Russian mafia can't help you deal with pesky CIA officials. You won't get close enough with your people. I can do that for you."

Kalugin swallowed his food before emptying his shot glass of vodka.

"I also need a little extra money for retirement. My government pension won't cover all my expenses."

Kalugin furtively examined the room. The nearest table was empty and, close by, a couple was more focused on each other than anything else at the moment.

"This is not the kind of conversation I want to have at this restaurant. Why did you choose it, anyway?"

"Because it's only two miles from your embassy, and I knew a lot of your people frequent this establishment. Plus, the vodka is superb."

"You're right on one account, the vodka here is the best

in town. I'm sure you know you're playing with fire. Our people did some investigating on you. As you say, you were an accomplished officer of the CIA. A man of many talents. You left your employment several years ago, correct?"

"Yes, but I've been working with the Agency in a different capacity from the outside."

"I see. Since we don't khave much to establish your bona fides, perhaps you can prove your usefulness to us in some other way."

"Lovely. What did you have in mind?"

"Consider it a test assignment, if you will."

"I'm listening."

"The focus at the embassy these days is on one matter in particular. Moscow is determined to find out what khappened to Iranian Qods Force chief, General Kalantari. You've probably read about this. He disappeared from the Ritz Carlton Hotel in Moscow."

General Kalantari, the QF chief, had not disappeared. Janusz had killed him in Moscow, but the Russians were not about to admit that they had failed to protect a visiting VIP. So, they concocted a story about his *disappearance*.

"And you think Washington was involved?" Janusz said, trying to keep a straight face. It was almost comical. If he told this man the truth, he was certain Kalugin would not believe him.

"Obviously, the Mossad had its own interest in the matter, but that's not my concern. If you can help me shed light on this case, you'll khave a rewarding experience working for us."

Deep down, Janusz wished he could beat the truth out of the Russian. But that was out of the question. He had to become a trusted asset before he could get some answers.

"Am I to assume you're with GRU or SVR?"

"You can assume whatever you like. It should make no difference to you. Both organizations answer to the same authority in Moscow, which is not your concern."

Kalugin got up and pulled a card from his wallet, "call me at this number when you learn something. We'll meet in front of Peirce Mill and khike together through Rock Creek Park. Make sure to wear you khiking gear."

They exchanged goodbyes before Kalugin walked out of the restaurant. The Russian left him to pay the check.

10. VIENNA, VIRGINIA

December 05

K im drank her second cup of coffee as she fidgeted with her phone. Damn thing would not accept her password. On the fourth try, she recognized that her fingers were inputting the password to her computer.

Kim usually enjoyed listening to classical music to relax, but not today. She eyed the bowl full of milk-drenched cereal sitting in front of her. As the butterflies grew restless in her stomach, she got up and threw the entire meal in the trash. Kim turned on the TV. She switched back and forth between the various morning news shows but nothing grabbed her attention. It seemed like ages since she had a decent night's sleep.

Kim had taken melatonin in addition to various other sleeping aids with no luck. The entire experience was new to her. As far back as she could remember, she had always been on the side of the stronger team. Whether with the FBI or the Unit, she had always been the one doing the hunting. Now, she was the prey.

How long had it really been since it all began? Was it a day, a week, or a month? Everything seemed a blur since Stan was killed and Tony left in the hospital. The image of Tony lying helpless on the hospital bed was all she could think of. She was unable to gather the strength to visit him. It was....it was just too much.

She shut out the image of Tony by reminding herself of the disappearance of Bill Turner. No one knew what had happened to him but, in all likelihood, he had not fared much better than

Stan. Would Bill's children become orphans now that their father was gone? Who was behind it all?

Kim had taken the job with the Unit to escape the dreadful bureaucracy. The politically correct culture, the cover your ass attitude, and the risk averse atmosphere was something she could no longer tolerate at the FBI. She had wanted to serve her country in an organization that rewarded initiative. Kim had no idea how things would turn out going forward.

Tom Stone had advised everyone to go underground until further notice. Tom was the highest-ranking member of the Unit that was still alive. He had also gone underground. Things were made all the worse with the departure of Donald Patrick from the SSCI. The president-elect had been the Unit's greatest advocate, but now he was in the middle of a transition into the White House, constantly under attack by the media. Tony was the one who had held it all together. Without him.... Without him, there would be no Unit 81.

Amidst the chaos, Janusz was the only operative looking for answers. If there was anyone in the Unit who could save them, it was Janusz. She had offered to help, but he told her to keep a low profile until he gathered more clues. So, here she was, trying hard to stay calm amidst a storm of insanity that swept over her life.

She had played enough with her phone, TV, and bowl of cereal this morning. The only thing standing between her and a straitjacket was her exercise class. She got dressed in her favorite leggings and top. Kim grabbed the car keys off the kitchen counter before combing through her purse in search of the phone. Oh, yes, she had left the cell on the dining table.

She was about to close the door behind her when a wave of panic worked its way down her legs. She had forgotten the most essential part of her new routine. Kim walked to the bedroom and grabbed the .38 revolver out of the top shelf of her dresser. She would not leave the house without it these days. It was her last line of defense in case the worst came to pass. If she was going to be outgunned, then so be it. Kim was not going down without a fight, even if it meant firing off only six rounds before the bitter end.

◆ ◆ ◆

"Come on, just a two more minutes, you can do it," the instructor yelled.

Kim was drenched in sweat. Lactic acid filled every muscle. The sounds of her rapid breath drowned the blaring music from the speakers. Extreme spin was her favorite way to decompress. After a heart pounding sixty minutes, she was ready to cool down. Kim was surrounded by eleven others, all of them women, including the instructor. She grabbed the towel off the handlebar before immersing her face in it. As she wiped the perspiration off her skin, she was completely rejuvenated. From behind, someone sent Kim hurtling forward. Kim grabbed a stationary bike to break her fall.

"Watch where you're going?" Kim snapped.

She caught herself by surprise with the outburst.

"I'm sorry. I wasn't paying attention," the woman replied with a smile. She stood no more than a mere five feet two inches with auburn hair. Her brown eyes were full of arrogance, and her complexion was light. She wore a tight white top along with tight gray leggings. Kim had to admit she was thin and in great shape.

"That's the problem with everyone these days. Too self-absorbed to be mindful," Kim said.

Was a hidden ventriloquist giving expression to pent up frustration?

"I'm very sorry," the woman repeated.

Her classmates tried hard not to notice the unfolding scene. Kim nodded and went off toward the locker room. Fifteen minutes under steam, and she was off to shower. Under the reinvigorating frosty water, she took a moment to reflect. She should not have been so curt with her classmate. This gym was her only refuge from the stormy seas of her life. The last thing she needed was to become a pariah among her classmates.

Kim made a mental note to apologize to the woman as she put on her clothes. On her way out the locker room, she was momentarily incapacitated by fear. She raced back to the spin room, which was currently being cleaned. Kim found the bike without much effort. She checked under, over, and beside it. Kim also checked the water holder and side slots. No sign of it. Her keys could be anywhere. Between the lack of sleep and the shattered state of her nerves, Kim would misplace her own head if it was not attached to her body.

"Looking for these?" the voice asked.

"You found my keys. How can I ever thank you?" Kim said.

"I saw them on your bike after you left. I knew you'd be back for them soon enough."

"I was about to lose my shit. I didn't mean to—"

"It's okay. I understand. We all get frustrated every now and then."

"I'm sorry. I owe you an apology. It's been a—" Kim stopped herself before going further. She was talking way too much, but it was the only way to deal with her grief over Tony.

"It's been a rough morning. Can we start over?" Kim said.

"My name is Lesley. Nice to meet you," the woman said with an extended arm.

Kim shook her hand. "Nice to meet you, too. I've been attending this class most weeks for the past year. I don't recall ever seeing you here before."

"It's my first day. To tell you the truth, I wasn't sure if extreme spin was for me."

"You know what, there's cool little coffee shop on Church Street. How'd you like to join me for some caffeine?"

"I'd love it," Lesley said with a strange Cheshire grin.

Kim hated herself for being so judgmental.

11. MANHATTAN, NEW YORK CITY

December 06

Janet finished typing the last sentence in the article. At a little over a thousand words, it was the first installment in a series she had to write about Octavio Souza's contributions to America. It was the perfect immigrant story. A young man arrives in San Francisco with little more than pocket change. Several decades later, he is a billionaire dedicated to making his adopted country a better place for everyone. What could be more inspiring?

Someone called her from another room, but Janet reflexively blocked it out like she always did. She took a sip from the glass of wine before placing it on a coaster. She wouldn't dream of placing the wine glass on the bare surface of her eighteenth-century English burl walnut secretary desk. It was grandmother's favorite, appraised at over a hundred thousand dollars. The desk, just like the apartment on East 70th near Central Park, was left to Janet in her grandmother's will.

Grandma was strict, an old school disciplinarian with little patience for those who did not respect her wishes. When mother and father had refused to send Janet to private school, Grandma had threatened to cut them off from the family trust income. Grandma had paid the tuition for Janet's entire eight-year tenure at Dalton while cutting her parents out of the will.

It was at Dalton where Janet had made her most important friendships, connections that had helped her land the job with *Impressionable Magazine*. Unlike the backward swamps where most Americans were educated, Dalton taught its kids to be *woke* before anyone had really heard of the term, at least anyone who mattered. The school had a long tradition of progressive politics, which had over the years touched every institution in America. Dalton students were at the forefront of protests against the Vietnam War.

They had fought valiant battles against their conservative headmaster to usher in a new era in America where dressing down, taking drugs, and opposing American imperialism would become mainstream. Her own parents had been oblivious to the new politics sweeping the land. They were too immersed in their privileged professional lives to care about the plight of those less off.

Thanks to some friends who were now teaching at Dalton, Janet had learned a great deal about white privilege and implicit bias. She had learned about gender pronouns and the beauty of non-binary people. For thousands of years, closed-minded societies had brutally divided humanity into either males or females without regard to the countless masses who have no sex. It was the epitome of oppression. Most important of all, grandma's decision to send her to private school had educated Janet about diversity and inclusion. The racist slaveholders who had founded America were only interested in one thing, money. The price paid by those they exploited never entered their head.

Janet's open-minded instructors taught her another way to see the world. They taught her about the great wise men who had ushered in the age of wokeness. White privilege was an epiphany that came to the imminent Harvard scholar, Noel Ignatiev. Without him, American media and academia would still be ignorant of the horrors bestowed on the world by white people.

Critical Theory emerged from the founders of the Frankfurt School. They were immigrants from Germany who had arrived in America before the Second World War. Chief among this group were the giants of the New Left. They were some of the first men to plant the seed of doubt in academia about America's racist past.

Critical Theory taught a new generation of scholars that the failures of certain marginalized groups in America was not their fault. Those failures were not the result of lack of initiative or lack of effort but rather a failure of a system set up to persecute non-whites. Not only was the American system created to oppress them, but science itself was a tool to subjugate minorities. In reality, the Enlightenment and its reliance on rationality was a system of oppression. Likewise, mathematics, physics, chemistry, and worst of all, the English language, were at their core tools of white supremacy.

Noel Ignatiev and the wise Frankfurt School Germans understood American society had been established to take advantage of minorities and was, therefore, irredeemable. Their work on Critical Race Theory, White Privilege and Systemic Racism enabled Americans to see the evils of their ancestors. For centuries, Americans had believed that freedom of speech, protected by the outdated First Amendment, was a most cherished right that had to be protected at any cost. Myriad Supreme Court decisions, filed by plaintiffs from both the right and the left, always served to protect free speech. The troglodytes on the high court believed hate speech was protected speech. Thus America, alone among the great democracies, is the only country without laws banning hate speech.

Janet remembered fondly that day she had been assigned to read Herbert Marcuse's treatise on *Repressive Tolerance*. In it, the father of the New Left had brilliantly explained, "True pacification requires the withdrawal of tolerance before the deed, at the stage of communication in word, print, and picture. Such extreme suspension of the right of free speech and free assembly is indeed justified in our society."

It was fortunate that the ideas of Marcuse and the Frankfurt School were able to penetrate the top strata of American society. Now, the race was on to spread these eye-opening truths to the canaille. The ignorant mass of racists and fascists who still clung to their guns, God, and their flag needed to be educated. From behind, the door to her study creaked open.

"Sorry, miss. You said I clean the china. So, I clean, but one of them broke, miss."

Juanita's strident voice unraveled her focus. Her hands trembled as her blood boiled. If not for the wine, Janet would have lost her cool.

"Juanita. Oh, my God. How often have I told you to be careful when cleaning the china? That collection was a gift from my grandmother," Janet said raising her voice, "do you know how expensive that is? That set costs more than, well, more than you make in a year."

"I'm sorry, miss. I didn't mean it. I lost my balance on the ladder and fell. I hurt my hand. Look, miss," Juanita said, holding her hand out.

The side of her wrist had swollen to twice its size. Perhaps it would teach this petulant immigrant to be more careful.

"Why didn't you call, you clumsy oaf?"Janet said. The uneducated Mexican, or wherever she was from, probably had no idea what the word *oaf* meant.

"I did miss, I did call you. You no answer. I said, 'Miss Janet, please, come help.' I said five times, but you no answer."

That was probably the voice calling her name earlier. The voice she chose to ignore.

"I should call the police. Better yet, maybe I should call immigration, you know ICE?"

"Oh, no, miss. Please, no. I have a family, little kids. I'm so sorry, miss, I'm very sorry," Juanita said with tears rolling down her eyes.

"Don't cry, Juanita. It makes you look like a spoiled brat. You go home and think about what you did. I'm not going to pay you for today, so you learn your lesson. I'll call you soon for our next appointment, okay?"

"Thank you very much, miss. Thank you," Juanita said as she tried to kiss Janet's hand.

Janet pulled her hand away in horror. "There is no need for that, Juanita. Now, pull yourself together and grab your coat."

Juanita wiped her face, grabbed her purse and coat, and made her way to the foyer. Janet locked the door behind her and returned to the study. She opened the browser on her computer before navigating to her favorite search engine. Within seconds, she found the number to the local ICE field office in Manhattan. She picked up her cell phone and dialed the number.

12. ELLICOTT CITY, MARYLAND

December 07

"**M**a, you home?" Jake said.

He entered the vestibule before taking off his coat. He had come to visit his parents. Between parties and his new commitment to DC Antifa, there was rarely any opportunity for the forty-mile trek up to Ellicott City.

"Jake, is that you, honey?" Mother said as she walked over from the kitchen. "My dear boy, you finally remembered you had parents?"

"Oh, Ma, don't start that again. I've been busy."

"Doing what?"

"Busy studying and trying to find a job. I graduate next semester, you know?"

"Yes, your father and I know all about it. We're just wondering what you're going to do with a sociology degree."

"Don't worry so much. You'll get wrinkles."

"Too late for that. What's this?" Mother said, pointing to a large duffle bag Jake had dropped on the kitchen floor.

"Oh, that. That's my laundry. I thought you could take a load off my shoulders."

"You should be taking a load off *our* shoulders. Instead, you bring laundry? I work, too, you know?"

"I know, Ma, but you're a teacher. All you do is boss around a bunch of silly high school kids and grade their papers. I mean, how hard can that be?" Jake said.

"Boy, I oughta..." Mother said, slapping him behind the neck.

"I'm going up to my room. See ya."

Jake grabbed a huge chocolate chip cupcake from the fridge. Once inside his room, Jake closed the door and sat on his bed. After devouring the cupcake, he opened the front of his jacket and removed a stack of letters, placing them on the nightstand next to his bed. They were letters from the bank underwriting his loan. Almost four years at Georgetown and he had accumulated over a quarter million dollars in debt. Tuition alone was now approaching sixty thousand dollars a year.

If he decided to go to graduate school, the number would only balloon to something more grotesque. With a bit of luck, when all was said and done, he would only be in debt for half a million dollars. But he knew people who owed much greater sums. His father, an engineer at NASA, and his mother, a local schoolteacher, made good money, but they could not afford the high price of tuition at Georgetown.

They were spread too thin on their mortgage and car payments as well as school for Bobby. Jake's younger brother attended a private school which consumed the bulk of his parents' disposable income. Jake had been a good student in high school, but his scores were not high enough to earn a scholarship at Georgetown. Given the combined salary of his parents, he also did not qualify for financial aid. The only remaining option had been to borrow against his future from a bank. The US Government had made it all too easy for the universities to keep hiking tuition by guaranteeing all those outstanding loans. By one account, student debt in America now stood at over one and a half trillion dollars.

As Jake bounced a Nerf ball against the headboard of his bed, he resented the reality of being burdened with a mountain of debt. The sobering numbers had only served to solidify his support for politicians promising to forgive the monstrous amount of student debt burdening America's future. And what of that future? He had no interest to work for a militarist government his father had served so willingly. The private sector was no better. An assortment of greedy corporations would place him in an office cubicle for the next forty years in exchange for a measly salary that would barely pay his rent.

Jake had zero interest in entering the rat race like his parents. He wanted to travel, see the world, learn about new peoples and cultures. The corporate world offered none of that. There was only one semester left before graduation. The more he thought about it, the more pointless it all seemed. The ball fell off the bed. His eyes grew heavy and—

"Jake, get up dear. Your father is waiting at the dinner table."

Jake brought his hand up to wipe the saliva off his chin. "What time is it?"

"Half past six."

"I've been asleep for four hours?"

"You must've been tired. Splash some water on your face and come down. I know you don't want to miss a juicy steak."

"Thanks, Ma. On my way."

Jake trudged toward the bathroom before turning on the lights. His reflection in the mirror resembled a zombie. His hair was a complete mess like usual, and his clothes were disheveled. His nose was unremarkable, but he was damn proud of his manly chin. He wore contacts over his blue eyes. His goatee could use a trim. He was ready to ditch his boring piercings for the trendy disc earrings embedded inside the earlobe. They looked so cool, but Jake feared he would be attacked for cultural appropriation on campus. After all, didn't that trend start in Africa? He took a moment to clean up before joining his parents in the dining room.

"Well, look who it is. You must be studying extra hard these days if you can't stay awake," Father said.

"Let him enjoy his dinner, dear. It's not too often we get to have dinner as a family."

"Where's Bobby?" Jake said.

"Your brother's at band practice. He's staying at a friend's house tonight," Mother said.

"What a spread! Juicy filet mignon, fancy vegetables, asparagus, mashed potatoes. Wow, and Merlot imported from France. A table fit for a king. Too bad there are millions of people around the world, heck even in this country, who are starving."

"Now, don't start that bullshit again, Jake. Let's just try to enjoy our meal."

"Dear—" Mother said to his father.

"Don't excuse his behavior, he needs to learn some gratitude."

"Tell me, Dad, how much do you think a feast like this costs? I mean, what is the street value of this sumptuous meal?"

His father held his gaze before snapping at him, "what the fuck are they teaching at the university these days?"

"Calm down, dear."

"It's okay, Ma."

"I just want to know what kind of an education you get for over sixty thousand dollars a year nowadays?"

"What are you worried about? It's not like you're paying for it."

"That's not fair. I paid top dollar for you to go to a fancy private high school for four years. I'm trying to do the same for your brother, although I don't know why anymore," Father said.

"No one asked you to."

"If it wasn't for that private school, you wouldn't have even made it to community college."

"Good, but I probably would've been happier."

"Let's change the subject," Mother said.

"Dad, how much does a house like this cost?" Jake said, pointing toward the walls and ceiling. "Not how much you guys paid for it, but how much does it cost now?"

His father's jaw moved rapidly as he placed greater pressure on the knife to cut his stake. Jake's father held the steak tipped fork in midair, examined it for a second, and said, "probably around a million."

"A million dollars?"

"Roughly, in that neighborhood. Why, you wanna buy it from us?"

"You see, that's exactly my point. Who the hell can afford to buy a house coming out of college? My generation is hundreds of thousands of dollars in debt from the start," Jake said.

"Is that my fault? If you'd studied harder, you could've gotten a scholarship. Perhaps if you worked instead of partying you could pay your own tuition," Father said.

"In other countries, tuition is paid for by the government. A college education should be free."

"Here we go again with the leftist propaganda."

"It's not propaganda. How much do you think they're going to pay me when I graduate? Do you really think I'll be able to afford a house at these prices?"

"Hey, I didn't tell you to get a degree in sociology. We talked about this for hours. I said over and over again you should get a degree in electrical engineering or computer science. You have no useful skills for the modern economy."

Jake stood up and slammed his fork down. "I-I-I have no interest in participating in the modern economy. I-I-I have no interest in buying a million-dollar home in your bourgeois community. Most of all, I have no interest in supporting an oppressive economic system. There are better alternatives."

"What does that mean?" Father said.

"It-t-t means what it means. Ma, is my laundry done?"

"Yes, dear. I folded everything and placed it in your bag."

"G-g-great. I'm going back to Georgetown."

"But you haven't finished your dinner."

"Let him go. He's a loser," Father said.

"I'm not interested in your bourgeois food. I--I'll grab some pizza in Georgetown," Jake said as he walked toward the laundry room. Destruction was right. The only alternative for the future was the world Antifa wanted to build.

13. BAKUNIN FARM, BELTSVILLE MARYLAND

December 09

"**C**ome on people, keep pushing. We're not done yet," Destruction said as he let out a gas bubble that had been bothering him all morning.

Each pair, one man and one woman, pushed the heavy tires over and over again through the spacious converted barn. There were twelve of them in this class, including Jake, who had made a formal commitment to the cause. Despite the moderate temperature outside, heating fans in the barn had been turned up to heighten the intensity of the experience.

"You may think it's safe to give up in here, but out there giving up could make the difference between life and death when fighting against the capitalist pigs," Destruction barked at the group.

They had been in the barn for five hours straight, without breakfast. Each man and woman was thoroughly drenched in sweat from head to toe. They were being worked to complete exhaustion, but that was necessary to attain the desired level of dedication. From the tire lifts, it was on to another obstacle course. After that, it was on to hand-to-hand combat drills. At this point, they were ready to collapse on each other. On to the listening comprehension part of the exercise. He had them all lined up in rows as he stood in front of the group.

"Can we get something to eat or drink?" Fiona said.

"You're welcome to leave whenever you like," Destruction replied before pausing for effect, "but you'll remain the same lost soul in search of meaning. Antifa gives your life purpose. It provides the kind of fulfillment you'll never get from the consumerist culture of America the exploiter. All I ask in return is your complete dedication. Ya think that's too much?"

"Absolutely not," came the roaring reply form Jake, who took the initiative to answer for his partner.

"That's what I want to hear. Some of you are about to be reborn. By that, I mean you'll no longer be referred to by the names your parents gave you, the names our pig-infested capitalist society uses to control you," Destruction said.

The group was mesmerized as they tried to replenish their strength from the words that emanated from Destruction's parted lips. It was a true and tested method perfected over hundreds of years. Hunger and sleep deprivation had a counter intuitive effect. By keeping them tired and disoriented, they were deprived of wayward thoughts that might challenge the group's orthodoxy. They would then come to accept his teachings more passionately.

"I've been asked why I'm called Destruction. My birth name was Sean Sutherland. DC Antifa has given new meaning to my life. I was reborn with a destiny to destroy America the exploiter. Thus, I became Destruction. Those of you assigned a new name will acquire an identity with meaning."

His trusted assistant stood beside him in front of the group. "My story is slightly different. I injured an off-duty police officer as he stood in line to buy a sandwich late one night after his shift. I knocked him out using brass knuckles from behind and ran away. With the benefit of black bloc fatigues, surveillance cameras were of no use to the police. I did the same thing to three other officers before they all stopped going to fast food restaurants late at night. You could say I was hazardous to the health of those protecting the capitalist system. Thus, Destruction named me Hazard."

The group sat motionless. It was hard to tell if they were impressed, or just plain hungry.

"You, in the front, with the sweaty shirt and the clenched

jaw," Destruction said, pointing to Jake. "In you, I see anger. The fury that churns inside you is from the emptiness that surrounds us. You're going to be reborn as Rage."

The man formerly known as Jake unclenched his jaw while relaxing his fist. A wave of contentment seemed to wash over his entire body with his new identity.

"Ya may be asking what we're doing out here in the hinterlands of the decrepit state of Maryland. A generous donation from one of our benefactors paid for this farm. It's named in honor of the great Russian anarchist, Michael Bakunin," Destruction said.

Stomachs growled as he spoke to prolong their food deprivation. Destruction placed a hand in his pants pocket. With his thumb, he pushed a button on the remote that turned the heat in the barn even higher.

"This facility is great because it allows us to practice with firearms on the outdoor range, which is exactly what we're going to do once we eat. Ya may be wondering why Antifa even needs guns. After all, weapons of war were invented by the racist capitalist exploiters. To you I say, it's not going to stop until we stop it with our own guns. Let me remind you of the actions of a great hero. John Brown understood speeches, petitions, and protests were never enough against the enemy. He knew violence was necessary to defeat the racist exploiters that govern this country. That's why he risked his life to attack the federal armory in Harper's Ferry West Virginia. An act of bravery for which he was subsequently tried and executed. Take a look around you—" *buurp*, "you're all John Brown's children," Destruction said.

He wondered if the group had noticed his nervous burp. Most of these volunteers were not going to survive the attack on the White House. It didn't matter. Destruction wasn't going to help Octavio write a constitution for a new government. The entire story was a ruse to get the old man's money. What mattered was the influx of new recruits following the offensive. That meant only one thing. More women.

Hazard straddled beside Destruction. "We're not the first group of anarchists to take up arms, but we'll be the best at it. All across this country, there are numerous John Brown Brigades and gun clubs. Our brave brothers and sisters in the Redneck Revolt militia groups have been spreading firearms knowledge among anti-fascists from Kansas City to Seattle. Don't let media disinformation fool you. Antifa is well-armed and trained to fight against the capitalist enemy."

"Are we far out enough?" Rage said.

"Far out enough for what?" Hazard replied.

"For shooting outdoors. We're only about five miles north of the beltway. A stray bullet may enter someone's property or hit a passing car," Rage said.

"Destruction took special care when choosing this property. As you probably noticed on the way in, we're surrounded by woods and quiet a distance from the nearest road. But that's not the main reason we're here. It has to do with our upcoming mission to change history," Hazard said.

Hazard positioned himself to face north before pointing. "If you drive straight down Powder Mill Road, past the parkway, you'll arrive at the James Rowley Training Center for the United States Secret Service."

They all straightened their backs, focusing more intently.

"Now that I have your full attention, you'll be happy to know that we're not just here for the fresh air and the fancy shooting range. Across the street from the Secret Service is the Beltsville Agricultural Research Center, part of the US Department of Agriculture. We have contacts with access to this facility. We've placed hidden cameras along the tree line to monitor the comings and goings of the Secret Service," Hazard said.

"How's that going to help us?" Rage said.

"We have sources in the Department of Motor Vehicles in Maryland, Virginia, and the District of Columbia. Footage from the vehicle plates will be sufficient to dig up names and addresses of those working there. We can match those against a classified organization chart to see if anyone we are interested in comes through," Hazard said.

"What then?" Rage asked.

"As much as I hate the intelligence services, I'll borrow one of their phrases. Need to know. None of you has a need to know at the moment. If you're chosen for the mission, you'll be briefed on your part and your part only," Hazard said before pausing to read the room. "Let's break for lunch. Eat quickly and make your way to the shooting range."

Outside the air was crisp and the sun bright. Destruction observed as several of them proceeded to collapse and vomit from exhaustion. Rage immediately ran to assist his teammate. Fiona dry heaved. There was not much to throw up.

"Let her be, she's not a baby. She'll be fine in a few minutes," Destruction yelled.

"It's heat exhaustion. She needs help," Rage replied.

"Nothing we haven't seen before. Part of the exercise to toughen you up."

Rage ignored him and continued to hold Fiona's head as she took deep breaths to calm herself.

"I said leave her be and walk—"

Rage rose to his feet and grabbed Destruction by the collar before pushing him back against the barn. "li-li-li-listen, you sick fuck—"

"What you gonna do, Georgetown boy? Ask Mommy to sue me?"

Rage punched Destruction in the face before pushing him to the ground. What came next was a surprise to the young recruit. Destruction kicked him in the groin. Rage slumped forward and fell to the side. A metal pipe rested against the barn several feet to the right. Destruction grabbed the weapon, raising it in the air. Rage's kneecap looked mighty tempting. Destruction tightened his grip in preparation for a devastating blow. Just then, his arm no longer moved. Something pulled against the metal rod.

Destruction twirled toward the obstruction. It was one of

the other recruits. Another burly young volunteer from the Army. An image of Lutz popped in his skull. These military shits were out of control. He could see nothing but red now. Destruction reached under his shirt and removed a Glock 19 from his waist. Everyone was attentive as if still in the classroom. This was no longer an academic exercise. A life lesson had to be imparted.

Pow...pow...pow...pow.

Destruction pulled the trigger again and again. Each bullet hit its mark on the young recruit's chest. Jaws dropped open all around. The army boy fell backward toward the earth. Destruction calmy walked over to stand over the writhing man's body. *Pow.* Destruction fired one more round into the man's head. As the blood dripped down the side of his face and onto the ground, Destruction turned to Rage once more, "Grab the keys to one óf the trucks and help Hazard get rid of this body."

Destruction immediately focused his attention on the other recruits.

"The rest of you have a choice to make. You can devote yourselves wholeheartedly to the cause or end up like him," Destruction said, pointing to the corpse.

No one dared move a muscle. Destruction proceeded to order everyone to eat lunch before turning to Fiona. He grabbed both her arms, pulling her off the ground. The color had not yet returned to her face. He was certain this exhibition of resolve would only magnify his stature in her eyes.

"How you doing?" Destruction said.

"I'll be all right," Fiona replied in a daze.

"Good. Come by the recreation room tonight around seven. I want you to meet a few of the other women."

Fiona was ready for the next phase.

14. ROCK CREEK PARK, WASHINGTON D.C.

December 09

Kalugin placed a nervous hand in his pants pocket. Before long, he removed another cigarette, lighting up his second smoke in the past ten minutes. The Russian paced impatiently back and forth as if he was a caged Siberian tiger. Janusz observed him from the parking lot on the other side of Tilden Street. Every operational meeting Janusz remembered, the Russians always arrived late.

Since he was not here to recruit, and was furious about the attacks against Unit 81, Janusz decided to return the favor. He was going to be exactly fifteen minutes late, which was quite generous considering that he had once waited over an hour to meet with a Russian. When he was satisfied, Janusz locked the door to his vehicle before crossing Tilden Street. When Janusz reached the other side, indignation was plastered all over Kalugin's face.

"You're late."

"Sorry, there was a lot of traffic on Connecticut Avenue."

"Khow about leaving earlier?"

"Fifteen minutes. You can't be upset about that?"

"Life and death decisions are made faster than that out in the field."

"Irascibility is a completely Pavlovian reaction to this unfortunate situation. May I suggest a daily routine of meditation to calm your nerves," Janusz said, waiting for the Russian's face to explode. Kalugin clenched his jaw and smiled.

He was not going to give Janusz the satisfaction of getting under his skin.

"Let's take a walk," Kalugin said, pointing toward the trails next to the old Stone Mill. "What do you khave for me, you said it was important."

"Indeed, I've talked to my contacts in the Agency. Several individuals with intimate knowledge of the Eurasia Mission Center, and—" Janusz said before falling silent.

"And...and...what did they say?" Kalugin was anxious.

Janusz was more confident now.

"It was not us. The United States is definitely not behind the assassination of General Kalantari."

"Khow can you be so sure? Perhaps it was another agency in your intelligence community? Maybe the DIA, or a branch of the military? What about a special forces unit from your SOCOM?"

"One of my sources is a Russian affairs country director on the National Security Council. Something like this would surely be discussed at an NSC meeting."

"Khow do you know your source had the proper access? The discussions may khave been confined to a compartmented program."

"The same can be said for you. How do you know President Putin did not order a clandestine group in Russia to dispose of the Iranian General? We don't know what we don't know, we must base our judgments on what is most probable."

"I suppose you're right."

"Notice I said our government was not responsible. I'm not ruling out the possibility a secretive unit or a criminal organization in America was involved."

"What, you mean like the old Blackwater?"

"Something like that. Maybe some rich American paid a group of mercenaries," Janusz said.

He was searching for a change in Kalugin's demeanor and facial expressions. It was similar to walking a tight rope. Not wanting to reveal the existence of Unit 81, while also fishing to see what the Russian knew about it.

"I need to do more research. If you start paying me, I can gather some data by spreading money around."

"We'll discuss that later. For now, I khave another job before we decide whether to take you."

"I'm all ears."

"I need you to accompany two guys."

"To do what?"

"The two guys will tell you all you need to know," Kalugin said.

It was not a good sign. Janusz wanted to avoid a blind assignment for the Russians at all costs. But he was in no position to turn it down. In order to get to the bottom of who was targeting the Unit, he had to get in deeper with Kalugin.

"Where should I go?"

"I'll text you the information shortly," Kalugin said.

They walked back toward the mill in silence.

"Here, have a drink. It'll cheer you up," Sasha said to his comrade.

Janusz sat in the back seat of a Cadillac Escalade with tinted windows. The cigars being smoked by the thick necked Russians in the front seat were getting on his nerves.

"Do you wanna tell me what the fuck we're doing here?" Janusz said.

"Patience, dear friend. Patience," Sasha said.

Dimitry, the driver, quietly puffed out several smoke rings. He eagerly cranked up the catchy Russian pop music. On Massachusetts Avenue, near Dupont Circle, they waited next to an ornate stone building as the traffic passed by. These men were certainly not with the GRU. They wore expensive suits and had a slight New York flavor to their Russian accent. He had noticed their New York plates before entering the

Escalade.

"You two come to DC often?" Janusz said.

The front row was silent. Every passing minute convinced Janusz more and more that his new companions were part of the Russian mob in New York. Minutes later, a tall red-haired man emerged from the building they were observing. Red walked down a few steps toward a private driveway. The twinkling lights of the cell phone danced on Red's face as he stood on the stairs.

"There he is," Dimitry said as he put the car in gear and charged full throttle toward the front door of the building they were surveilling.

Red was still alone as the Escalade pulled in front of him. The front passenger window came down.

"You're not my ride," Red said with a thick Russian accent.

"Get in!"

"Why?"

"Get in!"

Sasha pointed a gun at Red's face as Janusz opened the back door. Red entered after contemplating his options. He took a seat next to Janusz as the Escalade catapulted toward Dupont Circle. With little traffic on Massachusetts Avenue, they drove past American University in no time. The homes here were among the most stately and expensive in all of DC. The Escalade whizzed through several residential streets as it finely pulled into the driveway of a brick mansion. What the hell were they doing here, and who was the man next to him?

"Let's go, everybody out," Dimitry said as he opened his door.

The rest of the group followed his lead up the stairs toward the front entrance. Janusz was the last man in the procession. To his surprise, Red did not protest much, seemingly resigned to his fate at this point. The front doors opened, and they entered a marble foyer with a double winding staircase leading to the floor above. Through the foyer was a main room with an exquisite Fazioli grand piano. Ornate columns topped with gold, Louis XIV furniture and still life oil painting surrounded them. This house was meticulously decorated to fit Russian tastes.

"Take a seat, Gennady," Dimitry said to the captive.

Gennady looked at the other two before staring at Janusz. He then took a seat on the small piano bench. Dimitry stepped forward. Janusz noticed he held a small sports bag in his hand. He flung the bag beside Gennady's feet.

"Go ahead, open it," Sasha said.

They had switched to Russian now, likely assuming Janusz would not understand. Gennady unzipped the bag and gazed at its content. It was full of cash. Crisp one-hundred-dollar bills wrapped by rubber bands into thick bricks.

"That's yours. Take it and go back home, or if you prefer you can go to Europe. Whatever you do, leave the US immediately," Dimitry said.

Janusz had no idea what was going on, but he was praying that Gennady would take the money and agree to their terms. These men would not react well to disappointment.

"I don't need money," Gennady replied.

Fuck, this guy wants to die. Janusz walked toward the stairs to do some research on his cell phone. From the tidbits of information in the conversation, where they had picked up Gennady, and several other clues, he was able to piece it all together. Gennady was a dissident who had fallen out of favor with the Kremlin. At one point, he had been a close advisor to Putin. Gennady had lost a hefty sum in a business transaction from which the Russian president had emerged unscathed as usual.

Gennady was getting revenge by airing Moscow's dirty laundry in the West. The *Siloviki* security men would have none of that. Not wanting to get their hands dirty, they had hired the Russian mob to get rid of the problem. Janusz walked back to find the two mobsters standing over Gennady. The Russian dissident was rubbing his own cheeks. It was not a good sign.

"What is this?" Janusz said.

"Gennady has something to tell you," Dimitry said, switching to English.

Turning to Gennady, Janusz said as calmly as possible, "what's the problem?"

The dissident remained silent.

"I guess he does not like you either," Dimitry said, laughing.

"What's happening here?" Janusz said.

"We need a promise from this man to do something. He's not willing to give it. We must change tactics," Dimitry said.

Why had Kalugin gotten him mixed up in this? Suddenly Dimitry used his left leg to deliver swift kick to the side of Gennady's face. The dissident was thrown to the ground. Dimitry then picked Gennady up by the collar and slapped him across the face.

"Are you going to leave, or do we have to hurt you?" Dimitry asked in Russian.

"Perhaps I should try," Janusz said.

"Be my guest," Dimitry said.

"Why don't you make it easy on yourself and take the money," Janusz said.

He was sympathetic to Gennady, but the goons from New York would not take well to disappointment. Gennady then spit into to Janusz's face. The warm saliva trickled down his nose as the Russian mobsters laughed. Janusz stood straight to wipe himself as Dimitry pulled out a Heckler & Koch VP9 semi-automatic pistol out of his coat pocket and pointed it at Gennady. He was certain the Russian would pull the trigger.

Without thinking through the implication of his actions, Janusz delivered a roundhouse kick that jolted the VP9 out of Dimitry's hand. Sasha was startled but swiftly moved to open his own jacket. Janusz lunged and tackled him to a grand chaise. Just then, Gennady made a run for it. Dimitry ran after him. It gave Janusz better odds to deal with the problem at hand. They wrestled onto the floor as Sasha grabbed Janusz's throat with his meaty hooks. The massive fingers dug into

Janusz's flesh with the intention of removing his larynx.

Janusz used his left arm to block the Russian's powerful hold while he used his right to grab a key from his pants pocket. Sasha foamed like a rabid animal, screaming obscenities and promises of death. He did not notice the weaponized key Janusz had maneuvered to the side of his face. It was a costly mistake. Janusz jabbed the key straight into the Russian's left eye. His screams must have reached his masters in New York, if not in Moscow.

The gargantuan mobster leapt to his feet in agony. He was dripping blood all over the fancy furniture. Sasha stumbled back a few steps as Janusz grabbed an expensive vase from a side table, smashing it against his head. The man plodded a few more steps before collapsing to the floor. Janusz turned him over, putting his column sized neck in a chokehold. He squeezed with all his might until Sasha was completely limb.

There was no explanation for killing one of these men that would satisfy Kalugin. He had to go two for two. The sound of a struggle emanated from a nearby room. *Where the fuck is the gun?* Janusz searched high and low for the weapon he had kicked out of Dimitry's hand. Perhaps the fucker had found it himself. If he waited any longer, Gennady would be dead. Janusz ran toward the noise and tripped, falling flat on his face against the marble. Beside his foot he saw the obstruction. It was Dimitry's pistol. He grabbed it as he pushed himself off the floor.

Through a hallway, he made it into the kitchen. A metallic pan flew across the room almost hitting Janusz on the arm. Dimitry was chasing Gennady with a long kitchen knife as the Russian dissident ran around a marble topped island for his life. Janusz raised his weapon and walked straight in. Gennady and Dimitry stared daggers at him.

"What the fuck are you going to do with that thing?" Dimitry said.

Janusz said nothing as he tried to pull the trigger without success.

"Huh, looks like it's not your night," Dimitry taunted before charging at Janusz with the raised knife.

Dimitry screamed at the top of his lungs and Janusz had to act swiftly. As the Russian closed the distance, Janusz ducked to grab him below the waist. He proceeded to lift the Dimitry into the air, flipping him over on his back onto the floor. The kitchen knife flew into the air. Gennady ran after it. As Dimitry struggled to catch his breath, Janusz wondered if Dimitry' pistol had a round in the chamber. Janusz swiftly racked the slide.

"Let's see if this does the trick," Janusz said.

Janusz pointed the VP9 straight at Dimitry's chest. The mobster had an idiotic expression plastered on his face as he waited for his fate...*pow...pow...*

"Just as I thought, you're an idiot," Janusz said.

The aftermath of two shots swiftly determined the outcome. While blood trickled out of Dimitry, Gennady stood motionless with the knife in his hand.

"What are you going to do with me?" Gennady asked.

"I was trying to help you earlier," Janusz said in Russian. "I just saved your life, so you owe me. Take the money in the other room and disappear for a while. I need to figure out who is behind all this. I can only do that if you're out of the picture. Can you do that for me?"

Gennady nodded in agreement.

"There were several cars in the driveway when we pulled in. Find the keys and leave with the bag of money. Consider it compensation from the Russian Government," Janusz said.

The place was a mess. Janusz had no choice but to clean up and collect the bodies. He knew exactly where to take them.

15. BAKUNIN FARM, BELTSVILLE MARYLAND

December 09

T hey had all changed from their work clothes into casual attire. Dressed in jeans and T-shirts, they drank wine to relax. The ten individuals gathered here tonight were the top women in DC Antifa. They were the cream of the crop, the most loyal and dedicated to the cause. Destruction had even given them a Latin name, Mulieres in Servitium, MIS for short. Most importantly, Lesley was considered the leader of this little coven. She had earned her stripes through dedication and, of course, enduring pain.

The women in DC Antifa and its inner sanctum, MIS, had been recruited personally by Lesley either through Georgetown or through her network of friends. She had taken to this calling through *his* vision. From the first night she met him at a gathering of anarchists, she had fallen in love. Destruction was bigger than life. He was the first man to transcend human limitations and become fully evolved.

Like Nietzsche had so eloquently put it in *Thus Spoke Zarathustra,* Destruction was the world's first true *Ubermensch* or Superman. Lesley was a feminist through and through, but she did not see Destruction as a man. He was the key to an era where America would transition to anarchy. DC Antifa was going to save the world.

Lesley walked over to make sure that Dr. Johnson did not partake in the drinking. Allison Johnson had been Lesley's gynecologist. Her idealism and proclivity toward progressive issues had made her a perfect candidate for the group. Dr. Johnson was exempt from many of MIS's requirements given the important nature of the service she provided.

"Is everything ready, Doctor?" Lesley said.

"Yes, all we need is the new recruit."

"She'll be along shortly."

"Is she aware of our requirements?"

"No, she just passed the physical and mental stamina trials. Don't worry, she'll be ready."

As Lesley finished her sentence, she spotted her latest prospect coming through the door of the recreation room. Fiona had colored her hair purple this evening. She wore her signature dark lipstick along with a nose piercing. Come to think of it, she was the perfect candidate for the procedure.

"Fiona, glad you made it."

"Hi, Professor."

"Call me Lesley. We don't retain lofty titles here."

"Of course, Lesley. Where's Destruction?"

"He'll join us later. For now, I want you to meet and mingle with the top women of DC Antifa."

Lesley walked around the room with Fiona, introducing her to the other women of MIS before asking them all to be seated. Two rows of upholstered gray sofas faced each other. In between the rows, Lesley took center stage.

"DC Antifa is the most important chapter, not just in the US, but also the world. I say that not because we are based in Washington or because we have the most dedicated people. No, our group will lead this country to a new world order because of *his* leadership. Sean Sutherland, aka Destruction, is not just our leader. He is also our master," Lesley said as the other women clapped and cheered.

Lesley took a moment to pick up her glass of wine from a nearby tray, taking a sip before continuing, "We make this bold statement because Destruction has given meaning to our lives. This is not just a revolutionary movement. It is a self-empowerment group. All of us in this room are better off for being entrusted with the responsibility of ushering Destruction's vision into reality. Tonight, we celebrate by inducting a new sister into our inner circle."

Lesley turned toward Fiona, "Make sure to drink plenty of wine. As a matter of fact, you should be working on your third glass by now."

Fiona looked at her before grabbing a glass of wine. She quickly swallowed the fermented grape juice and asked one of the women to fill her up once more. Lesley nodded approvingly before continuing to ramble on for another twenty minutes in this manner. The whole point was to make sure the group, including Fiona, was drunk enough for what came next.

Dr. Johnson moved through the group to pass out the surgical face masks. She came to the center of the room to provide one to Lesley before giving one to the purple haired recruit. All the women donned their masks with enthusiasm, all that is, except Fiona.

"Fiona dear, put the mask over your face," Lesley said.

"But why?"

"You'll find out in a second."

Lesley motioned for her coven to move toward the back of the room where a surgical table had been placed. Above the table was a round ceiling mounted surgical light. A four wheeled metal instrument table and several accompanying carts sat on either side of the surgical table. On top of one of the carts was a panel with a variety of metal instruments.

"Dr. Johnson, please do us the honor," Lesley said.

"What's all this?" Fiona said while giggling.

Her reaction indicated the wine was doing its job.

"This is all for you. Go ahead and lie down on top of the table," Lesley said, pointing her finger.

"Sure," Fiona said as she handed her glass to Lesley.

Before she had a chance to jump on the table, Fiona was stopped by Dr. Johnson. "Not like that. Please, remove all your clothes."

"Are you kidding?"

"Listen to what she says, dear. Please disrobe," Lesley said.

"Here? In front of all of you?" Fiona replied.

"What's the matter? Are you shy? A prudish Catholic girl perhaps?" one of the women said.

With the challenge laid down, Fiona proceeded to take off all her clothes. Off came her boots, then her sweater, followed by her jeans, and finally her panties. When she was stark naked, Dr. Johnson looked her over.

"Good, you're shaved. Lie down," Dr. Johnson said.

Everyone in the room knew what Fiona was going to go through as they had all dealt with it themselves, including Dr. Johnson. Poor Dr. Johnson. She was the only one who had the procedure performed by a non-specialist. Lesley shook her head as she remembered the night of Dr. Johnson's initiation. The procedure had been done by none other than Lesley herself. She still remembered the overpowering stench.

"Wow, these lights are so bright. Can you dim them just a bit?" Fiona said, half-drunk.

"Of course not. We wouldn't want Dr. Johnson to make a mistake, would we?" Lesley replied.

"What are the straps for?"

"We won't be using those," Lesley said.

As soon as the words exited her lips, the group descended upon Fiona. Two women grabbed each of her arms and legs while Dr. Johnson maneuvered into position. Fiona's arms were held down above her head. The last woman walked over to the end of the table with a camera in her hand. She was going to tape the entire procedure for *him*.

"Go ahead and spread her legs," the woman with the camera said as the others complied.

"Let go of me, what are you doing? Let go of me!" Fiona cried out.

Lesley laughed on the inside as she remembered those exact words uttered by some of the other women around the table when it was their turn. As for herself, Lesley had uttered every four-letter expletive she could think of in the English language.

"Okay, girls, here we go. Hold her tight," Dr. Johnson said as the others tightened their grip over Fiona's limbs.

Lesley was the closest to Fiona's head. She leaned to whisper in her ear, "Try to enjoy the experience dear. This is an honor you should celebrate for the rest of your life."

Fiona's skin was turning red under the pressure of being squeezed. Dr. Johnson held the cauterizing pen at arm's length near Fiona's torso. The needle tip glowed red from the heat. Dr. Johnson placed her left hand over Fiona's upper thigh as she moved the scalding pen in her right hand over the delicate skin of Fiona's shaved mons veneris. Before Lesley had an opportunity to blink, Dr. Johnson had finished carving the first S.

"*Aaaaaaaahhhhhhhhhh*, please, stop. God, please, make it stop," Fiona cried out.

"God? I didn't know you're the religious type," one of the women mocked as the group burst out laughing.

"This is not the place for jokes," Dr. Johnson immediately chided, "unless you want my hand to slip."

The girls stopped laughing as they used their weight to hold down the flailing recruit on the table. The nauseating whiff of searing flesh grabbed hold of their olfactory neurons before overpowering their senses. This was always a problem during this portion of the procedure. Despite the best efforts of Dr. Johnson, they could never block the powerful odor of burning flesh. There was only so much the masks could do for them.

Lesley recalled how nothing in the world compared to the fire that tore the delicate skin of her own pubic mound. The sensation of her flesh singed open, second by second, was a nightmare that wouldn't end. Fiona continued to wiggle under the combined strength of eight women. It was as if she was possessed by an alien force. At one point her right leg broke free causing Dr. Johnson to stop in anger. The girls responsible for that limb immediately reasserted their control. Since they were all a bit tipsy, they could not stop giggling like schoolgirls.

"*Eeeeehhhhhhhh, Ooooohhhhhhh, Aaaaarrrrrrhhhh,* the pain. God, the pain. I can't stand the pain," Fiona continued to cry.

"It's almost over, darling. Just hold on," Lesley said.

Dr. Johnson stepped away from the table. Beads of sweat covered her hair and neck. "There, we're done. That wasn't too bad, was it?"

Lesley cast her eyes on Fiona's mons pubis. A wave of joy washed over her body from head to toe. Two raw marks in the shape of SS were clearly visible. The wound was so fresh it oozed blood. Dr. Johnson moved in to clean the area with an antiseptic infused gauze. Fiona was still. She had almost passed out from the pain. A stream of tears ran down her face, a stream Lesley dried off with Kleenex. Fiona was dazed but coherent.

"Welcome to *Mulieres in Servitium* or MIS, dear sister," Lesley cried enthusiastically.

"What does it mean?" Fiona said in a weak voice.

"It's Latin. It means women in service. It's a double entendre for both women in service to Antifa and to our wonderful leader, Destruction. Since its pronounced *miss*, it also refers to women in general. We're the top layer of the women of DC Antifa. We take our orders directly from Destruction and convey them to the rest of the troop, the female members, that is. Every woman in DC Antifa wants to be a member of MIS, but only a chosen few earn that honor. You should consider yourself lucky," Lesley said.

"What did you do to me?"

"We branded you. That's why it hurt so much. You'll see for yourself soon enough."

"Branded... You branded me?" Fiona said.

Her voice was weak now. Dr. Johnson injected her with a sedative immediately *after* the operation. The point was to make sure she remembered her initiation into MIS for the rest of her life. It also helped to bond Fiona to the other women standing around her as they all shared her pain, thus increasing their loyalty to one another.

"Yes, we branded you with the initials SS, which stand for Sean Sutherland. That's Destruction's birth name. More than two letters would be too painful, while a D for Destruction would look weird. So, we all get the SS instead," Lesley explained.

"All right, everyone, let's cart her off to recover. She needs sleep to heal," Dr. Johnson said as one of the other women pushed Fiona's cart to a cordoned off area of the room.

With that out of the way, it was on to the formal MIS meeting. Destruction would be down any second.

They sat around him in a circle on the floor of the recreation room. Each woman enthralled by his presence. He wasn't the tallest man in the world, nor the most handsome, but he had an unmistakable aura that exuded confidence.

"Ladies, you know what to do," Lesley said.

All ten women in the room immediately disrobed. They sat back down on the floor in their birthday suits, ready to absorb every word from the master.

"Each and every one of you has the power to change the world within you. My job is to release that power using my unique and unparalleled genius to guide you. Every day that you're a part of DC Antifa you become empowered. In order to keep negative thoughts from sapping your strength, we'll begin this evening's confession session," Destruction said.

He scanned the room, making eye contact with his targets.

"Let's start with you," Destruction said, pointing at Dr. Johnson.

The physician looked to her left, then to her right, seeking encouragement from her MIS sisters. They each nodded approvingly, including Lesley. This was a difficult journey. You had to bare your most private thoughts as well as your most embarrassing transgressions to the master in order to unburden your soul to achieve its full potential.

"*Ahem.*" Dr. Johnson cleared her throat, "This is not easy for me to admit. There's a man in my office building. He comes to the local diner every day for lunch. He's very tall, perhaps six feet four inches, with dark hair and broad shoulders. He wears the classiest suits, cut perfectly to fit his body. He has the most amazing eyes and most beautiful smile. I guess what I'm trying to say is that I'm attracted to him. I've also tried to grab his attention by flirting."

The group gasped in unison at the admission by Dr. Johnson.

"He took the bait and came over. At first, I was very aloof, but soon enough we exchanged phone numbers. We had dinner once but that was it—"

"Enough," Destruction blurted out. "What does this well-dressed man do?"

"He's a financial planner."

"It's not enough that you embarrass yourself by cavorting about in this manner. To top it off, you do this with a man in charge of enriching people who don't need more money. This man represents everything wrong with the capitalist system."

"I didn't mean to. It just sort of happened without much thought. I stopped responding to his texts after that first dinner. I swear!"

"Did you ever relieve your tension for him in any way?"

Dr. Johnson froze. Her chin quivered but she was not able to speak.

"For Christ's sake, it's not a difficult question. Did you ever masturbate thinking about him?" Destruction shouted emphatically.

Dr. Johnson's entire body shivered, "Yes! But I starved myself for a day and donated an entire month's salary to our organization."

"That's not good enough. You set a bad example for DC Antifa and for yourself. You know what that means," Destruction said with furrowed brows.

Everyone in the circle knew exactly what that meant.

"Lesley, get the paddle. One of you get me a pitcher of water."

When everything was gathered, they all gawked. Destruction poured water over Dr. Johnson's bare butt cheeks. He handed the paddle over to Lesley.

"Okay, bend over," Lesley said before smacking Dr. Johnson on the butt with all her might.

"What do we say?"

"Forgive me, Master, for I am weak."

Lesley smacked her once more.

"What do we say?"

"Forgive me, Master, for I am weak."

It went on this way for a good five minutes. Both of Dr. Johnson's butt cheeks were completely red. She would not be able to sit comfortably for a few days. That was precisely the point. After the confession and punishment session was over, Dr. Johnson was sent away. Destruction walked over to choose three girls for the next step of the ritual. He always chose three girls but alternated between them. Tonight, it was Lesley and two others. What an honor it was to participate in this ritual where the women could purify their souls with his essence. His seed was the gateway to the future. Once a week those fortunate enough were called into a foursome with Destruction.

As the anointed women pressed their naked bodies against his, an unpleasant thought emerged from his cerebral cortex. He needed Rage for the next assignment.

16. ROCK CREEK PARK, WASHINGTON D.C.

December 10

J anusz walked down the gravel path, staring straight ahead deep in thought. This could turn into a huge cluster fuck, if he wasn't careful. As long as he remained calm, there was no reason for Kalugin to doubt his version of events. He wasn't even worried about the Russians at this point.

If the SVR and the GRU were after Unit 81, they would have done things differently. They would not have sent him out with a couple of amateur mob men to track down a Russian dissident. No, someone else was behind these shenanigans. The question remained, who? Any number of actors had both the motive and the means. Janusz was certain the answer was staring him in the face.

Could it be the Iranians were out for revenge? It was certainly possible. Iran had a variety of capabilities at its disposal. They had deftly used their network to blow up the Argentine Jewish Center in 1994. They murdered the prosecutor looking into the affair, Alberto Nisman, in his Buenos Aires apartment twenty-one years later. There was also the assassination of Iranian dissidents all over Europe in the eighties and nineties.

A grisly example was the 1989 murder of Abdul Rahman Ghasemloo, the leader of the Democratic Party of Iranian Kurdistan. Ghasemloo and two assistants were brutally gunned down by the Iranian MOIS in a Vienna apartment. The killings occurred inside the very room where Ghasemloo had met earlier to negotiate a truce between his group and the Iranian Government. That was just the tip of the iceberg in Europe. According to expert estimates, the Iranian regime had killed at least three-hundred-thirty dissidents outside of its own borders.

The most notorious incident in the US was that of Ali Akbar Tabatabaei, an Iranian exile who had been the last press attaché to the Iranian Embassy in Washington. He was killed on his front doorstep in Bethesda, Maryland back in 1980. The assassin was delivering Tabatabaei's mail dressed up as a US Postman using a borrowed mail truck. After eliminating his target, the killer made his way back to Iran where he currently makes a living as an actor in Iranian movies and an anchorman for Iran's English language state media, Press TV.

"John, where've you been? I've been trying to get a khold of you for hours."

"What do you mean? I came as soon as I got your message," Janusz said.

"Where are Sasha and Dimitry?"

"How would I know? They work for you, remember?"

"I don't have patience for this bullshit. I can't get a khold of them anywhere."

Kalugin spoke rapidly now. Janusz just shrugged his shoulders.

"What about Gennady, what khappened to him?"

"Is this some sort of test? Is there something you're not telling me?"

"I assure you this is not a test. You're the last person to khave contact with all three of them. No one knows where they are?"

"I thought Sasha and Dimitry were with the Russian mob in New York, or at least that's what they told me."

"Idiots," Kalugin said.

"Doesn't the Russian mob know where they are?"

"No, the mob is breaking my balls about it."

"So, where's the money now?"

"You know about the money?" Kalugin said.

"They threw the bag of money at Gennady right in front of my face. Was I supposed to close my eyes?"

"Amateurs." Kalugin paused to gather his thoughts. "The money was supposed to be shown once Gennady *accepted* the offer. Tell me what khappened last night from the beginning. Assume I know nothing."

Kalugin's face was red, and his nostrils inflamed.

"We picked up Gennady and—"

"Where?"

"Near Dupont Circle."

"Go on."

"Anyway, we pick him up and drive out to this large house near American University."

"Good."

"We proceed to the house and the mobsters start talking to Gennady."

"This was before or after they showed him the cash?"

"At the same moment. They had the bag of cash on the floor as they talked."

Kalugin shook his head incredulously.

"Thirty minutes later things looked to be going well and—"

"What do you mean by well?" Kalugin asked.

"How do I know? I don't speak Russian."

"Then khow can you be so sure?"

"Everyone seemed happy, so I assumed things were going well. Then Dimitry gets up and tells me the work is done for the night, and I can go home. He tells me to wait by the car so he can drop me off where he picked me up."

"What about the other two?"

"They stayed in the house as far as I could tell. Dimitry dropped me off and I never saw him again. I suspect he went back to the house after he drove off."

Kalugin took a moment to evaluate the story. He debouched a cigarette from his pants pocket, lighting up with a metallic Zippo. Within seconds, his giant nostrils emitted a dragon like smoke. Kalugin took several puffs before he resumed the conversation.

"You sure you didn't leave anything out of this story?"

"Positive," Janusz said, pausing to increase the tension. "You think they took the money and ran?"

"If they did run, they didn't take Gennady with them."

"I figured that to be the case."

"Still doesn't make sense. The money didn't come from Moscow. Our connections in New York put up the money and we were going to pay them back. Those two idiots stole from their own boss. Khard to believe they would be that stupid."

"How much was in the bag?"

"A million dollars."

"Ouch, that's gotta hurt. They probably ran off to Mexico."

"It doesn't matter if they're on Mars. The outfit in New York will track them down wherever they went. They're as good as dead."

"Sounds like it," Janusz said with a chuckle.

It was the only thing Kalugin had gotten right so far.

"The remaining question is what khappened to Gennady? You sure they didn't tell you anything else?"

"Why would I come here and talk to you if I was hiding something?"

"I guess you're right. I'm sure Gennady will turn up sooner or later."

"I still haven't gotten paid for my efforts," Janusz said.

"Yes, absolutely. When we meet again, I'll khave something for you, I promise. It shouldn't be too difficult to find something for a man with your abilities."

Janusz was at a dead end. He could tell there would be no more work with the Russians. He started walking back toward the car. Something was vibrating in his pants. *The phone.*

"Janusz, I've got a lead."

"Jason, I don't think the Russians are involved. I've been working this nonsense angle, and it hasn't panned out."

"Oh, it's them all right. You just haven't been looking in

the right place. I'll get you on the right track shortly," Jason explained before hanging up.

Janusz was relying too much on Jason, he knew that. It was amazing how all the Unit's contacts had gone underground as soon as they heard about the attack on Tony and Stan. Tony was the glue that held everything together. Then again, Stan's death was a huge blow to the Unit's network of contacts.

Due to his background in finance, Stan handled all the payments to the Unit's assets. With the senior leadership either dead or in hiding, agents were not getting paid. The entire enterprise was in shambles, and there was no one to turn to. There was a need for a serious shakeup and reordering of Unit 81. That would come later. For now, Donald Patrick was the Unit's most reliable ally in the US Government. Since he was transitioning to the White House, his senior staff assistant, Jason Osborne, was the only person left. Janusz was not happy about that.

17. BROOKLAND, WASHINGTON D.C.

December 12

Destruction eyeballed Rage fiddling with the car radio. It took a great deal of self-restraint to stop himself from slapping the stupid fuck-face. They had been driving for close to an hour through the DC traffic and he was ready to kick Rage to the curb. It was not enough that Destruction was doing all the driving, mostly because he had lost confidence in the Georgetown boy after Rage had challenged him at Bakunin Farm.

On top of everything else, the arrogant prick had to change the station every few minutes. They finally arrived at the house of Captain Roger Chambers of the Uniformed Division of the Secret Service. Discovering him had been like finding a needle in a haystack. The cameras he had placed on Powder Mill Road, across the street from the James Rowley Training Center, had photographed every license plate that entered and exited the Secret Service training facility.

Destruction had relayed the plate numbers to paid sources inside the Department of Motor Vehicles for the states of Maryland, Virginia, and Washington DC. The plates had yielded names and addresses of the people entering the training facility. The last step in the treasure hunt was providing those names to another source who utilized a classified internal Secret Service database to identify the specific assignment of each name within the organization.

One of the vehicles that had visited the training center belonged to Chambers. He lived in the Brookland section of DC. As it turned out, Chambers was the special agent in charge of security at the White House. He was exactly the man they were looking for. The Department of Motor Vehicles sources were on Octavio's payroll.[1]

Destruction parked several houses down the street at a quarter before eight in the morning. It was quiet. A school bus passed them without making a stop. The howling wind blew mercilessly through the neighborhood, announcing the arrival of a cold front. The trees had long ago shed their foliage, the dead leaves scattered across front lawns.

"I don't like this, we're too exposed. One of the neighbors can call the cops. Why do we have to wait out in the open?" Rage asked.

"Because we need to learn his pattern of life. When he goes to work, what route he takes, when he comes home. Whether or not his house is empty during the day. Things like that."

"I think this is a terrible idea. We should ask the women of DC Antifa to do this. It would be less suspicious."

"No one asked for your opinion. I give the orders, and you obey. That's how things work—"

"Hey, there he is. He's coming out," Rage said excitedly.

Chambers walked out to his front porch to fetch the morning paper. Still wearing his pajamas, he quickly wrapped the bathrobe tighter to guard against the wind. He bent down to grab the paper before running back inside. His wife had driven their older daughter to school over a half hour ago. Even though he had the latest gadgets, to include smart phones and e-book readers, Chambers fancied himself old school. He enjoyed reading the morning news in paper format, the way his father used to do when he was a young boy. Chambers dropped the paper on the kitchen island before making his way to the coffee pot. He slowly poured the dark roasted elixir that gave him life every morning. He took his coffee black, with no sugar or cream.

The morning news was the usual mix of sensationalist rubbish used to agitate the American public. He was close to canceling his subscription. Chambers walked straight over to the garbage can in disgust and dropped the entire paper, minus the sports section, in the trash.

"Okay, Dad. I'm finished with breakfast. Can I have some money for lunch?"

"No need. I packed you a nutritious meal. Roast beef sandwich with a salad."

"Dad, they're serving spaghetti and meatballs today."

"That stuff's not good for you. I made you lunch last night when I got home from work. You're a growing boy, you should eat healthy," Chambers said, staring at the boy's left leg.

He could see the trembling had started again, so he instinctively changed the conversation.

"You going to wrestling practice today?"

"Of course. Why wouldn't I?" the boy said before catching himself, "the tremors haven't been that bad lately. The medicine seems to be working for now."

Despite his macho demeanor, Chambers could see the boy had a slight limp as he walked across the kitchen to the living room. He was only fifteen years old but, somehow, the poor boy was in the early stages of Multiple Sclerosis. They had taken him to the best doctors at Johns Hopkins Hospital. The medicine seemed to help, or at least slow things down but, every now and then, Chambers would detect a new symptom the boy tried to hide.

He was brave like his dad, but he certainly did not deserve this. Chambers and his wife went out of their way to make sure he had the best care. They also took turns taking him to school, driving him to athletic events, or to visit his friends. It was disgusting how some of the other kids at school had made fun of his limp and his trembling hands when it had all started last year. How could they be so heartless? Although those rotten kids were kids nonetheless, Chambers was ready to go to school and crush their heads. The only reason he had not done so, yet, was that it would only make things worse for his son.

"I'm ready, let's go," the boy said, holding his school bag.

As his son made way toward the front door, his leg gave out causing him to fall flat on his face with a loud *thud*.

"Jeezuz," Chambers said, running toward the boy.

His father pulled him off the floor only to find the boy's lip had been cut and was bleeding profusely. Chambers grabbed a paper towel off the counter and handed it to him.

"Here, put this over it." He was surprised the boy had not shrugged off his help as usual.

It was a stab in the heart. His boy was slowly accepting the fact that his body was deteriorating.

"You want me to throw you over my shoulders?" Chambers said half in jest.

"That won't be necessary," the boy said, leaning against the counter.

"Here, let me get you another paper towel," Chambers said. "How about a hand? Will you at least hold on to my arm, so you don't fall again?"

The boy just nodded before grabbing hold of his father's muscular arms. Observing his son's arms reminded him the boy needed to bulk up. But this was not the right occasion to bring that up. They made their way to the dining room where Chambers placed his son on one of the chairs. Chambers proceeded back upstairs to change. Fifteen minutes later, he returned and aided his ambling son out the door. Together, they made their way down the porch stairs before walking through the brick path to the car.

Chambers was so absorbed in his son, carefully studying him place one foot in front of the other, that he did not even bother to lift his head. He positioned his son in the passenger seat, checking his holster once more to make sure he had not forgotten the pistol. Five minutes later, they were driving down the street toward school.

◆ ◆ ◆

"Don't lose him now. Don't lose him," Rage said. "Why is the kid limping?"

"How the hell should I know? Maybe he fell at school and hurt himself."

Fifteen minutes later, they had arrived at the school. It was obviously late as there was no one else outside.

"I don't like this guy. He can't even get his own kid to school on time. How can he be of use to us?" Rage said.

"Are you retarded? You saw with your own eyes the kid is injured."

"I don't get it, why don't we just grab this guy and take him to the farm in Beltsville. Couple of days under lock and chain and he'll tell us everything he knows."

"And then what, arse-wipe? Don't you think his colleagues in the Secret Service will get suspicious if he disappears? Entire point is to catch 'em with their pants down. What do they teach you guys at Georgetown, anyway?"

Rage fell silent for a few minutes before resuming the conversation, "What made you want to start the DC chapter of Antifa, I've been dying to know?"

"Same as you. I was fed up with the consumer culture. I felt miserably empty inside. I was a community organizer and sold pot for a few years, but something was missing. I needed more out of life."

"I gotta figure out what I want to do when I graduate. That is, *if* I graduate."

"You've come this far, just finish the damn thing. We'll need experts of all kinds in our new society. Doctors, mechanics, you name it. The only thing we won't need anymore will be lawyers," Destruction said with a sinister laugh.

"What use is an undergrad degree in sociology?"

"You got a point. You may have a future with Antifa if you

can prove yourself on this assignment."

"You serious?"

"We'll see how you do," Destruction said warily. He was still not sure if the kid was more of a liability than an asset. "There he is, he's getting in the car again."

"Let's go," Rage shouted.

Destruction fired up the engine. Chances were high that Chambers was headed to the White House to report for duty. Within minutes, they were stuck in a sea of cars going south on Seventeenth Street. Chambers was several cars ahead as they approached the intersection of Seventeenth and L. The light turned yellow.

"Stay on him. Stay on him, Destruction."

"I can't, there are too many cars ahead."

"Go around them. Come on, don't lose him."

"I'm trying, you arse-wipe. Light just turned red."

"Go, go!"

"O-o-okay, shut your trap. Oooooh, fffffuck!"

The impact of the airbag was the only thing Destruction remembered. There was smoke in the cabin. To his right, Rage's head rested on the passenger's airbag. Destruction coughed heavily.

"Ooooh, what the hell happened?" Rage said.

"Someone smashed into us. *Ahhhhhhhh,* my fucking neck. I shoudda never listened to you, shit-brain."

Destruction touched his midsection in search of the strap. He found and pressed the button to open his belt. It was much easier to breathe with that contraption off his chest. To his right, Rage was trying to do the same but with greater difficulty. Destruction decided not to help him. The accident was his fault, and he deserved his fate. Let him suffer until the paramedics arrived. A weird odor engulfed the inside of the vehicle. Destruction could not be sure if it was gasoline or smoke. A chill ran down his spine with the awareness it could be both. *Knock, knock, knock.* Someone tapped against his window.

"You gotta *wa wa wa*," the man said.

"What? I can't hear you," Destruction replied.

"Get out! Now...I mean now! Open the door?"

The meaning of the words did not register. Why did this man insist on them exiting the vehicle? The stranger waved a short black stick. It looked like a pen with a sharp tip. The pen magically smashed through the window. *Craaaacccccckkkkk.* Destruction put his hands over his face after the glass had already scraped his skin.

A powerful arm moved in around his waist. When the owner of the arm was satisfied Destruction was free, a second powerful arm connected with the first from his backside. In an instant, Destruction was pulled out of the car as if he were a Lilliputian plucked out by Gulliver. The large man to which the arms were attached ran several feet before gently placing him down. The asphalt pebbles pressed against his back. His savior had disappeared.

Destruction tried to make sense of it all. He was lying in the middle of an intersection. A large crowd had gathered. The distant wails of a siren grew closer. No one from the crowd came over to help. They just stood there. What were they staring at? They certainly weren't interested in him.

As he labored to catch their gaze, he finally discovered the source that drew their attention. His car was a total wreck. It lay in the middle of an intersection like a sambar torn open by a tiger. A hulking black SUV had T-boned the front of his vehicle, plowing straight through the engine compartment. Bits of mangled metal and shattered glass covered the street. A tire rested several feet away on its side. The hubcap was missing. Another casualty of this unnecessary conflict. His car was contorted into an unusual shape that could only be conjured up by the twisted imagination of an abstract expressionist sculptor. It resembled a grotesque architectural design worthy of Frank Gehry.

The flame caught the corner of his eye. A fire rapidly spread through the demolished engine compartment. Within seconds the fire shot up into the air. From behind the blaze a muscular man appeared. He held someone in his arms. Seconds later, the man placed Rage next to him on the asphalt. The sun was shining from behind. He couldn't see the face. This man had saved their lives as the rest of the world stood by.

"*Ahhhhh,* God that hurts," Rage screamed.

Serves him right, Destruction thought.

"Heads down, now," the muscular man said.

Baaaammmmm, something exploded. The mangled wreck was in flames now. If not for this man, Destruction and Rage would have been served as BBQ to the lunch crowds in DC at noon.

"This must be my lucky day, where the fuck did you come from?" Destruction said.

"I was on the other side of the intersection when I heard the impact. I checked the rearview mirror knowing it would be bad. I jumped outta my car and ran over."

"You saved our lives," Destruction said as Rage lay moaning next to him.

"You woudda done the same for me," the man said.

"Thank you."

"No worries," the man said modestly.

Destruction struggled to recapture his breath. Just then, two ambulances pulled right in front of them. A paramedic rushed out, going over to Rage. The next one approached Destruction, blocking the sun that blinded him.

"Gimme your arm. I gotta take your blood pressure," the paramedic said.

With the shade provided by the ambulance crew, Destruction finally got a good view of his rescuer. The man was catching his breath a few feet away. A jolt of panic shot through Destruction's body as the hairs stood on his neck. How could he have been so stupid? The man's face was unmistakable. The entire episode was surreal. Destruction had his pulse taken while he looked nervously away from Chambers.

18. MARY'S MISSION, WASHINGTON D.C.

December 16

O ne by one they came with their bowls. Kim poured the soup as they each passed by. She had been volunteering at this soup kitchen for a number of years. The work gave her a sense of accomplishment. Kim also needed a distraction from the reality of being hunted.

She had joined the FBI to serve her country, but over the years she grew disillusioned with a bureaucracy that stifled initiative. She had been briefly engaged to a man, Todd, but that was not meant to be. He was too obsessed with status to suit her tastes. Kim left him, dedicating herself to work in order to dull the pain. She was grateful about the opportunity to travel the world on various assignments, but she was often too busy chasing enemies to enjoy life.

Volunteering with Mary's Mission in DC allowed Kim to connect with people outside of the Unit. People who were not scheming to attack America. These were people who the world had forgotten and who needed a second chance. What good was the effort to keep her country safe if her fellow Americans were hungry?

Until recently, Kim had only served at Mary's Mission during Thanksgiving, Christmas, and other holidays. Since work at the Unit had become a hazard, Kim dedicated more hours to charity. She found that it also gave her a way to connect with the memory of her own mother who had died of cancer. When she was alive, Kim's mother had devoted her life to helping those less fortunate. When mother was young, she had volunteered to be a nurse in Vietnam where she had seen her fair share of gore.

In her later years, mother had been president of the PTA and head organizer for the local church. More importantly, mother had founded one of the largest charities in the Commonwealth of Pennsylvania, using her connections with business leaders to collect vast sums for the poor. Come to think of it, Kim had never really made service to others a central part of her life like mother had.

That was the thing about starting down this path. Once you focused outside of yourself, you soon grasped what it was that made you tick. Why had she joined the FBI in the first place? Why did she risk her life after leaving the FBI to serve in Unit 81? Was it purely for love of country? Perhaps it was for the same reason she volunteered here today. Perhaps she was still in competition with her mother. A mother that haunted her subconscious. Yes, when it came down to it, Kim had to admit that, even today everything she did was motivated by a fear she would not measure up to a mother who had spent her whole life in service to others.

It drove her crazy that mother had known so early what she wanted out of life. Yet Kim was here today to avoid danger. She was just a shallow, self-absorbed woman with zero purpose in her life. *Goddamn you, Mother. Goddamn you!* Kim thought as she poured another bowl of soup. She took a deep breath to pull herself together. Why had she thought those terrible things about her deceased mother? She had never resented her before in this way. The fear of the unknown, the fear of being killed at any moment, the fear of a faceless enemy was affecting Kim in odd ways. *Maybe I should go back to Pennsylvania and become a teacher.* Imagine mother's face if she had been alive. Her disappointment with a daughter that ran away from the first sign of danger.

The vibration of an incoming text message broke through her thoughts. It was the woman from the gym, Lesley. She wanted to know if Kim was free. Thank God, Kim was in desperate need of a friend right now.

"What do you think of this?" Kim asked as she tried on a red sweater.

"It looks fabulous on you. You have the perfect complexion and body to pull it off," Lesley said.

They had been at the Tyson's Mall for the past hour hopping from store to store. After trying on a variety of outfits in the women's section of Nordstrom's, they drifted out into the main walkway of the mall.

"You know what would be fantastic right about now?" Lesley asked.

"I'm all ears."

"A facial and a massage."

"Well, you go right ahead. I'm worried about my job, so I'll pass. I'll wait for you in the food court," Kim said.

"Don't be ridiculous. A friend of mine was going to take her daughter but had to cancel at the last minute. She gave me these," Lesley said, pointing to two vouchers.

"Are you sure? Those vouchers are pricey. I don't think I—"

"What am I going to do with the other ticket? Invite an imaginary boyfriend that I don't have?"

The girls laughed as they made their way to the spa. Although she did not want to say so out loud, Kim was glad Lesley had the extra ticket. She needed a massage more than anything else right now. Kim decided to accept.

"Do you have a preference for your masseuse?" the lady at the counter inquired.

"I'm happy with whoever. My friend here is about to get married and she needs a massage from another man before she ties the knot," Lesley said with a devilish gleam in her eye.

"I think that can be arranged. If you ladies will kindly wait twenty minutes, I'll give you both exactly what you need," the clerk said.

Kim and Lesley looked at each other, holding the urge to grin. They sat down and waited until the clerk went to the back.

"I can't believe you said that. I didn't know whether I should slap you or hug you," Kim said.

"You just had that look in your eye."

"What look?"

"That look that says I need a pair of rugged hands to work me over," Lesley said.

Before long, Kim was laying partially naked on a massage table with her head down. She could barely see with the candlelight. The aroma of citrus danced in her nose as it slowly calmed her nerves. Seconds later, a warm layer of oil was generously applied all over her back and legs.

Kim gently drifted into ecstasy before his strong fingers grabbed the side of her neck. The faceless man soothed every muscle in her shoulders working his way down her spine. When he expertly squeezed the lactic acid out of her calves, she was embarrassed to acknowledge the obvious. Kim was getting wet for a man whose face she had not yet seen. She needed to distract herself before her panties soaked through. Kim tried thinking of the multiplication tables but could not even remember two times two at the moment. Her thoughts drifted to Pennsylvania.

Her grandfather had a cabin on the way to Harrisburg. He had bequeathed the property to her in his will. It was a great place to get away when life got too hectic in the big city. It was also the perfect location to hide out until Janusz contacted her. She would no longer have to worry if she was next on the hit list.

"Would you like me to cover you so you can turn around?" the man said.

Kim was no longer in a heightened state of excitement.

"That won't be necessary. Please, continue," Kim said as she turned face up.

Twenty minutes later, Kim was showered and dressed. When she stepped back out into the harsh fluorescent light, Lesley was waiting for her. Kim stepped forward and gave her a kiss on the cheek.

"Wow, you really needed that massage," Lesley said.

"I want to thank you."

"Why?"

"For inspiring me."

"To do what?"

"To go home. I'm going to Pennsylvania for a few weeks to rest. If not for today I would not have understood how much I needed it," Kim said.

Lesley's left eye twitched as she raised her eyebrows, "You're leaving? I mean that's great."

"I'll stay at a cabin by myself for a few weeks."

"Are you sure you should be alone? Can we still talk?"

"My family is nearby, and you can call me when you like. You wanna grab something to eat? I'm suddenly famished," Kim said.

"Yeah, I know a great place on the third floor."

19. BROOKLAND, WASHINGTON D.C.

December 18

T hey stood in the center of the living room near a bookcase. Destruction and Rage had come to gather intelligence on the Secret Service and steal a uniform from Captain Chambers. Although still sore, both men had mostly recovered from the accident on Seventeenth Street the week before. Fortuitously, their injuries were mostly superficial.

Destruction walked around the first floor to familiarize himself with his surroundings. He walked from the living room to the dining room then onto the kitchen. Destruction was disgusted by the lavish display of wealth. A humongous stainless-steel fridge was surrounded by marble countertops and white cabinets. Wooden stools sat behind a marble topped island above which were low hanging lights. He could see clear out to the spacious backyard through the white French doors in the kitchen. There was a swing set out there along with a playhouse and toys strewn about. Rage was milling about aimlessly.

"Rage, what the fuck are you gawking at? This isn't a museum. Get moving?"

"I don't get it."

"Get what?"

"This guy is a government employee. How does he afford a place like this?"

"He's not just any government employee, Chambers is one of the supervisors in charge of security for the White House."

"Still, this is a really nice place."

"His wife is a GS-15 at the Department of Transportation. Put those salaries together, and there you have it. This should help motivate you. We need to overthrow this corrupt system so a guy like this doesn't live in the lap of luxury while countless Americans can't afford to buy a house."

"I still feel bad about all this. He did save our lives."

"He didn't do it for us, he did it because that's the type of guy he is. He would've done that for anybody."

"It's still wrong. Why can't we go to another agent's house?"

"Because Chambers is a supervisor at the White House and may have important information about perimeter security. We also don't have the time to follow another agent around and learn his pattern of life. If you hurry it up, we can leave before anyone finds out we were here."

"I'm hungry, I bet there's ice cream in that freezer."

"Hey, arse-wipe. Would you cut it out? We only have two hours before we earn ourselves a parking ticket."

Destruction was fuming on the inside. Rage had zero understanding of punctuality. He was a spoiled Georgetown dimwit.

"Instead of standing around all confused, go upstairs to his bedroom and take a uniform. Make sure to search for anything else that can help us," Destruction barked.

"What exactly are we looking for, anyway?"

"Anything with names and identifying information on his colleagues. Fuck it, you're quite useless. I'll go upstairs, and you can stay down here to keep an eye out for any unexpected surprises."

"All right," Rage said as Destruction made his way up the stairs.

On the second floor, there were several doors that led to bedrooms and bathrooms. Destruction walked through all of them until he found the master. It was rather spacious with dark wooden floors. The king-sized bed in the center of the room was covered with a white down comforter.

Destruction made his way to the nightstand. He rifled

through all the drawers but found nothing of value. Inside the top drawer of the left nightstand, he found an eight-inch dildo, which he assumed belonged to the wife. Next to the dildo was a romance novel with a bare-chested man on the cover.

Destruction made his way to the walk-in closet and carefully scoured the Secret Service agent's coat and pants pockets. There was not much there other than a few keys and loose change. From the look of things, the target was quite a neat individual. Suits and ties had been carefully placed on a hanger. Dress shirts were neatly folded in shelves that lined the closet. He immediately found what he was looking for. Three folded Secret Service dress uniforms and winter wear.

The black coat came with a matching ski hat, gloves, and undershirts. The black pants were wrinkle free and smelled as if freshly dry cleaned. Funny, without the Secret Service badges and insignia, the clothing looked eerily similar to their own black bloc fatigues. He took one pair of the uniforms along with matching black winter boots and walked out of the closet. Destruction had a tailor who would make six exact replicas of his new wardrobe. He checked the time. They had been in the house for over an hour. At the other end of the room was a makeshift office. A small desk with a swivel chair and a fancy two screen computer. Destruction shuffled through several folders and a book next to the computer. Disappointed, he inspected the shelves. Lots of loose change, several CDs, and a pocket calendar.

"What do we have here?" Destruction said as he meticulously leafed through the calendar. At the back of the calendar was a page with passwords. Next to each password was a note about the account. Destruction placed the calendar in his pocket and continued his search. On the right side of the bed was another nightstand. In the middle drawer, he found an intricately carved wooden jewelry box. He opened the lid and eyed what was inside. An exquisite men's Rolex. He had always wanted one. Destruction put the watch in his pocket and walked down to find Rage skimming through a few pieces of paper on the marble topped kitchen counter.

"You find anything?" Destruction said.

"Not much, What about you?"

Destruction extended the folded uniform to showcase his triumph.

"Very nice," Rage said.

"Why don't you check downstairs to see if there's anything else that can be of value to the mission?" Destruction said.

"Sure,"

Destruction had been training Rage for only a few weeks and at present regretted the decision to recruit him. He decided to follow Rage to make sure the shit-brain did not overlook anything. At the bottom of the stairwell, it was pitch dark.

"Where's the light switch," Rage said.

"How the fuck should I know, figure it out."

After another minute standing in the darkness, Rage finally discovered what they were looking for. Once the lights came on, they found themselves in an impressive man cave. There was a poker table not far from a pool table. Foosball and ping-pong sets accentuated the space. Rage made a sudden bee line for the pool table.

"What the fuck?" Destruction shouted.

"Pool is my favorite way to chill at the end of the day. I practically earned all my pocket money playing this game." The moron said before cueing up an eight ball. Rage positioned himself at the end of the table. He then proceeded to smack the balls around. Destruction wanted to shove the cue straight up Rage's ass.

"Having fun there?" a familiar voice echoed from behind.

Destruction's heart sank as Rage disappeared from view. Who the hell was this guy standing behind him? There was no choice but to face forward slowly.

"Chambers?" Destruction said.

"Christ. You're the guy I rescued from the car crash."

"But yo-yo-you're—"

"Not supposed to be here? Yeah, I came home a little early to this unexpected surprise."

Chambers reached under his sports jacket. Destruction knew exactly what he was searching for. There was nothing he could do. Destruction raised his hands before Chambers pulled out the pistol.

"You've got a lot to answer fo—" Chambers said before a loud *thud* sent him hurtling forward into space.

Chambers fell face forward to the ground. Destruction raised his eyes and found Rage standing with a wooden baseball bat. The bat was extended as if Rage had just hit a home run.

Destruction did the slapping. When the giant man finally opened his eyes, he found himself on a wooden chair in the dining room. His hands had been tied from the back with rope. Other than that, Chambers had been left unmolested. Chambers studied the two men standing in front of him, his eyes slowly bulging out of their sockets.

"We did our best to avoid this?" Destruction said.

"I should've known. You idiots were following me when you crashed. What do you want?" Chambers said.

"Sorry, we have no choice but to take you with us now."

"What do you mean take him with us? You said yourself that would ruin our plans," Rage said.

"Maybe if you hadn't been too busy cueing up the pool table, we could've avoided it. This is on all on you."

"Yo-yo-you're the one who asked me to search downstairs," Rage shot back, "why the fuck are ya blaming me?"

This was the second instance Rage had challenged him. Destruction's face felt hot as he clenched his jaw.

"*Ahhhhhhhh,*" Destruction screamed, galloping forth like a bull in Pamplona. Destruction tackled Rage to the floor before mounting his chest. A deluge of punches fell upon Rage as the

Georgetown boy maneuvered to protect his face.

"Wait, Destruction, wait. He's getting away."

The punches stopped as Destruction looked up. He sprang to his feet reflexively. Chambers was halfway to the front door. The only thing slowing him down was the fact that his hands were still tied behind his back. He had apparently broken the top half of the dining table chair and was dragging the wooden pieces of furniture behind him. Within seconds Destruction caught up and tried to tackle the Secret Service man. Chambers bumped Destruction to the ground.

"Help me, arse-wipe. Come quick before he escapes," Destruction cried.

He looked at the wall clock in panic. They had stayed over two hours. If their vehicle on the street was ticketed, it would create a record of their presence near this address.

"Rage, where are you?"

The Georgetown idiot finally jumped on Chambers. He was riding the back of the massive Secret Service giant as if he were a child. It would not be long before Chambers would throw him off. Destruction continued scanning the room for something to even the odds. Then he saw it against the dining room wall. The bat was exactly where Rage had left it when they tied up Chambers.

Destruction picked up the wooden weapon and ran toward the commotion. Chambers dragged Rage into the kitchen. Destruction was only a few steps behind as the Secret Service giant slammed Rage against the stainless-steel fridge. The impact was so powerful the fridge moved back into the wall. As Rage peeled off onto the floor, there was a crater sized dent on the steel door.

Destruction didn't know what to do. The only factor in his favor was that Chambers still had his hands tied behind his back. If he pushed through the French doors into the backyard, one of the neighbors would surely see him and call the police. But Chambers was not the kind of man to back away from a fight. Destruction was about to get run over by a Mack Truck.

He took a slugger's stance, ready to swing the bat. His hands turned cold as he tightened the grip around the tail end of the handle.

Destruction planted his legs several feet apart for better balance. His knuckles were numb as he continued to choke the bat. The only sensation in his body was the pressure of the bat pushing against his palms. Chambers charged. It was imperative not to swing too soon. On the other hand, swinging too late was also problematic. With Chambers only a few feet away, Destruction swung with all his might. He was not sure why everything was suddenly a blur. Somehow, Chambers managed to lower his head. The bat struck the top part of his back and bounced off.

As soon as he recognized he was fucked, Destruction was flying through the air. A hard smack from behind stopped his momentum only milliseconds before the cracking of bone. An electric current shot through his entire back. The bat was no longer in his hand as he looked up at the ceiling. Destruction was too afraid to move, fearing the worst from his fall. The approaching footsteps headed toward him.

"You little shit. I gotcha," Chambers yelled.

Rage appeared out of nowhere to stab Chambers with a kitchen knife, but the giant man had smacked the weapon out of Rage's hand. Chambers's hands were now free. The knife was lying on the floor only inches away from Destruction. He leaned over and wrapped his fingers around the handle. Destruction pushed himself off the floor with all his might and turned his head. The pain was excruciating but soon forgotten.

He inched closer to the unfolding scene of Chambers pummeling the crouching Rage. Something snapped inside Destruction. At that moment all he could see was the enemy. Destruction charged as fast as he could. He raised his arm just like that day at Bakunin Farm when he was about to strike at Rage. Only now, there was no one holding him back. Destruction plunged the knife into the giant's neck. The startled man tried his best to stop the bleeding. It was no use,

Destruction struck again and again, mercilessly stabbing the Secret Service captain.

"Jee-Je-Jesus! Enough, man, that's enough!" Rage yelled as he moved in to grab his arms.

The pool of red liquid grew larger by the second underneath their feet. Who could ever eat in this room again?

"How do you like that?" Destruction roared.

"There's so much blood? We're fucked," Rage said.

"How'd you like that?" Destruction continued to scream at the bleeding body. Why had he stabbed this man who had saved his life?

"Destruction, w-w-we gotta go. Come on, we gotta go before the cops get here."

Destruction was in a trance. Rage slapped him hard across the face. "Give me the knife, man. Give me the knife."

"What did I just do?" Destruction replied.

"Yo-yo-you killed him, and now we gotta get out of here."

Destruction dropped the knife. Rage ran to the kitchen to fetch a plastic freezer bag. He proceeded to shove the bloody knife inside before dropping it in a gym bag. It was the same bag they used to hold Chambers's Secret Service uniform. Destruction bent over to remove the dead man's wallet.

"What are you doing?" Rage said.

"We gotta make this look like a robbery. He didn't want to cooperate, so he was killed. It's business as usual in this city."

"How are we going to pull this off without alerting the Secret Service?" Rage wanted to know.

"I'll figure something out. Look outside to see if we have a clear path to the car?"

20. MANHATTAN, NEW YORK CITY

December 21

S he darted her eyes from face to face, studying each of them intently. It was odd. The closer Janet looked, the more similar they all appeared. It wasn't just because they had all attended the same prep schools, or got their degrees from the same journalism programs, or even the fact they all went to the same parties. It was something deeper.

As God was her witness, there was no denying the fact that the men seemed no different than the women and vice-versa. The phenomenon was definitely not physical as most of the men wore short hair with beards while the women were made up with long highlighted hair. No, it was much deeper than that. When had men become so weak and women so assertive? It wasn't just a New York thing as she had witnessed the same dynamics in cities as far apart from one another as Los Angeles and Seattle, or Chicago and Philadelphia.

Janet tried to purge the insensitive thought. Heaven forbid she ever spoke this way in front of the others. Besides being labeled a vulgarian, she would be banished from high society. Janet had gathered this coterie at the upscale Italian restaurant, Valentino's, in Manhattan. She knew everyone here for nearly a decade. She didn't exactly consider them friends, but they all looked up to her for one reason or another.

"Okay, which one of you is going to write the first hit piece on the new administration?" Monroe from *Society Magazine* said.

He was Harvard boy through and through. He had jet black hair and wore glasses. His trimmed beard was the hallmark of the hip millennial male throughout the country.

"Hey, the *Times* and the *Post* have been there done that," Taylor, the Yale graduate writing for *Yorktown Magazine* declared.

"Dear God, the *Times* and the *Post*? Those outlets cater to the masses. I'm talking about a literary piece for those with more refined tastes. How about you, Taylor? Why don't you write something?" Monroe said.

"President-elect Patrick is a veteran. Even though he is a conservative, I can't tear him down until he does something first. We need to wait a little," Taylor said.

"Lame excuse, you need to check your privilege at the door and do something to stem the tide of fascism taking over the country. How about you Janet, what you got up your sleeve for the new administration?" Monroe said.

"I'm working on a few things," Janet replied.

"There are rumors that *Impressionable Magazine* is about to be scooped up by one of the big boys."

"Oh my God, stop spreading lies, Monroe. Where did you hear that?" Janet said.

"Cross my heart and hope to fly, no joke. Some private equity firm out in San Francisco. It's owned by that old guy from Brazil," Monroe said as he snapped his fingers in rapid succession. "Souza Enterprises, that's it. Rumor has it Souza Enterprises has made an offer."

"I'd check my sources again if I were you, my dear. Anyway, I would strongly encourage all of you to stay away from that story for your own good," Janet said coldly.

Octavio had promised to bring her magazine into his empire quietly but, apparently someone had contracted verbal diarrhea. She made a mental note to inform the old man so he could deal with the fallout.

"What's with this guy anyway? They say he's behind the Freedom Coalition's efforts to change America," Taylor said.

"I'm surprised to hear you guys repeating rightwing conspiracy theories. First of all, Mr. Souza is one of numerous members in the Freedom Coalition. Second, it's just a group of civic-minded citizens who want to give back to their country. I attended one of their recent fundraisers. Since you're all so eager, I'll publish a piece on the entire affair in an upcoming issue of our magazine so you can educate yourselves."

"Looks like you have your ear close to the ground as usual, Janet dear."

"Why, Monroe, if I didn't know any better, I'd say you're jealous."

Monroe snorted so loud he almost spit out wine through his nose. She loved when he squirmed.

"Jealous? Only those with unchecked privilege are jealous. I'm however curious to learn more about the Freedom Coalition. After all, if they're going to shape our future, the people have a right to know more about them."

"There you go again spouting rubbish. Dear Monroe, it just so happens the coalition is a sort of charity, if you will," Janet said.

"So, anyone can donate?" Taylor said.

"In a manner of speaking, yes. Members are encouraged to contribute a minimum of ten million dollars annually. The Coalition then vets organizations it believes advance the value of its members to create a more just and equitable society."

"Really, Janet? Ten million dollars a year?"

"Is it a bad thing that rich people have finally acknowledged they owe something to the rest of us. Isn't it great that the cries for social justice and inclusivity have finally reached the ears of individuals with the means to make a difference?"

"Yes, but—" Monroe started before getting cut off.

"I think this kind of activity calls for celebration. We need to show how noble these individuals are in our articles so that more members of the top one percent join their ranks. You should be happy to know that one of the coalition's main goals is to increase voter participation among the young, women, and other disadvantaged groups," Janet said.

"I think that's fabulous," a voice from the other end of the table blurted out.

Janet was not sure who it was, "Another important objective is criminal reform. The Coalition will direct resources toward prosecutors and justices who will eliminate bail for violent criminals. We all know what's needed are jobs and education, not punishment. The entire justice system is racist, and the Freedom Coalition will help to dismantle it."

"What about Antifa? Is the Freedom Coalition going to sponsor organizations that bail out Antifa members burning down our cities?"

"Monroe, have you been reading rightwing propaganda again?" Janet said to boisterous laughter around the table.

"Of course not!"

"Then what's gotten into you? Antifa stands for anti-fascist. These are virtuous individuals who want to do good."

"Really? Most of the mug shots on TV are of privileged white students," Monroe said.

"See what I mean about propaganda? For your information, I've interviewed members of DC Antifa. I've even attended one of their gatherings in the bowels of a DC church. Let me tell you, these guys work harder than anyone around this table to create positive change."

"Can you give us an example?" Taylor said.

"I'd be happy to. The head of DC Antifa is a man by the name of Sean Sutherland. He has devoted his life to create a more equitable society in America. He works hard to recruit new members and he believes in women's empowerment. He teaches how to resist injustice and how to fight back against the system. He is a community organizer of the highest degree who helps give meaning to the lives of those who work with him. Sean Sutherland is a man of the people. Sean Sutherland is the future of this country. That is exactly the kind of person the Freedom Coalition wants to groom," Janet said, raising her voice while gesticulating for effect.

If this conversation had not convinced them to write positive stories about the Freedom Coalition, and the groups it sponsored, she did not know what would. Janet's thoughts drifted off to her next assignment. She had to tie Octavio's accomplishments with her editor's request for a pro-immigration story, while also scaring the public against the threats of racism. The only thing missing was the perfect event to bring it all together.

21. BLUE SKY CLUB, MONTANA

December 24; Christmas Eve

Octavio shifted in his seat as Placido took the final turn a bit too quickly on the ice. Ordinarily, he would provide a long lecture for careless lowlife behavior. Placido was a bit hot headed, not to mention he was the man in charge of his personal security, so he said nothing. The Maybach 62 came to a halt under the vaulted ceiling of the wooden porte-cochere.

Octavio pressed the button in the center console, automatically lowering the footrest of his leather seat. Despite the fact that he no longer enjoyed travel like he used to, the Blue Sky Club was one of the few places on Earth for which he was willing to abandon the comfort of home in San Francisco. The resort was about an hour drive from Bozeman International Airport and four hours from Jackson Hole, where his confidants owned vacation homes.

The main reason for this trip, besides an opportunity to breathe fresh mountain air, was to ask for a favor. There was no better place to talk business. The Blue Sky Club was a rare private mountain resort. Forget Aspen, open just about to anyone with enough cash. It took a million dollars upfront to join this Montana paradise. Then there was the three hundred thousand in annual dues.

On top of that, every member had to purchase a home in the resort with a starting price tag of ten million. His own villa, the most expensive by far, was worth over a hundred million dollars. If all that wasn't enough, one had to fill out an application and get accepted as the club capped membership at five hundred individuals and their families.

What made it all worthwhile was the convenience of a private police force staffed by former special forces operators. In addition, there was a private hospital with a paramedic service and a fire department, all within a tightly guarded territory. This meant that club members did not have to tow their bodyguards as was the custom in such quotidian locations as St. Moritz, Courchevel, and Aspen. Placido was here mainly to help with the bags. Octavio was getting too old to carry heavy luggage.

"Would you like me to accompany you, *Chefe*?" Placido said.

"That's not necessary, you can drive back to the villa. I'll call you when I'm done," Octavio said as he walked toward the front door of Mountain Lodge 22.

Inside, he was greeted by the warmth of wood burning fireplaces and fancy stone walls. There was a flurry of activity in the lobby as some of America's wealthiest families converged on the resort for Christmas. Normally a reserved man, Octavio was not in the habit of mingling with strangers.

Although everyone here was a member of the oligarchy, It was awkward having to wave at people not part of his immediate circle. He blamed unfair publicity. The media had recently taken to accusing him of every single ailment in America. It was a bad joke. Whenever there was a spike in crime, his name was mentioned. Whenever unpopular politicians were elected with dark pools of money, his name was mentioned. He was the central figure of every right-wing conspiracy in the country. This was the thanks he got for trying to make his adopted land a better place.

Octavio quickened his pace to make it difficult to engage him in an unsolicited conversation. Out of the corner of his eye he spotted the famous Hollywood actor Chandler Ellis surrounded by his kids. Chandler was talking to someone. Octavio could not be sure, but it appeared that Chandler was bantering with Luke Fontana, the famous quarterback for that team from Texas he couldn't remember.

Oh, yes, Luke led the Dallas Cowboys to four straight Super Bowl rings, earning him the adulation of dimwitted Americans. A recent article had mentioned that Luke was worth approximately four hundred million dollars. He was certain most American couch potatoes could not fathom that kind of money, but to Octavio it was mere chump change.

The only things Luke had that he wanted were youth, strength, and good looks. For that, Octavio was willing to pay billions, but medical science was not there yet. A prodigious amount of gas churned in his bowels as he stood by the elevators, waiting to descend to the piano room below.

With a loud *dinggggg*, the doors flew open to a most unexpected sight. The founders of the world's largest social media platforms, who managed companies worth trillions of dollars, were gathered in a circle. On the outside of their circle were five leggy blondes who Octavio assumed to be either their wives or mistresses. It did not matter which. There was an understanding among club members that whatever happened within the boundaries of the resort was to be held in the strictest of confidence.

The risk of ostracism from this community was something none of them wanted to contemplate. As the raucous circle entered the lobby, they exuded the same careless bonhomie that permeated the entire resort. Why shouldn't they be cheerful? They were not risking everything to secure a new future for America, like he was. One of the women in the group, wearing a low-cut black dress with stiletto heels, paused briefly to study him. Not sure if she recognized Octavio, she promptly turned without acknowledging his presence. *Good riddance.* He was relieved to have avoided another pointless interaction.

After stepping onto the dark-wooded floor of the piano room, he finally released the bubbling gas that was bothering him. The smell reminded him of the burger he ate for lunch. Down here, the atmosphere was more private. He strolled toward a stone fireplace surrounded by leather chairs. An ebony grand piano in the corner masterfully churned out Chopin. The familiar tune from the Steinway sparked a sense of euphoria that flowed from his head down to his toes.

He rolled with a gait that exuded confidence from every pore. And why not? He was a man about to transform America. A man about to recreate the world in his own image. His companions were presently seated. T.B. Shuster, also a member, had arrived from Jackson Hole. John Millhouse was there, too. These men were his closest confidants, fellow billionaires who had little reason to be jealous. He rarely did anything without consulting them. They were fully reclined with drinks in their hands.

"Vel, looks like you mendicants started without me," Octavio said.

"You finally decided to show. I should be the one now walking in. I had to get here from Jackson Hole," T.B. said.

"Looking good Octavio, you back on the Viagra?" Millhouse said.

"Could be. You should ask your girlfriend."

All three laughed as Octavio asked an attendant for a scotch on the rocks. He then turned toward his friends, letting out a long sigh before adjusting his position.

"So, what's so important that you called us out here the day before Christmas?" T.B. Schuster said.

"I've missed you guys. It's been a while since we all got together," Octavio replied sarcastically.

"Uh oh. Here it comes, Millhouse. What did I tell you?" T.B. Schuster said wagging his finger.

"Quit busting my balls, T.B. I need a little help. More specifically, there's a dangerous news story that needs to go away," Octavio said.

"Which one?" T.B. Schuster said with a smirk before turning to wink at Millhouse.

"The one about the Secret Service guy—"

"Oh, you mean Chambers? The poor SoB stabbed to death in

his house?"

"Yeah, that one. I need the story of that lowlife to go away?"

"Gee Octavio, that story is gold. There's a lot of interest, which means ratings and revenue."

"I know, it would be a personal favor."

"Go away how?" T.B. Schuster said in earnest.

"Let's get down to it, go away completely."

"That'll be tough, I'll see what I can do. What's your connection to this story?"

Octavio grabbed his scotch off the tray. When the attendant was gone, he took several sips with a loud *slurp* as he brought the glass to his lips. The crackling fire combined with the scotch eased every muscle. The piano player gracefully switched to Beethoven's Moonlight Sonata. Outside, a colorful display of fireworks kept the guests entertained. Octavio examined his surroundings. Besides the pianist and the attendant across the room, they were alone.

"Vel, I'm afraid I haven't had the chance to fill you both in on my vision for America's future. This evening is an opportunity to do just that," Octavio said, taking another sip.

His companions instinctively drew closer in anticipation of something juicy.

"The election of Donald Patrick as president, after that awful Robert Adkins, made me think. The kind of change we need will not come rapidly enough through the ballot box. I've supplemented my political operations with a bit of street activity," Octavio said.

His friends were speechless. Octavio was quick to add, "I've sponsored a branch of Antifa, the cell in DC to be more precise. They're low lives and mendicants, but they'll accelerate the process to change the country. They're also tied to this unfortunate episode with the Secret Service."

T.B. Shuster and Millhouse seemed startled by this admission. They had always known him to be a man of action, but for some reason they appeared surprised.

"Why did you get involved in this?"

"We're all involved to one degree or another T.B. Aren't you and your friends in Hollywood involved with providing bail money when these same groups get arrested?"

"That's different. The majority of college educated Americans now believe the justice system is corrupt. Supporting this cause allows us to score points with the intelligentsia while also winning over a significant portion of the minorities."

"What about the instances when your news network characterized the burning of American cities as peaceful protests?" Octavio said.

"That's called public relations. You of all people should know that!" T.B. Schuster snapped.

"Is that so? As I recall, Ed Bernays, the father of public relations had another name for it. Propaganda!" Octavio said.

T.B. Schuster moved back in his seat, turning his head rapidly from side to side, "Octavio, please...I know you grew up in Brazil, but never use that term here in America. Especially when it comes to our own media."

"Spare me the indignities T.B., we both understand that effective propaganda is not about lies. You know as well as I do it's about manipulating reality to fit one's needs. You magnify certain details to resonate with the public while minimizing facts you don't want the public to care about. Plain and simple. That's what you do on your network every day. That's all I'm asking for now. You don't have to lie about the stabbing of Chambers in his home. Just never mention it and ask the other network executives, some of whom are at this resort at the moment, not to mention the story either."

T.B. Schuster picked up a glass of cognac that had been sitting on the coffee table in between them. He emptied the glass in one sip. He then motioned for the attendant standing on the other side of the room to bring him another. Millhouse sat back in his chair while observing the two of them. He seemed content to let the others do the talking for now.

"Look, I'm sympathetic to what you're trying to do. But

direct involvement with the murder of police and federal officials is a step too far. I'm not sure I can—" T.B. Schuster said before he was cut off.

"You can what?" Octavio growled as if that's not exactly what the networks had done for months during recent protests where police precincts were burned down, while federal and local officials were attacked in cities all across the country. If he recalled it correctly, all the coverage had been adulatory.

"Vel, you know the average American can't be trusted. They are still too patriotic. I didn't start this war against them, but I'm just as committed to its success as any of you," Octavio said.

"Shhh, keep your voice down," Millhouse finally chimed in. He appeared more eager to participate in the conversation now.

"What war are you talking about?" Millhouse said.

"Vel, let's get down to it. I'm talking about the war against the middle class. As Marx would say, the war against the bourgeois. Of course, some would categorize us as members of that same group. But we all know there is a great chasm between the petty bourgeois and ourselves." His companions sat quietly as Octavio emptied his glass of scotch placing it on the table.

"The British journalist David Goodhart is calling it the war of the Anywhere's against the Somewhere's. We're the Anywhere's given our education, wealth, and ability to move from place to place whenever we like. The Somewhere's are the miserable fellows still tied to the concept of America for their identity. Their allegiance is to their religion, their flag, and their guns. They stand in the way of the free movement of capital and labor with their outdated national attachments," Octavio said.

"You mean the people we've labeled as far-right extremists and white supremacists?" T.B. Schuster said.

"Sure, if that's what you choose to call them. But we're

among friends now, you can drop the pretenses. This is why I always call for open borders and equate patriotism to fascism in all my interviews. The fact is the entire globe is one big market today and we can't afford to have national governments, whether in the West or anywhere else, enact protectionist policies that'll hurt our businesses. As far as I'm concerned, democracy as practiced in the West for the past three centuries no longer works. America needs a new Constitution, and I can't sit by any longer."

"I agree whole-heartedly, Octavio, but that has to come about organically, if you know what I mean? Our job is to mold public perceptions so voters will demand those changes themselves," Millhouse said.

"Vel, I'm tired of the slow lane. How long do each of us have left anyway?"

"You can't approach it that way?"

"What way?" Octavio asked.

"As if you are in a hurry. Revolutionary change will sweep us away and everything we hold dear along with it," T.B. Schuster said.

"What about the two of you? It's not like you're not doing the same thing by promoting the post-modernist agenda. Oh, excuse me. I meant political correctness," Octavio said.

"Our approach is more gradual, and thus more stable. I learned about the appeal of post-modernism by reading Herbert Marcuse, Jacques Derrida, Michel Foucault and the rest of them back in the 1970s. By masking our struggle against national interests under the guise of social justice we'll make more progress. America has a long history of racism and lots of guilt among the intellectual class to go along with it. What better way to eliminate every obstacle in the way of a truly global market than by painting all protectionist policies of the US Government as a vestige of its racist past," Millhouse said.

"Octavio, take a second to marvel at what we're doing here. We've combined the teachings of Karl Marx and Antonio Gramsci, the Frankfurt School and post-modernism, turning them on their head in service to global capitalism. We've coopted the leftist agenda in service to our own interests. We are the new face of the left because, in modern day America, right has become left and left has become right. By promoting the policies of the feminists, gays, transexuals, critical race theorists, defund the police lunatics, and what have you in corporate boardrooms, we've gained powerful allies," T. B. Schuster said.

"Don't forget, we get the added bonus of destroying class cohesion. This way, middle class whites, blacks, browns, and immigrants can never unify against us," Millhouse jumped in.

"Since we ourselves benefit from legal loopholes and lower capital gains tax rates, the cost of our welfare state falls squarely on the middle class. We get an added bonus of an alliance with the poor. The best part is, if anyone objects, we paint them as a racist in the media. We've now completely blurred the lines between nationalism, patriotism, protectionism, white supremacy, and fascism. Eventually, the majority of the public will push for the very policies we support through Congress and their state legislatures. As I said, you just have to be patient my dear Octavio," T. B. Schuster said.

"This is exactly the point I was making about a war. He crafted it in those exact words."

"Who crafted what?" Millhouse said.

"One of those lowlife scholars critical of American ruling elites. He died a few years back. Christopher Lasch, that was his name," Octavio said.

"What did he say?" T. B. Schuster said.

"The title of his book was *Revolt of the Elites*. He described a scenario where American elites are no longer bound by obligations to their own country and fellow citizens. Where the richest Americans don't care about overcrowded schools, crumbling cities, crime, and unlimited immigration. Lasch argued we send our kids to private schools, live in gated communities, and utilize private security and bodyguards.

Therefore, the policies we advocate don't really affect us," Octavio said.

"To that, I would only add Mr. Lasch is missing the best part," T.B. Schuster said.

"Which is?" Octavio said.

"That we can attack anyone who disagrees with us as a white supremacist and a fascist. With a little help from the guilt-ridden members of the intelligentsia, we've turned twenty-first century capitalism into a struggle for social justice. We've learned to use the language of the oppressed as a bludgeon to silence our critics. We've turned the struggle for social justice into a vehicle to increase our own wealth. That's how power works in America these days. How's that for irony?"

The pianist was back to Chopin. They finished their drinks and seemed ready to retire. Now to wrap things up.

"So, you don't think I should support Antifa?" Octavio said.

"That's not what we're saying. You can support them behind the scenes, like we do, by funneling weapons or contributing to bail funds. Just don't get directly involved in activities where you're forced to protect them by asking us to bury profitable news stories. Having said that, I don't want this thing to blow up in your face, so I'll do my part to help you," T.B. Schuster said.

All three men stood to shake hands.

"It's done. I bought you as much distance as I could from the media. The rest is up to you," Octavio said.

He was back inside the warm villa perched in front of the fireplace. In his hand was a glass of scotch.

"No need for concern. We decided to flip the script," Destruction said.

With every passing hour, Octavio grasped that Placido had been correct in his assessment of DC Antifa.

"Vel, what the hell does that mean?"

"It means, we're going to blame the entire affair on this Janusz fellow you're so keen to get rid of. We're planting the murder weapon on him."

"You don't think he's going to defend himself in court. He may have an alibi."

"He won't be able to defend himself from the grave. If you'd let me finish, I could've told you that we'll plant the knife, which is still in our possession, in his car, *after* we kill him. That way the FBI will go down the path of a criminal investigation like we wanted."

"The man worked for the CIA. He has a clean record. Do you think anyone will buy this? It's quite risky."

"Doesn't matter, it'll provide a buffer to carry out the attack on the White House."

"Fine, do what you think is best. But if they trace this back to you, I'm not bailing you out," Octavio screamed before hanging up.

If Destruction fucked this up, Octavio would let Placido clean up the mess the way he did best.

22. LAFAYETTE SQUARE, WASHINGTON D.C.

December 29

"Hell no, we won't go. Hell no, we won't go," Rage screamed, holding his hands up in the air.

"Defund the military! End American imperialism now!" Hazard said with the rest of the group. Half of DC Antifa was here today in a sanctioned protest to test the enemy's defenses.

It was interesting to see the slaying of Captain Chambers had not visibly affected security around the White House in any discernible way. Perhaps the feds had attributed the killing to the rise in urban crime, which was perfect. Destruction observed the entire scene from the edge of the park standing near the Rochambeau Statue. He had obtained permission for this gathering from city officials.

Learning what the Secret Service would tolerate from protestors, how quickly they reacted to different incidents, and what kind of force they would use against various provocations was the real intent. The only factor they hadn't given much thought to was the frosty chill that had descended on the nation's capital. Although not one of the coldest cities in America, Washington was known to throw a nasty curve ball at its inhabitants every so often.

His breath vaporized as if he was inside a meat locker. Destruction regretted choosing this day to test the Secret Service. The sting of countless needles on the tip of his numbed fingers was a distraction from the task at hand. He shifted back and forth to stimulate his circulatory system. The silver lining was that the extra clothing provided protection from hidden cameras using facial detection software. True to his word, Octavio had dissuaded the press from covering the Chambers story. That meant less pressure on the Secret Service to beef up security.

The uniformed division of the Secret Service had three cruisers and around a dozen men on bikes keeping a vigilant eye on the pedestrians passing through Pennsylvania Avenue. The street had been closed off to vehicular traffic after Timothy McVeigh blew up the Alfred P. Murrah federal building in Oklahoma City back in 1995. Over the years, Pennsylvania Avenue had become a staging ground for protestors. Destruction moved toward the crowd to blend in.

A pack of five smartly dressed young women passed to Destruction's right, completely oblivious to his presence. Inside Lafayette Square, a row of picnic tables was occupied. His eyes moved from face to face looking for him without luck. A brick pathway crisscrossed the park. He made his way cautiously down the trail. On a wooden bench facing the White House sat his most unruly recruit, Smash.

He resembled a cancerous growth on the wooden slats for which there was no cure. Smash had a bad habit of attacking police officers and destroying property. He rarely followed instructions and was quick to violence. His only redeeming quality was his fearless enthusiasm in the face of danger. Destruction was purposely inundating him with surveillance work to keep him out of trouble for the fight ahead.

To his surprise, Smash was surreptitiously filming the area in front of the White House like he was supposed to with the aid of a hidden camera. Destruction's team of professional protestors drew most of the attention toward themselves. Destruction cautiously observed the perimeter before lowering himself on a bench next to Smash. If they did this while facing away from each other, like they had practiced on Bakunin Farm, no one would be the wiser to their interaction.

"How ya holding up?" Destruction said.

"I had the camera pointed on the president's storm troopers approaching our group. I believe I also captured their reaction to our advance toward the main gate. We should have plenty of footage detailing their procedures against a rowdy crowd," Smash said.

"Excellent work. I knew I could count on ya. Have any capitalist pigs come forward to talk to you?"

"Not yet. The pigs seem fixated mostly on the crowd. Don't worry. If they bust our balls, I'll show respect as you instructed."

Destruction took out his cell phone, staring at it to deflect any interest in the conversation between himself and the man sitting next to him.

"You're making fantastic progress. Well on your way to fulfilling your full potential," Destruction said.

"Are you serious?"

"Does this look like an occasion where I would crack a joke shit-brain? I've been waiting for the right moment, but I think you're ready," Destruction said while playing with his phone.

"You're finally showing your ability for leadership. As of next week, you'll be a lieutenant, just like Hazard. It'll mean more responsibility, but I'm sure you'll handle it," Destruction could sense Smash staring, "Don't acknowledge me directly, ya arse-wipe. Eyes down."

"Sorry, got caught up in the moment."

"The organization puts a great deal of trust in ya. With trust comes a great deal of sacrifice."

"I'm aware of that."

"Good, then I'm sure you won't have any objections to your next assignment. You're going to be one of six men who'll dress up as a Secret Service officer on the night of the attack. Your job will be to fire on the crowd as soon as things heat up. It'll be a chaotic atmosphere, allowing you more freedom to shoot at protestors. We'll fire back with our artillery, so make sure to take cover. Think you can handle that, fuck-face?"

Smash threw his head down while shaking it from side to side.

"You want me to fire on our brothers and sisters?"

"What did I just say about a great deal of sacrifice?"

"But…but…how can I—"

"Are you developing a stuttering problem like your girlfriend, Rage? That's what it'll take to win this war. You can either sit at home and complain about the evils of the system, or you can step up and make a difference. Take a good look around, your sacrifice is about to bear fruit," Destruction said before getting up and walking away.

He needed to check in on the rest of the operation. Out of the corner of his eye, he saw two uniformed agents walking toward him. It was a good opportunity to test their alert level after the death of their boss.

"Gentlemen, some guy physically assaulted me in the park," Destruction said.

"Do you remember what he looked like?" one of the uniformed Secret Service officers asked.

"No, but I think he may have stolen my keys."

"There are a lot of people here buddy. Sounds like something for the Metro Police. We deal with threats to the White House."

"Yeah, but I really need those keys. What about surveillance. I'm sure you have multiple cameras focused on this park. Can't you pull up the footage to see if the guy who threatened me was the one who took my keys."

"Sorry, buddy, can't help you."

"Aren't your cameras able to detect an incident like this?"

"Like I said, sir, it's best if you take this matter up with DC Police."

"What if the guy had pulled a gun on me. Would you arrest him, then?"

"Sir, are you saying that someone in this park has a gun, and they threatened you with it?"

"I noticed he had a bulge in his pocket. I figured it's something sharp, a weapon of some sort. Not sure exactly what?"

"If you didn't see anyone with a gun out here, then there is nothing more we can do for you."

"I appreciate your help, Officer," Destruction said as he walked away.

The Secret Service officers were professional and composed. It was obvious that they had the duty and authority to arrest anyone with a firearm in the vicinity of the White House. What was still not clear was whether they would actively move through a hostile crowd in search of weapons during a large protest. The question about the cameras focused on the park was a long shot but worth the effort.

The one thing he was certain of was that they would be hesitant to use dogs against protestors given the optics. No American president would want to have images of barking German Shepherds outside the White House. It would invite easy comparisons to Nazi Germany and the era of the Jim Crow South. Without the presence of the dogs, they could more easily sneak in the explosives, although there was always the possibility there would be machines with the same capability.

Destruction made his way deep inside his crowd. They were still chanting at the top of their lungs.

"No justice, no peace! Fuck your police!" the crowd said in unison.

Destruction couldn't find the man he was looking for. They were all in black bloc with their faces covered. After several minutes, he finally identified Hazard. Destruction maneuvered behind the man so he could whisper in his ear.

"You're one of the six. You'll be joining Smash and Rage in Secret Service uniform."

Hazard turned to gaze with wide open eyes. "Don't know what to say?"

"Can you handle that, jack-off?"

"Of course."

"You're not squeamish about killing our own like Smash, are you?"

"A true revolution cannot succeed without bloodshed."

"Good, you were listening," Destruction said proudly. "Did ya ascertain the coordinates I asked for?"

"Not yet. To be honest, I think it may be a little risky to use a laser range finder around here," Hazard said.

"I didn't ask you to think shit-brain. Who has the equipment now?"

"I do."

"You're pissing me off."

"What if they have sensors that can detect our beams?"

"You remind me of Lutz and the other dead guy from the Army. You wanna end up like them?"

"Of course not."

"Good. Make sure to memorize the distance to target from the predetermined points on the perimeter. I need those coordinates for our artillery on the night of the assault."

23. LETTERKENNY TOWNSHIP, PENNSYLVANIA

January 01; New Year's Day

T he red-throated finch chirped above her head before gliding gently onto a branch, like an F-14 Tomcat kissing the deck of an aircraft carrier. Its beak was smeared with a gooey brown substance. The finch lowered its head, rubbing the beak side to side against the wood in a futile effort to wipe it clean. Back and forth it went, grinding the beak, then pounding it to no avail. It was a slimy morsel of goo from the depths of Hell. A gob of the brown goo hung perilously from its beak, battling against gravity's attempt to pull it down. The gleaming dangling brown substance was the only thing she could think about.

Kim wanted to snatch the bird with one hand before wiping its tiny, pointed beak with the other. Slowly she raised her right arm. Less than two feet away, Kim pictured using her handkerchief to give the little bird a much-needed facial cleanse. As she closed the distance with steely focus, dried twigs snapped under her sneaker. The finch instantly flew off with the pendulous brown goo flapping in the wind.

Disappointed, Kim made her way toward the cozy wood cabin, a family treasure for generations. To be more precise, it was the land that had been passed down for all those years. Ten acres in one of Pennsylvania's most secluded regions. Letterkenny Township, in Franklin County, was one of the quietest places in the world. Her own father had lived up here for a year when she was a little girl. He had used the solitude to write a novel about the first members of the Jennings family who had settled these parts back in the late 1700s. In reality, the cabin was better suited as a backdrop for a horror novel. If an axe murderer ever decided to attack any of the families that lived off the dirt roads in these parts, hacking them to death, no one would be wiser for weeks.

Worse yet, no one would hear their agonizing cries for help. That's why she'd come prepared. Having traveled with Janusz on one too many missions, Kim never went anywhere without guns. In addition to the .38, Kim had brought along a compact SIG P365 9mm pistol. She placed both guns in the glove compartment of her car in preparation for her evening drive to town in search of food. Kim locked the doors behind her.

When she reached the cabin, her legs weighed a ton, while her stomach ran on empty. Once inside, she took off her shoes. Kim had been hiking through the woods for nearly four hours. Her undershirt was drenched, and the bottom of her feet were raw. She grabbed a small bottle of water from the fridge along with a humongous hamburger she had picked up at a diner in the nearby town of Greencastle the night before. Too famished to heat her food, Kim ravaged the burger stone cold.

Her only compromise was to waste several seconds pouring the ketchup in between the bun and the meat. She attacked the sandwich similar to a ravenous lion tearing into a freshly slaughtered wildebeest. Kim took successive bites, diving in as her eager teeth pulled meaty chunks into her anxious maw. Food flew out as drops of ketchuppy-mayo ran down her chin and onto the floor. She was too hungry to care.

Upon catching her breath, Kim washed down the masticated food with water. Her phone rang several inches away. Reluctantly, she placed the burger on the table to sneak a peek at the caller ID. She was faced with a vexing decision. Should she answer Lesley's call or should she continue to replenish her depleted energy? The smart choice was to let the food settle before diving back in.

"How goes it, Lesley?"

"I called to ask the same question, how's life in the country?"

"It's only been a few days, and I'm calmer. Not sure if it's the fresh air or the hikes."

"What do you do all day?"

"It's not that bad. I have electricity, a water heater, and satellite internet connection. The nearest town is a fifteen-minute drive so I can get everything I need. I spend most mornings hiking or chopping wood. The evenings are dedicated to reading and meditation. The whole thing is kind of therapeutic."

"I was going to ask if you wanted some company, but it looks like you're doing quite well by yourself."

"What's the matter, don't you have friends nearby?" Kim said.

"They're all up in Connecticut. I've been in DC during the past four years. With my teaching job at Georgetown, I'm too busy to meet new people. Anyway, I don't want to bore you with my life. I'll let you get back to it—"

"No, no, you're not boring me," Kim said hesitantly. Although she was enjoying the seclusion, she saw no harm to having Lesley over for a short stay. It would be a good change to her routine.

"You wanna join me for day or two?"

"I don't want to impose."

"No imposition. It's only a two-hour trip for you—"

"Since you insist," Lesley jumped in before Kim could finish, "I'd love to. What do you want me to bring?"

"Just yourself. I've got everything else we need up here."

"Perfect. Text me your address. I hope the GPS can find you."

"Oh, don't worry. It's not that hard to find this place," Kim said before describing the best way to reach her cabin. She finished her meal and laid on the couch to rest her eyes.

Her chin tickled as a warm liquid ran down the side of her face. Placing her left hand over the wetness, she immediately knew what it was. Kim wiped the drool before opening her eyes. She had no idea where she was. With her head aching, she wondered how she had gotten here.

Her first instinct was to get up and run. Upon closing her eyes to focus, it all came back. The drive up from Virginia, the family cabin, the four-hour hike, the gigantic hamburger, and lying down to rest her eyes. Kim walked to the sink to wash her face. She strained to remember something important. What was it?

For no particular reason Kim opened her laptop, typing *Lesley Gantz* in the search engine. A slew of articles populated the page one after the other. She hated herself for not having done this before amid the chaos. With the Unit under attack, she had overlooked the basics of her training. Lesley had mentioned she was a professor at Georgetown University, but what did Kim really know about this woman? *Oh, God, I gave her my address.*

Kim reassured herself that Lesley had shown kindness on numerous occasions. Lesley had found and returned her key. *God, what if she took them herself when she bumped into me?* Why was all this doubt hitting her now? She scrolled down the page, opening the articles authored by Lesley one by one. Paranoia was a debilitating affliction if left unchecked.

The Consequences of American Imperialism. Or was it? She read through the first paragraph of the article and opened another. *The History of Racism in American Politics.* What the fuck was all this? *The Legacy of White Supremacy and Fascism in America.* There had to be a mistake. Why was this woman so eager to be with Kim? *Thump...Thump...Thump...Thump.* Too late to ask.

"Kim, it's Lesley. Are you home?" the voice came from outside as Kim considered her options.

"Just a minute, I'll be right there," Kim said as she closed all the tabs on her browser before folding the screen. She opened the front door.

"Hey, stranger. Wach ya up to?" Lesley said. The hairs on Kim's neck stood, she was not sure why.

"I was napping,"

"Oh, I'm sorry I didn't mean to—"

"Don't worry, I'm up and awake now. Come on in," Kim said, suddenly aware she had left the guns in the car before her nap.

"It's a real cozy place you've got. Where's the fire?"

"Haven't turned it on yet. I usually do that later. For now, the space heater is sufficient."

Lesley gazed awkwardly around the room before focusing her eyes back on Kim.

"Please, have a seat. I don't have much food, but I can get you some water."

"Maybe later," Lesley said as she moved toward the couch. "What you wanna do?"

"We can enjoy movies on my laptop. I think I have some hot cocoa."

"How about a short walk before it gets dark? The secluded woods are perfect to reconnect with nature."

"I just got back from a hike before my nap. Maybe tomorrow?"

"Do you keep any weapons here?" Lesley said out of blue. "I mean, for hunting. There must be lots of game to hunt around here."

"Season starts later in the year, closer to fall. Besides, I don't have a license and I don't enjoy killing," Kim said as Lesley raised an eyebrow and threw her head back.

"You need a license to hunt animals?"

"What do *you* think? Anyone could just go out and hunt whenever they like?"

"I just assumed—"

"You assumed there are no regulations regarding the hunting of animals in the country. Maybe you thought people who own guns just like to kill things?"

Lesley stood there with a blank expression on her face. It

was obvious she wanted to reply but did not know what to say. *Maybe I'm being too harsh,* Kim thought.

"Sorry, Lesley, I just woke up and am a bit grumpy," Kim said with a forced smile.

"Oh, don't worry. I understand."

"It's just that—"

"Just that what?"

"Oh, it's nothing."

"No, go ahead. Get it off your chest."

"It's just that I was reading some of your work before, and man—" Kim said before stopping herself.

"Yes, what did you think?"

"I know you're in academia, which is traditionally left of center, but don't you think you're being a bit harsh?"

"I didn't come here to argue, but no. I don't think critiquing the exploitive system that governs the United States is harsh."

Kim studied her intently. What was this woman after?

"I'm surprised then that you enjoy hanging out with me. I think I mentioned that I worked for the FBI before transitioning to private equity."

Lesley beamed a fake smile and glanced her timepiece once more. She quickly turned her head toward the door before returning her attention to Kim. Lesley was rapidly tapping her shoe on the floor.

"Am I holding you up from an important engagement?"

"Not at all," Lesley said, trying to avoid eye contact. Beads of sweat accumulated on her forehead right below the hairline.

Thump...Thump...Thump

Both women turned to face the door. Kim's heart sank into her stomach. A shiver ran down her back as her throat suddenly turned dry.

"You expecting anyone, Kim?" Lesley said.

"Absolutely not. I have no idea who—"

"Go on, see who it is," Lesley said.

Kim's legs were glued to the ground. Her body was cold. She breathed heavily. There wasn't enough air in the room.

"All right, I'll get it," Lesley said as she opened the door.

Kim was unable to stop her. A young man stood outside wearing jeans and a puffy Hoyas jacket with a bulldog insignia over his heart. His breath was visible with each exhale.

"Don't just stand there, come in," Lesley said as if she owned the place. "This is Kim," Lesley continued with a weird smirk, "What's the matter, dear? Did you see a ghost?"

Kim could not say anything. She kept thinking of a way to get to those guns. Lesley and her guest were standing in front of the door.

"Don't worry, Rage. She doesn't have guns with her."

The man studied Kim without saying a word.

"Why don't you make yourself comfortable," Lesley said staring menacingly at Kim.

Kim's legs froze. *Get yourself together, do something.* The man reached into his coat pocket, pulling out a Beretta M9 pistol. Kim's body was starting to shut down.

"Don't worry, we don't want to hurt you. We just need a quick favor," Lesley said.

This was ridiculous. Kim wasn't going to let these people get the best of her. She maneuvered toward the couch and sat.

"That's better," Lesley said.

"Why did you call him Rage?" Kim asked.

"Because I asked her to. I have a tendency to get angry, and my brothers thought it would be the perfect name for me," the man said.

"Your brothers?"

"Yeah, my brothers in Antifa."

Kim's eyes darted back and forth between the two of them.

"Don't strain yourself trying to figure it out, dear," Lesley said.

Her newly acquired pedantic tone was quickly getting annoying.

"Like I was saying. We need a favor," Lesley said.

"Go on," Kim said, anger bubbling in her stomach.

"We need you to use your phone to call a friend. Ask Mr.

Janusz Soltani to join you for the evening. I'm sure the thought of fucking you must have overtaken him more than once," Rage said.

She was staring at the culprits that were systematically killing off her colleagues. She had not seen it coming until it was too late.

"You want me to turn a man I trust with my life over to you?"

"You have too much faith in this man. Remember dear, every relationship has an element of exploitation."

"Go to hell. Better yet, go fuck yourselves," Kim said raising her voice.

"I told you she was going to be trouble. You should've just let me finish her," Lesley said looking at Rage.

"This Janusz guy is a high priority for us. We need to use her to draw him out. Now, let me do this my way—" Rage stopped mid-sentence.

Kim jumped over the couch toward the kitchen. There was sharp bread knife under the sink.

"Stop right there, you bitch," Rage yelled.

Pow...pow. the second bullet tore through a cabinet door inches from her face. Kim froze with her hands up. She dared not turn. The clatter of the footsteps grew closer. Which one of them was it? The blow pounded her head before she stumbled to the ground. The back of her neck grew hot, then cold, then hot again. It was as though someone had placed her cranium inside a water mattress before jumping up and down on it. Seconds later, something fell on her back. She turned slowly so her cerebrum would not spin out of control.

"How'd you like that you privileged bitch?" the high-pitched voice said.

Kim tried to focus through the blur. Lesley stood above her. She had smashed the laptop over Kim's head.

"Take it easy. I need her functional so she can make that call," the man said as he placed the M9 back inside his coat pocket.

He put his hands out to help her up. She decided to grab onto him.

"Easy now, easy," Rage said as he helped her stand erect. "Let's walk back over to the couch. Don't just stand there, Lesley. Get her some fluids."

Lesley's face turned red, "how often should I repeat myself. I don't take orders from new recruits."

"What's your problem?"

"You can give her your own fluids."

"Okay! Okay! Will you please get this woman something to drink?"

Kim sat on the couch. The water mattress containing her cranium was no longer spinning. If she made it out the door it would take at least seven seconds to reach the car. The SIG P365 and .38 were in the glove compartment, but she was not sure if she had locked the doors. It was likely given force of habit. In that case she was in for another beating.

"Are you going to call this guy, or not, you stupid bitch?" Lesley shouted while handing her a small water bottle. Even during her college days, Kim could never figure out why these progressive activist women were always so angry. Perhaps they didn't get laid enough.

"Go over there and let me handle this," Rage said, his head turned toward Lesley.

Kim gathered all her strength to deliver a Krav Maga punch straight into Rage's testicles. The man immediately crumbled as she stood to face the lunatic Lesley. The crazy bitch threw a punch that Kim deflected before counter punching her jaw. The stinging sensation worked its way from Kim's knuckles toward her wrist and down her arm.

Lesley took several steps back but was still on her feet. An intense pain shot up Kim's body straight to her skull. She looked down to see Rage biting her leg like a madman. She used her other leg to kick him in the stomach before lunging for the doorknob. The cold handle pressed against her palm. She tried turning it but it would not budge. Any second now, they would pull her back.

What the fuck is up with this knob? She was turning left. She immediately reversed direction, and the door opened. Out of the corner of her eyes someone was approaching. Kim pulled the door with all her might, throwing it fully open before jumping outside. To her surprise, she ambled with a gimp. She shut the pain out, pushing forward toward the car. Before long she would even the odds. She grabbed the handle. *Fuck, it's locked.* Footsteps approached from behind.

"Come back here, you bitch!" Lesley screamed.

Kim focused on the dense tree line up ahead. If she could get far enough into the woods, she might be able to lose them. Someone grabbed her wrist. She turned to punch Lesley on the nose. Kim immediately ran toward safety in the woods. As she passed the tree line, there was buzzing by her ears. Strange for bees to be flying around in the winter. Chunks of tree bark landed on her face.

Holy Shit. A hot burn seared her flesh. Perhaps a colony of bees were stinging her. Seconds later, another bee stung her leg. If she had trampled on a beehive, she was paying the price. She pushed forward, deeper into the woods. Her heart now beating against her ribcage. Kim gasped for air but did not stop. Her entire body burning now from the bee stings. She ran out of breath.

Strange, Kim usually ran ten miles a week for exercise. She hadn't even run a mile yet. The forest started spinning around before a debilitating chill overwhelmed her body. *Why the hell am I nauseas?* It did not matter, she had to keep moving. Just a bit farther, and she would rest. Everything turned black. She gasped for air, trying hard to stay on her feet. She collapsed face down into a pile of decaying leaves.

"She got away! She got away! Come on, we gotta go after her," Lesley said.

"She's not going anywhere," Rage said annoyed. Lesley was pissing him off, it was all he could do to keep from slapping her.

"How do you know?"

"Because I've grown proficient with this M9, and I squeezed off a good five or six rounds right at her. Pretty sure I hit her at least once, maybe twice, judging by her reaction."

"Where the hell is she then?"

"It don't matter. You see this?" Rage said, pointing toward red stains on the leaves.

"She's bleeding. She can't be that far, let's get her."

"What for, she won't be in any condition to call this Janusz guy if we do find her. She'll bleed out and die in the woods. Judging by the distances between property lines, it may be weeks, hell, years, if she's ever found. You know what, that's fine by me," Rage said.

"What do we tell the others?"

"The truth. She wouldn't cooperate and tried to escape. So, we killed and buried her in the woods," Rage said.

He was looking for the slightest indication of protest. He would enjoy killing this arrogant slut more than the other one.

"Sounds good to me," Lesley said with a smile.

"Come on, let's get out of here before it gets any darker," Rage said, placing the M9 in his pants.

24. MAZATLÁN, MEXICO

January 05

Monroe stood at the edge of the patio under a palm tree. He was staring out into the blue waters of the Pacific Ocean. Down below was a two-hundred-foot drop to the Malecon de Mazatlán boardwalk along the rocky coastline. To his left stood his buddy, Taylor, another pesky high society reporter who had made life difficult.

The two men were accompanied by two other journalists for what was promised to be a working vacation in paradise. They were all gathered near the pool where generous amounts of Mexican food, alcohol, and fruit were available for the guests. They had come to learn how Mexico's business community sought to combat climate change.

The invitation had promised exclusive access to some of the top business leaders in Mexico to cover their efforts to reverse global warming. The unique alabaster compound perched against the side of a cliff in Mazatlán was rumored to be the largest in the city. In addition to the pool and Jacuzzi, there were numerous palm trees adding to the resort like ambiance of the fifteen thousand square foot main residence.

Scantily clad local women in bikinis frolicked among the guests with a mischievous glimmer in their eyes. Their behavior was partly the result of cocaine and partly that of the money these escorts had been paid to entertain the American journalists.

After waiting several hours for his guests to absorb some sun and fun, the host invited the four correspondents to a question and answer session in one of the recreation rooms.

This chamber was a converted dance studio which, at present, was empty with the exception of a row of four folding chairs that had been placed in front of a makeshift podium. The lights were dimmed and there were no windows down here as the entire floor was carved into the hillside away from the beach.

They waltzed in one by one, still dizzy from the champagne and margaritas. The group was comprised of three men, Monroe, Taylor, and Bradford and one woman, Darcy. The reporters entered the darkened room uneasily, not sure what to do with themselves.

The host monitored the group through a bank of infrared cameras hoisted on the walls.

"Please, take your seats, your host will join you in a moment," an ominous voice commanded through the speaker system.

When he was satisfied that they had waited long enough, their host entered the room. Two large floodlights on the ceiling shined brightly on the faces of the reporters, making it impossible for them to see who stood at the podium in front of them.

"Dear friends, so nice of you to come down to Mexico on such short notice. I hope you're enjoying the accommodations so far?"

"The view of the ocean by the pool is fabulous, which is why it's so hard to understand why we're meeting in this darkened room? We could easily discuss—" Monroe said before he was cut off.

"Yes, but I didn't want any distractions from the business at hand. This won't take long, I assure you," their host said.

"So, where's the rest of the group?"

"The group? What group?" the host replied.

"The invitations offered a Q&A and possible interviews with leaders of the Mexican business community committed to combating global warming. Where are they?" Taylor jumped in.

"They'll be here shortly," the hidden voice replied.

"And you are?" Monroe said.

"We'll get to my name in a second, first I want to review a few items."

"This is such bullshit. I knew we shouldn't have come here. I don't trust businessmen in America and my expectations for their counterparts down here are even lower. I think we should leave right now," Darcy said in a high-pitched voice.

"Let's not be rash, Darcy. We should give our host the benefit of the doubt before jumping to conclusions," Bradford broke in.

"Dear lady, I promise you'll get exactly what you came for momentarily. Please, relax so we can begin," The host said.

The four reporters sat back in their seats as the doors from which they had entered screeched shut. The room was completely dark with the exception of the two floodlights that blasted the American journalists. Darcy folded her arms under her chest while the men guarded their eyes from the harsh lights.

Monroe was the first to raise his arm. "I'd like to start by asking what Mexican corporations are doing to reduce their carbon footprint and what alternatives you're developing to transition away from fossil fuels?"

"Vel, before I answer that, I'd like to ask you a question that has been bugging me for the past two weeks."

"Sir, could you at least step into the light so we can see your face," Taylor said while raising his voice.

"My face is irrelevant. Now, who told you that Souza Enterprises is purchasing *Impressionable Magazine*?"

A deafening silence fell over the underground recreation room. Their faces contorted into a mix between incredulity and horror. Octavio always enjoyed these moments before the kill. He had bought this property in Mexico as a place to decompress in complete anonymity. It was registered to an offshore holding company no one had ever heard of or had reason to investigate further. Although he preferred to shoot game in the open, he was excited about the opportunity to kill more than one person during a hunt. It would be an entirely new experience.

"What kind of a sick demented joke is this? I demand to know who the fuck you are or else we're leaving immediately."

"Monroe, I can assure you that you're in no position to make demands at the moment. Please, save yourself the agony and answer my question."

They gazed at each other not knowing what to do. Finally, it was Bradford who stood up. "That's it. Open these doors immediately and let us out. We're going back to the airport."

"My dear spoiled brats, this is not an American university where you make demands and the administration immediately surrenders," Octavio said before closing the breech of the Browning Citori.

He had loaded two three-inch slugs into the weapon and had several more in his pocket. He also had the advantage of shelter in the darkness.

"I don't like this. I don't like it one bit," Darcy said with trembling hands. The color drained from her face.

"Who tipped you off about the purchase of *Impressionable Magazine*?"

"You won't get away with this, our editors will be looking for us."

"Really? Who did you come down here to see? Who owns this property? Hundreds of Americans disappear every year in Mexico, many of them kidnapped and killed by the cartels. Who is to say you won't be another statistic?"

"Please, sir, don't do this," Bradford said.

"*Noooooo*, I don't want to die," Darcy cried out.

"Get a hold of yourself, he's just bluffing," Monroe said, holding her by the shoulders. The sounds of the host's footsteps were audible from the dark outer perimeter of the floodlights. *Tap...tap...tap* was the pattern of his steps as he circled the group. *Tap...tap...tap.*

"God, where is he?" Darcy wanted to know as she made a run toward the darkness. One of the floodlights followed her every step of the way.

"Darcy, noooo, don't," Taylor yelled out.

Pow... the blast from the Browning roiled the entire room. The explosion was immediately followed by a *thud* as something hit the floor.

"Holy *fuuuuuck*," Monroe yelled.

"Dear Jesus, Dear Jesus, Dear Jesus," Taylor kept repeating.

"Mommy please, please, please," Bradford said in shock.

They stared at the mangled body of the woman known as Darcy. Her corpse was still after her cranium had exploded.

Even Octavio was surprised by the sight. This was his first head shot on a human being, and it took a little getting used to.

"So, who was your source?" Octavio repeated.

"Fuck you, you crazy bastard," Taylor said.

"Wrong answer," Octavio said aiming his shotgun. With the pull of the trigger the blast blew off a portion of Taylor's upper thigh. The man screamed in agony as he crashed to the floor.

"All right, all right. It was Tom McMillan. Are you satisfied you sociopath?" Monroe said.

"Who the hell is that?" Octavio shot back.

"One of the editors at *Impressionable Magazine*. The staff at the magazine does not want to work for Octavio Souza due to his involvement with fossil fuels. They were hoping to scuttle the transaction once word got out," Monroe replied.

"I'll deal with them later," Octavio said.

"Are you going to let us go?" Monroe said hesitantly.

"I'm afraid that's impossible," Octavio said as he broke the shotgun open to load two more shells.

Monroe was so nervous he had wet his pants. He turned his head from left to right, and then left again looking into the darkness. He didn't know which way to run.

Octavio closed the shotgun and took aim. "Come now, the least the two of you could do is to make this more sporting for me by scattering."

Monroe turned and ran toward the darkness, only to have the floodlights follow his every move. He was screaming at the top of his lungs. This prompted the other survivor, Bradford, to scream as well while frozen in place.

I guess I have to make this game more challenging for myself, Octavio thought as he raised his Browning. He took direct aim at Monroe's back and pulled the trigger. Without waiting to inspect his kill, Octavio instantly turned the barrel to where he expected Bradford to be standing. Octavio pulled the trigger again. The interval between the two shots was barely a second, just like a skeet competition.

When the smoke cleared, Octavio opened the breech allowing the ejector to push out the two empty shells. With the Browning broken in half over his right shoulder, Octavio walked toward the carcasses. Bradford's scrotum had been blown wide open as he lay still. His lips were parted, and he had a blank stare in his eyes. Gobs of his testicles were scattered all around. Octavio proceeded to shuffle across the floor like a graceful dancer. Monroe lay face down with a crater sized hole in his back.

The lights came back on before Placido entered the room. He had been operating the floodlights for Octavio. Placido was oblivious to the carnage all around. "What are we going to do about this McMillian character?"

"Don't worry about him. Clean up this mess and dissolve their bodies in the acid tank. Release a statement on behalf of one of the cartels that they have killed four American reporters for digging into their business operations. Once we drive back to San Francisco, no one will ever know we were down here."

"Ahhhh…ahhhhhhhh…help…help me…."

"Who is that?" Octavio said staring at Placido.

"That's Taylor, *Chefe.* You only blew away the side of his thigh. It appears he's still alive."

"I'm too tired for this. Finish him off."

Placido pulled out a six-inch folding knife from his pants pocket. "With pleasure, *Chefe,*" he said as he made his way to the mangled mess trying to crawl away in haste.

25. GEORGETOWN, WASHINGTON D.C.

January 10

From M Street, he turned onto Wisconsin Avenue headed toward the waterfront. Janusz made a right turn on K Street under the bridge. It was ten minutes to midnight and the place was devoid of human activity. Past 33rd Street, K turned into Water Street, so on he went.

With scant lighting, a heavy darkness enveloped this corner of Georgetown. The area had changed quite a bit over the years, the most obvious difference was the surrender of parking space for the ubiquitous Capital Bikeshare racks. This was one part of DC that reminded him of the industrial sections of Philadelphia and New York where pedestrians seldom ventured late in the evening.

Jason's instructions had been clear, "go to the end of Water Street, passing under the Key Bridge. Park in front of the boat house where they rent out the canoes and someone will meet you there at midnight."

It had been a month since his last meeting with Kalugin and this was their first new lead. The men who were scheduled to meet with him were students, according to Jason. They were walk-ins who had informed the FBI that they had been approached by Russians to monitor a private equity firm in Herndon, Virginia. According to the students, the Russians were interested in the employees of High Risk Capital, which was the outward cover for the Unit.

Since the FBI was unaware of the activities of Unit 81, Jason said they had recorded the tip and had thanked the students for coming forward. That was apparently less than a week ago and, so far, nothing had come of the investigation. Jason had come across the intelligence from a friend in the FBI who had provided the contact details for the Georgetown students. Jason's FBI source had arranged this meeting for Janusz.

He pulled up against the railing in front of the boat house. Although crowded on the weekends, there wasn't a single parked car around. The students had gone out of their way to meet somewhere quiet. He understood their apprehension not to be spotted in public with him. It would've been nicer to meet in a dorm or hotel room, but beggars can't be choosers. It was his most promising opportunity to learn about the people who had killed Stan, the people who had made Bill disappear, and the people who had put Tony in the hospital.

The Russians were not usually in the habit of eliminating US citizens on American soil. But given the debacle surrounding the death of General Kalantari in Moscow, anything was possible. Did the Russians know Unit 81 had no direct ties to the US Government? How they had pieced all this together, he was not sure. Perhaps there were Congressmen who were only too happy to be rid of the Unit. Maybe someone in the intelligence bureaucracy had found out. Any one of the sixteen intelligence agencies could have been angered by Unit 81's activities. The possibilities were endless, which is why this meeting was essential.

Janusz kept the engine running for heat. Outside, it was twenty degrees Fahrenheit and the temperature was only going to drop further before daybreak. He took the SIG P226 pistol out of the glove, placing it on the passenger seat next to him. There was a distinct possibility the Russians could have followed these students without their awareness. A stray criminal popping out of nowhere was another reason to keep the Sig close by. Janusz was blinded by a sudden flash.

A pair of headlights approached rapidly. He looked away to check the clock on the dash. It was exactly midnight. It had to be them. Their punctuality was the only thing out of the ordinary. College students were not known for respecting other people's schedule.

The headlights came to a screeching halt about six feet perpendicular to the driver's side door of his BMW. Janusz pulled his window down. The other vehicle kept its lights on and the engine running. Several seconds later, a silhouette emerged from the passenger side. The man appeared to be in decent shape.

When he got within a foot, Janusz could see the man was wearing a puffy Hoyas jacket with a bulldog insignia over his heart. He had a goatee with messy hair. The man carried a backpack on one shoulder. Perhaps he had documents to show.

"Are you Janusz?" the man said.

"I'm sorry, our mutual contact did not provide your name."

"We'll get to that in a second. Are you Janusz Soltani?"

"Yes, I am," Janusz said hesitantly, desperate not to miss an opportunity to learn more about the people who had shot Tony.

"What's your name?"

"For the purpose of this meeting you can call me Rage," the man said.

It was an odd nickname for a Georgetown student, but whatever.

"Who's the guy behind the wheel?"

"That's Hazard. We've both been looking forward to meeting you."

Janusz studied the man looking for anything out of the ordinary. Georgetown boy had a weird smirk on his face, as if he'd just caught a roommate with his pants down. His demeanor was cocky, a bit too relaxed for someone who had gone out of his way to avoid Russian surveillance for this meeting.

"What's in the gym bag?"

"I've got some evidence I want to show you."

"You wanna come inside my car so we can talk?"

"I can talk from here," Rage said with a chuckle.

"Aren't you cold?"

"Not at all. This won't take long."

"And why is that?" Janusz said.

He was starting to get annoyed with this kid.

"Because you'll be dead in about a minute," the kid said, pulling out a M9 Beretta 9mm pistol.

The Sig was too far to grab now. The kid moved closer. He placed the cold metal of the muzzle against Janusz's forehead. It was an unexpected twist to this meeting but then again Janusz had ignored all the warning signs. If this was the end, then so be it. His poor brother, Ben, hadn't seen the end coming either. The only difference was, unlike his brother, he could turn this around with just one mistake.

"I've never shot anyone up close, but I'm willing to give it a try," Rage said coldly.

Janusz peered into his eyes with steely determination, which seemed to unnerve the kid. The index finger moved but the trigger did not. The stupid motherfucker had forgotten about the manual safety. Janusz used his left arm to push the M9 down to the edge of the window. With his right, he pulled the Beretta away from Rage with overwhelming force.

The pistol fell on the ground outside his car. So did the gym bag. The man named Hazard approached from the side. Janusz had to finish this before it became a two on one situation. He grabbed Rage by the collar, pulling his face forward into the top of the driver windowsill.

"*Aaaaaahhhhh,*" Rage cried as Janusz shoved him back into street.

Rage fell as Janusz grabbed the SIG P226, pointing the weapon at Hazard. The man immediately ran back toward his car. Rage ran after him, leaving the backpack on the ground. Janusz was hesitant to shoot. He needed these two assholes alive to get some answers. The doors closed before he was blinded by the intensity of the high beams.

Janusz had less than a second to move out of the way as the lights closed in on him. He jumped onto the hood of the BMW just as their vehicle smashed into his driver's side door. The impact sent Janusz crashing onto the asphalt on the opposite side of the car. With the pistol still in his hand, he pushed himself off the ground and turned. The other vehicle raced down the street in reverse.

Janusz aimed dead center of the engine compartment and fired three rounds as the driver made a one hundred eighty-degree turn. The first shot hit something, but the next two must have missed their mark.

There was just enough light for him to recognize that they were driving a Dodge Charger, which was bad news. The other piece of bad news was that his driver's side door was completely smashed. It was hanging on to the chassis by a hair. Janusz pulled the door off before throwing it inside his vehicle. He then jumped inside, taking Rage's gym bag with him. Within seconds he had put the car in gear and was rocketing down Water Street in hot pursuit.

Whoever the fuck these guys were, they were definitely not professionals. Janusz turned left on Wisconsin, several seconds behind the Charger. Driving this fast through the arctic air was no longer a picnic without a door. He cranked up the heater to the maximum setting and took a hard left onto M Street. The Charger was a lot further ahead than he expected. Janusz floored the pedal determined to catch up. At the Key Bridge, the Charger turned left to cross the Potomac into Virginia.

On more than one occasion in his early twenties Janusz had been pulled over on these very same roads for speeding. Why were the cops never around when they were needed the most? The view from the Key Bridge passed by like lightning. Without the seat belt, he would have fallen out several miles back.

The approaching high rises of Rosslyn had the aura of a financial district. In reality, Janusz was in the heart of government contractor heaven. He recalled with amusement flying back to Reagan Airport several years earlier. In the seatback of the next row was a brochure advertising the allure of Rosslyn. Manhattan on the Potomac they had called it. The author of that piece must have fancied himself a comedian.

He sped through several red lights on Wilson Blvd. Janusz was only a car length behind. He revved the engine and turned the wheel aiming for the driver's side of the rear bumper. A properly executed PIT maneuver at this velocity would send the Charger careening out of control. He missed the mark again as someone popped out of the sunroof. It was the same twit who had tried to kill him, Rage. Janusz frantically turned the wheel, zigzagging between lanes as soon as he saw the first muzzle flash.

There were several more bursts before his front passenger window shattered. A million pieces flew into the cabin grazing the exposed skin on his hand and neck.

"Fucking bastard," Janusz screamed while launching toward the rear driver side bumper.

The motherfucker fired twice more, leaving two distinct spiderweb patterns on the front windshield. The Charger immediately turned into a small side street. Janusz suddenly caught up and rammed the rear bumper with maximum force. The Charger swerved out of control making a full U-turn in front of his BMW. The Dodge continued veering backward slowly with its front driver-side wheels next to Janusz's doorless cabin.

Janusz held the Sig in his right hand, shooting out the Charger's front tire. The damaged Dodge crashed into a parked car in the residential neighborhood. He tried jumping out to no avail. The fucking seat belt was fastened. After releasing it, someone shot out of the Charger's sunroof and ran the hundred-meter dash down the street. Out of the corner of his eye he saw the driver's door fly open.

A stumbling man emerged turning to face Janusz. He held a pistol, which he clumsily raised without warning. Instinct took over as Janusz grouped three shots into center mass, hitting his target straight in the chest. The man collapsed backward, hitting nothing but asphalt.

Seconds later, Janusz stood over a man he did not recognize. He promptly sat behind the wheel of the BMW in hot pursuit of Rage. He needed someone alive to answer questions. It was dark and every home had a yard. He went down the street several hundred yards before coming around the block to sweep the street once more. Rage was nowhere to be found, but Janusz had his gym bag.

26. BAKUNIN FARM, BELTSVILLE MARYLAND

January 11

"How could ya be this ffffucking careless, ya arse-wipe? Tell me? First Chambers, and now this? On top of that, the fucker we're chasing is still alive," Destruction said as his forehead sizzled.

"You're the one who killed Chambers."

"Only because you started playing pool instead of doing your job."

"You shouldn't have stabbed him. I told you it was wrong to take advantage of the guy who saved our lives. It was karma."

A bamboo baton used for combat training was resting against a nearby wall. Destruction was inclined to smash it against Rage's head but decided against it for the moment.

"We'll get him next time," said the arse-wipe standing within striking distance.

"What next time? Ya think this Janusz guy is going to sit around so you can take another crack at him?" Destruction waited for a reply. "Do ya?"

"No, but...but...but—"

"But...but...but what, ya stuttering fucking fool? What about Hazard? He certainly can't help you on your next attempt."

Destruction suddenly grabbed the baton and lobbed it at the shit-brain standing in front of him. Rage ducked instinctively.

"Why didn't ya bring the fucking knife back?"

"I was trying to escape," Rage replied.

"The knife we used to kill a Secret Service captain in charge of security at the White House is just out there somewhere. Do you have any idea what this means?" *Buurp.* Rage aggravated him.

Destruction took a deep breath. "Now, we have zero leverage. When the police connect Hazard's body to our organization, they'll request assistance from the FBI. Where things go from there, no one knows."

"I'll get this Janusz just like I did the other bitch in Pennsylvania."

"You're not listening. I built this organization from the ground up and—" *Buurp.*

Destruction took another second to catch his breath. Too many scenarios raced through his head. He needed Lesley and Fiona for relief.

"Why didn't ya just kill that fuck-faced capitalist pig before things got out of hand?"

"I told you, my gun jammed," Rage said.

"Did ya follow my instructions about cleaning your weapon and testing it before the operation?"

"Of course!"

"You sure your weapon wasn't on safety?"

"Absolutely not."

Something about Rage's answers irked him. Destruction's head hurt too much to put his finger exactly on what it was. The gas bubbles churned in his stomach, making their way up to his throat. The shootout in Arlington had made the news despite Octavio's efforts to suppress the story. Destruction considered moving up the date for the attack on the White House.

There were too many loose ends, and he needed to tie them off quickly. Should he send another team to finish off Janusz and the remaining members of Unit 81? That would only waste precious resources needed elsewhere.

Out of the corner of his eye he spotted Rage moving toward the door. "Where do ya think you're going?"

"To the apartment. I'm worn out."

The words coming out of Rage sounded like gibberish. Destruction had to act fast to salvage the plot. Rage was still standing by the door, with an idiotic expression plastered on his face.

"That sounds good, get some rest. You're going to need it," Destruction said as the shit-brain walked out. Destruction searched for a number on his computer. He was about to tie off those loose ends.

Rage sat on his bed staring catatonically at the wall. His studio apartment was one of a large collection of properties paid for by DC Antifa through front companies. The apartments were purchased to house new recruits. Rage was desperate to prove his worth. He was sapped of energy, but he could not fall asleep. Whenever he closed his eyes, he was under the bridge in Georgetown with Janusz. The Beretta M9 was right up against the man's forehead. He pulled the trigger, but nothing happened. *The safety, release the safety,* he shouted in his head.

He was being chased through meandering streets in Arlington. The gun shots still echoed in the deep crevices of his mind. He had been too far out to see the carnage, but he was haunted by images of Hazard. The fucker lay there on the asphalt as the blood drained from his corpse. Antifa had allowed Rage to find new meaning in his life and what had he done with the opportunity? He had squandered it through incompetence. Destruction was on the verge of ushering in a new era. Rage was not about to let this chance pass him by.

He walked toward the closet at the other end of his studio. Hidden behind his clothes against the wall was a freshly cleaned M-16 rifle. He had taken it from the armory at Bakunin Farm without telling Destruction. It was part of the large cache of weapons they had stolen from Fort Belvoir. Rage had been tasked with inventory for the weapons and had decided to take one for himself. He was glad he did. Rage would use this rifle to finish the job. Destruction had provided a home address for the target, Janusz. It was for surveillance purposes only.

Destruction had warned them not to attack Janusz at his home. Rage no longer cared. He would wait for Janusz outside the bastard's townhouse. He was going to finish the job no matter what. With the recent uptick in crime around the country, he was not worried about getting caught. Rage admired the weapon, patting the M-16 gently as if it was a child. On the floor of the closet was a loaded magazine he shoved into the rifle. He sat on the ground for several minutes admiring his toy while turning it from side to side. *It's not going to be on safety again, my friend,* he kept repeating while conjuring up images of Janusz.

Knock...knock...knock.

Rage gazed at the front door, clutching the rifle tightly. He was not expecting visitors.

Knock...knock...knock...knock...knock.

"This is the FBI. We have a warrant to search the premises."

Was this some sort of dream? How did the FBI know to come here? Perhaps it was Janusz who had tracked him down to this location. Didn't matter now.

"Ju-ju-just a minute," Rage said as he pointed the muzzle at the door.

He flicked the selector lever to a three round burst mode. Peering through the rear sights, he aimed for an area between the peephole and the handle. What would his parents think if they could see him now? Probably would disown him, that's what. Would he ever see them again? His muscles tensed as he placed an index finger over the trigger. *Tat, tat, tat...tat, tat, tat...*

"Aaaaahhhhhh," came a scream from outside.

Rage immediately hit the ground as the return fire tore through wood and dry wall all around. How many of them were out there? It had to be the FBI. He was not about to back down from these obsequious agents of capitalism. Shards of glass flew through his kitchen. His front door resembled an unfinished project in woodshop.

The dust penetrated his nostrils. Rage clenched his jaw to avert a sneeze. From the prone position. *Tat...tat...tat tat... tat...tat tat...tat...tat.* He fired at the dry wall in the living room which abutted the hallway outside. Within seconds the return fire was a cacophony of sounds the greatest maestro could never choreograph. *Bings* and *bangs, splatters* and *shatters* in stereo. Furniture filling flew through the air as if a chicken had just been plucked. A light fixture crashed several inches in front of his nose. He tried pushing his head lower but there was no place to go. An eerie quiet interceded as the firing stopped.

"It's your last chance, Jake. Come out with your hands up," the voice from outside shouted. How did they know his name?

The only thing he could say was, "A-a-all cops are bastards —"

Baaaaaaaaaannnnnnnng. The explosion shattered his ear drum. Within seconds a roaring hiss rattled the apartment. The noxious odor pierced his nostrils at the same moment the gas cloud descended on him. His eyes teared as a wave of nausea ran through his stomach. He could not stop the dry heaving. Rage pressed against the floor and stood on his knees. Between the smoke and the moisture in his eyes, he was almost blind. Tat...*tat...tat tat...tat...tat* Rage shot off aimlessly in every direction.

"*Aaaaahhhhhhh,*" someone yelled before something smacked against the floor shaking the ground beneath him.

A scalding pain shot up from the top part of his leg to his sensory cortex. A hammer-like object crushed his balls.

"*Ooooooohhhhhhhhh,*" the groan came from himself. The taste of blood. He was lightheaded. The piercing pain hit every point on his body, he couldn't hold on any longe—

The singsong of the cardinal chirp is what finally did it. He opened one eye, not wanting to emerge from the restful slumber. The blazing rays of sun penetrated the slats of his venetian blinds, illuminating the myriad dancing specs of dust above his head. Destruction reluctantly sat up. Fiona and Lesley were still asleep next to him.

None of the other women in MIS could match their enthusiasm and dedication in the bedroom. Destruction proceeded to place his feet on the icy hardwood as he trudged toward the window. There was never an easy way to do this, so he just pulled down on the chord until the blinding light filled the room from end to end.

Once his eyes adjusted, he gazed at the clear cerulean sky outside. It was a most excellent day. Destruction brushed his teeth before jumping in the shower. When he came out, Fiona and Lesley were still cuddled into each other's bosoms. He walked over to the kitchen. Destruction placed two pieces of wheat bread in the toaster, took out the organic peanut butter and loaded the coffee maker with his favorite rejuvenating hot liquid.

Destruction lowered himself on the sectional, and with the flick of a finger, fired up the wall mounted TV. Any channel would do this morning, but just for shits and grins, he decided to turn to one of the conservative outlets. The volume raged at full blast. He was hoping to wake the sleeping bitches in the bedroom:

We take you back live to DC, where we're following developments in a shootout that occurred last night:

Federal agents tried to serve a warrant on a suspect believed to be responsible for the brutal murder of Secret Service Captain Chambers. Authorities had received what they're calling a credible tip from an anonymous source on the whereabouts of Jake Van Dorn, 21, a student at his final semester in Georgetown. University officials tell us that Mr. Van Dorn had stopped attending class last December and did not sit for his end of semester finals. They have no update on his whereabouts.

Sources tell us that when the joint FBI and Secret Service team arrived on the scene, they announced their intention to serve a warrant. Due to months of protests across America, where the practice of no-knock warrants had come under intense criticism, the agents were hesitant to storm this apartment without warning. A spokesman for the FBI told us that their reticence cost two more lives.

A Secret Service agent was killed in the hallway as Van Dorn opened fire with his M-16 rifle on the unsuspecting officer through the wall of his apartment. An FBI agent was also gunned down during the hard entry raid with flashbangs and tear gas. The suspect was killed in the ensuing shootout. Sources in the FBI tell us they believe Van Dorn's M-16 may have been stolen. The serial number on the rifle was a match for an M-16 that belonged to the Virginia National Guard, whose armory in Fort Belvoir was recently ransacked in a brazen late-night attack. That investigation remains open with no suspects in custody.

Last night's shootout follows a string of unexplained battles around the nation's capital after the election of Donald Patrick. It all began with the attack on the Virginia National Guard Armory. Then there was the murder of Captain Chambers, followed by a bizarre chase and shootout in the streets of Arlington, where one man was killed, and another remains unidentified. Authorities are starting to wonder if these incidents are related. The tragic shootout last night has created more questions than answers in what increasingly resembles a free for all around our nation's capital. Back to you in the studio.

Destruction lobbed the remote at the image of Rage on the sixty-five-inch mounted LED display. A large spiderweb fracture now covered the center of the screen.

"What *was* that?" Fiona said from the other room.

"Cocksucker! Still gives me grief from the grave," Destruction screamed.

"Do you need us master?" Lesley cried out.

"I need ya to shut the fuck up and let me think ya shit-brain," Destruction said.

Destruction had provided the tip to the FBI in order to throw them off the trail. It was a stall tactic in preparation for the attack on the White House. Once that happened, the authorities would be so busy none of this would matter anymore. All payments to Rage had been made in cash, and there was no paperwork tying the moron to Antifa. Destruction had taken care to maintain only face to face contact with Rage over the past few weeks, but any mistake, even the tiniest oversight, could bring the feds to his doorstep.

What he had not factored in was the possibility the idiot Rage had taken one of the weapons intended for battle against the Secret Service. There was no way Destruction was going to let this set back ruin his plan. He had to ditch the cell phone and hunker down in Bakunin Farm where everything was registered under a front company. From there, he would coordinate the attack on the White House.

The only problem was the head of *MIS*, she was not part of the assault on the White House. He would just have to order Lesley to stay away from Bakunin Farm until Inauguration Day. By then, it wouldn't matter anymore.

27. ARLINGTON, VIRGINIA

January 12

"*M*adar Jendeh*," son of a whore,* Janusz yelled morosely. He leaned into his leather executive chair. The morning news had taken a sour turn. The man who called himself Rage, Jake Van Dorn, had joined the ranks of the dead with his accomplice, Neil Bakke aka Hazard, the driver of the Dodge Charger. Their faces, etched in his memory, were plastered all over the news. Janusz tossed a tiny nerf ball on top of the mahogany desk before putting his feet up and nearly knocking over his beloved collection of gilded fountain pens.

The only bit of good news in this disaster was Rage's gym bag. Inside, Janusz had found a bloody knife. It had to be some sort of murder weapon which Rage was probably hoping to plant in Janusz's car. Were these the men who had stabbed the poor guy from the Secret Service, Captain Chambers? Janusz kept the evidence in a safe place. The pieces of this puzzle would fall into place sooner or later.

Staring at the novels on his bookshelf, he was tempted to pack up and move to a bucolic town in rural Virginia to write. What good would come of it? He would get bored soon enough. Janusz wondered if there was anyone he could trust now. Jason Osborne, senior staff member on the SSCI, had betrayed him. There was no way Jason would answer questions about why he had turned rogue or who he was working for. After years of collaborating with him, Janusz was not willing to use coercive tactics to get answers. At least not yet.

There was always the possibility that Jason was acting

under duress. All of that would have to be flushed out. If the two dead men were connected to terrorists in any way the news would have mentioned it by now. Janusz desperately needed good intelligence but had nowhere to turn. There was no guidance from any quarter, and no one knew what to do.

To make matters worse, the Unit had never created a continuity of operations strategy for a scenario such as this. That was one of the things they would have to work out when, and if, they ever made it out of this mess. He texted his wife to see how she was doing. She was busy at her office.

He racked his brain for answers before grabbing the car keys. His BMW was in the shop. He was now dependent on a rental car. Perhaps a slow drive through scenic back roads would enable him to decompress. Janusz considered stopping at the hospital to check in on Tony, but the thought of his helpless mentor on life-support was too depressing. There was nothing he could do to help him now.

At least Tony was less likely to be attacked since Jennifer had arranged round the clock security for his room. Outside, a few of the neighbors were shoveling the invisible snow from the previous storm that dusted their driveway. It never ceased to amaze Janusz how the tiniest flakes would lead to a federal government shutdown around the capital of the world's most powerful country. If the rest of America operated this way, nothing would ever get done.

He inhaled the crisp air, shooting vapors out of his nostrils on the exhale. Within seconds of entering the car, the inside windows fogged up. He set the defrost button to the highest setting before adjusting his rear-view mirror. At first, he thought it was a shadow. He jumped out of his seat as the figure tilted its head. Janusz lunged toward the glove compartment to grab his Sig.

"Relax, Janusz, it's just me," declared the husky voice in the back seat.

His heart pushed through his ribcage as he tried to steady his hands on the dashboard. His rapid breathing filled the cabin with clouds of moisture as he turned to face his backseat passenger.

"Jesus Christ, Kim. What the fuck are you doing sitting here in the cold?"

"Just drive. We don't have much time."

Once the windows cleared, Janusz took the scenic route on the George Washington Parkway with a view of the Potomac River. As he checked the rear seat, he noticed her pallid complexion. The normally vivacious gleam in her eyes had been replaced by an ineffable expression that bordered somewhere between fear and sorrow. Not wanting to rush her, Janusz kept quiet.

"I came to see you as fast as I could. They almost killed me, and I'm sure you're next."

Janusz clenched his jaw while tightening his grip on the steering wheel. "They tried and failed with me, but we can reminisce about that later. What did they do to you?"

"I should've seen it coming. I just, I just wasn't thinking clearly after," she lamented as her voice faltered ever so slightly.

"It's okay, Kim. It's okay. Take deep breaths and exhale," Janusz said as he prodded her to finish her thought, "after what?"

"After Tony was—"

"Don't take it too hard. There was nothing we could do."

"You don't understand Janusz, I am..." she said as her chin quivered.

There was a long pause before she spoke again, "I am in love with Tony, we've been seeing each other for a while. We kept it a secret so there would be no distractions at work. Tony was going to announce our engagement when you and Jennifer returned from your vacation. But now—"

The devastating sadness was visible on her face through the rearview mirror. It all made sense now. If Tony had not been distracted with thoughts of Kim, he would never have allowed himself to become ambushed. Kim herself was a master operative. It was not like her to be so grief stricken. Now, he understood why. Janusz tried to distract her with a new line of inquiry, "What happened to you?"

"I was lightheaded, the trees spun furiously around me. Next thing I remember I was at a hospital. The nurse told me it was a miracle. A couple of hikers found me bleeding face down in the woods. They wrapped a tourniquet around my leg and drove me to the nearest emergency room. The doctors pumped me with God knows how much blood."

"Where was this?"

"At my family cabin in Pennsylvania. I went there to clear my head, to try to forget that I'm being hunted. To try to forget about Tony. Amid all the confusion, I befriended a woman in my gym—"

"Oh, no," Janusz said reflexively before shutting his yap in embarrassment.

"Yes, I should've known it was a trap. But—"

"You're not the only one, Kim. They tricked me, too. Please, continue."

"This woman was always there when I needed her. She called me at the cabin and guilted me into inviting her over. When the alarm went off in my head, I was staring at the wrong end of an M9 in the hands of a boy wearing a puffy Hoyas jacket."

Janusz was about to explode, "What did you say?"

"I was staring at—"

"No, no, what was the dude wearing?"

"A puffy Hoyas jacket," she repeated.

"With the bulldog insignia over his heart?"

"How did you know?"

"That's the same son of a bitch that tried to kill me. He's dead now so it doesn't—"

"Wait what?"

"The guy with the Hoyas jacket was killed by the feds last night. Who is the woman?" Janusz said as she shifted in the backseat.

Kim dug through her purse before handing him a crumbled piece of paper. He fumbled with it on the steering wheel until he found himself staring at an address.

"Lesley Gantz, a professor at Georgetown," Kim said.

"Sounds like someone is using Georgetown University for nefarious purposes."

"That's not all."

Her last sentence sent his heart into tachycardia. The other shoe was about to drop.

"The dude with the Hoyas jacket. He claimed he was a member of Antifa."

"Antifa? Are you sure?"

"DC Antifa to be exact."

Janusz took a moment to chew on the new revelation. "This is getting weirder by the minute."

"What do you think?"

"Don't know, but it might be worse than I expected," Janusz said staring stoically at the passing landscape.

"I need you to make me a promise, Janusz," she said emphatically.

"Anything!"

"Once we find out what's going on, that Lesley bitch is mine!"

"You got it," Janusz said while stopping at a red light.

Janusz turned to face her. "Where ya staying?"

"At a hotel in Tyson's. I pay in cash, and no one knows I'm there."

"Good, you should rest. I'll take it from here."

"Hey, wait a minute—"

"This isn't about how capable you are. You lost a lot of blood and your body needs to recover. Last thing we need is a mistake because you're not thinking clearly," Janusz said.

She nodded with obvious hesitation before the honking cars indicated the light had turned green.

28. NEW YORK CITY, NEW YORK

January 16

O n January 16th, the following article appeared on page six of *Impressionable Magazine*:

EXTREMISM & THE ENEMY WITHIN
By Janet Smears

A specter haunts America, it is the specter of white supremacy. Am I taking creative license by paraphrasing Karl Marx? Hardly! A series of brazen shootouts around the nation's capital, the likes of which we have not experienced since the days of Al Capone, have recently rocked our beloved republic. Two men driving down Route 28 near Dulles Airport are gunned down in broad daylight. Then, the Virginia National Guard's armory in Fort Belvoir is suspiciously raided in the middle of the night.

With the cooperation of the fascist Sergeant Adam Lutz, 27, and the fascist Specialist Tucker Evans, 24, the attackers hauled away a large cache of military weapons. Not long after that, Secret Service Captain Roger Chambers was brutally murdered in his dining room. He was found lying in a pool of blood by his wife and son. Finally, a car chase worthy of a James Bond movie unfolded through Georgetown and Arlington five night ago. One suspect was killed on the street while a second is still on the loose.

What do all these horrendous tragedies have in common? White supremacy! It's hardly a coincidence that violent actions such as these have skyrocketed since the election of Donald Patrick. You may be skeptical about this assertion, which is why I will dissect it further. Take for example the president-elect's claim that we need to increase border security. We must first assume the people who risk their lives to seek asylum, similar to our own brave ancestors who landed on Ellis Island, are all criminals.

This is a lie perpetuated by racist police departments across the nation who make a habit of arresting people because they can't speak English or they can't obtain a driver's license. Second, we must assume the newcomers will take jobs away from Americans once they're settled. This is another patently false assumption. No American wants to work for minimum wage on a strawberry farm in Oxnard or a meat packing plant in Des Moines. We have to face the reality that, as Americans, we have become fat and lazy.

Third, we must assume that immigrants are here to take advantage of our essential public services, such as our schools and hospitals. This assumption immediately evaporates under careful scrutiny. Migrants risking life and limb to sustain our standard of living as domestic servants and restaurant workers are here temporarily. Most return home after earning a little money during their stay in America.

In reality, the best way to deal with this issue is to give full citizenship to every asylum seeker who has risked everything to cross our border. When evaluating the above assumptions, note that they are intended to incite the extremists who want to destroy our democracy. These are the very same people that voted for Donald Patrick in the last election.

While we're at it, let's not forget to mention what makes these white supremacists dangerous. More than anything else, it's an outdated interpretation of the Second Amendment of the Constitution, written for another era. The reality is that America, at the dawn of the twenty-first century, has become a dangerous country due to an outdated Constitution. A Constitution that allows the most violent elements in our society to amass vast arsenals in their homes. A Constitution that places no limits on gun owners nor requires a national level registration of firearms. Such a Constitution is no longer valid for a modern country.

We must make radical changes to our Constitution or, we

will soon find our democracy subverted into something none of us recognize. It's reassuring to know that in this troubled day and age, there are those actively working to bring about positive change. I recently traveled to the San Francisco home of a camera-shy businessman who wants to help America evolve into a more enlightened nation.

His name is Octavio Souza, founder of Souza Enterprises, one of the largest private equity firms in the world. While no longer involved in the day-to-day management of his eponymous conglomerate, Souza strives to make America a better place. Souza's vast holdings include everything from the popular chain, Ice Cream King, to the pharmaceutical and petrochemical giant, Souza Plastics, the crown jewel of his empire.

Souza has recently taken a personal interest in politics. The Freedom Coalition, a nonprofit organization, collects money from rich mega donors, channeling the proceeds to promote a more just society. An idea that had been germinating in his head for a number of years, Souza finally put the wheels into motion at dinner one night in San Francisco, early December of last year.

"He had been talking about making a difference for years, so finally, I said 'Octavio, why don't you put your money where your mouth is' and, doggone it, he did," T.B. Schuster, a close friend of Souza's, told me over the phone.

With close to three hundred million raised since that auspicious dinner overlooking the Bay, Octavio Souza is an example of the kind of migrant that risks life and limb to journey to these shores. Despite the specter of white supremacy that haunts America, we can all rest a little easier knowing that our newest citizens are tirelessly working to make this a better country.

29. ECKINGTON, WASHINGTON D.C.

January 19

J anusz detoured for coffee and pastries before driving to the townhouse in the Eckington neighborhood of DC. He had no idea where Lesley was or when she would return, which is why he parked down the street to conduct surveillance. It always came as a shock how hungry he could get sitting motionless in a car. Perhaps it was boredom, or perhaps the nervousness that accompanied the unexpected.

He ate the chocolate filled Danish with alacrity, finishing off the entire treat in several impressive bites. He didn't even need the coffee to wash it down. The hot beverage did however serve to accentuate the taste of buttery cocoa on his tongue. To his delight the professor arrived within an hour, seven minutes before noon.

Lesley Gantz was a rather petite woman. She wore a black coat with jeans. Janusz had found a number of articles about her online. Lesley was pretty but hardly ever wore makeup in her pictures. She walked toward the front of her house with a seductive gait, quite unexpected for a radical feminist.

Besides teaching, Lesley was a director at an Islamic Studies think tank in DC. It was a job that paid two hundred and fifty thousand dollars a year on top of the hundred-and twenty-thousand-dollar annual salary Lesley received from Georgetown. Why a person with so much to lose was allied with the Unit's enemies was difficult to fathom. In order to get answers, he could either sneak into her house when she was gone or grab her off the street for an enhanced interrogation. There was a third option. Follow her around and see where she would lead him.

Several cars passed by as he pretended to read from a book, throwing a gaze up every now and then. Fifteen minutes later she was back out walking toward her car. A blinding ray of sun reflected off her right hand. Was that a knife or the car keys? It was impossible to tell from this angle. She got behind the wheel and drove away. He counted off twenty seconds before following.

Janusz tailed Lesley north on Baltimore Avenue through College Park. This was the main campus of the University of Maryland. Once they crossed the bridge over the beltway, the professor took the first left toward a roundabout. Sensing her unease, Janusz stopped on the side of the road. Lesley circled the roundabout twice before heading toward the sprawling parking lot of IKEA. Was this woman really here to buy some furniture?

He kept his eyes on her car as he drove down the same path. She drove to the far end of the lot, facing some trees. Janusz was at the opposite end, observing Lesley's car. He pulled out his binoculars and, sure enough, he could clearly see she had pulled up next to another vehicle with DC plates. He memorized the plate number. Moments later she exited her own vehicle to enter the adjacent one. It was impossible to see their faces from the back.

He continued peering through the powerful lenses. As five minutes turned to fifteen, they were still immersed in conversation. Finally, Lesley got out of the other car to get behind the wheel of her own vehicle. Sensing she was here to report to someone important, Janusz was no longer interested in Lesley.

Lesley approached his position on her way out. Janusz ducked below the steering wheel for thirty seconds until he was sure she had passed. When he popped back up, Lesley was nowhere to be found, and the vehicle with DC plates was still parked facing away from him. Janusz was not about to let this car and its driver slip away.

Twenty minutes later, the taillights of the new target vehicle came on. The car made a hundred- and eighty-degree turn. Through the binoculars, the face of Sean Sutherland was unmistakable. He was head of DC Antifa. There were several articles about him in obscure online magazines that Janusz found while conducting research on the topic after the conversation with Kim. As Sean drove down the path Lesley had traversed moments earlier, Janusz ducked below the steering wheel again.

Moments later, he popped up and turned his car to follow. Before long Janusz found himself several cars behind, headed north on Baltimore Avenue once again. His target proceeded to turn right on Powder Mill Road with Janusz close behind. He was overwhelmed by déjà vu. Anxiety gripped his stomach as he tried to remember why he had driven down this same path before. Steering cautiously through the winding road, he tapped the brakes as the target vehicle took a right onto a narrow country path.

Bakunin Farm, read the sign that cautioned drivers not to enter the private road. He continued down Powder Mill, needing to satisfy the urge to remember why he had been here before. Past the Baltimore Washington Parkway, the light went off in his head. *9200 Powder Mill Road, the Secret Service.* Janusz remembered the days he had come here for a training exercise while employed at the CIA. Suddenly, multiple thoughts connected at once. Captain Chambers. The bloody knife in the gym bag. Michael Bakunin, the Russian anarchist. Antifa, another name for anarchism. Janusz decided to return later that evening with the tactical gear.

30. BAKUNIN FARM, BELTSVILLE MARYLAND

January 19

It was a quarter past eleven in the evening. Janusz looked through the thermal binoculars once more. To the best he could determine, there were at least three people in the house, maybe more. Two of them appeared to be viewing TV in an open room and the third was by a desk in another part of the house. Janusz could not be sure if any of the bedrooms were occupied. He stood by a fence that surrounded the pool in the backyard.

Kim had dropped him off a half hour earlier. She was nearby, waiting for the signal to pick him up. He had passed a shooting range on his way down the gravel path from Powder Mill Road. The compound was likely DC Antifa's training facility. Closer to the house, an arsenal of heavy caliber weapons and ammunition was loaded inside four large minivans. Janusz rushed to search one of the vans. It appeared DC Antifa was better armed than most terrorist groups.

The house was a good thirty yards away. Janusz used the darkness to camouflage his approach. Dressed in black fatigues, Janusz had also painted his face the same shade of ebony. All his equipment, including the handle of his knife, his sidearm, as well as his Sig Sauer MPX 9mm were also black. Would Sean still be here tonight? It was a gamble Janusz was willing to take.

Although he had read a variety of articles about Antifa over the years, he never had reason for a personal interaction, until now. Janusz viewed himself as a live and let live kind of guy as long as a group was not a threat to him, his family, or his country. The more he learned about Antifa, the more it bothered him.

Antifa fancied themselves as antifascists, yet they were intolerant of all opposing opinions. They had a bad habit of labeling anyone they disliked as a racist or a fascist. On top of everything else, they were now in the business of silencing speech on university campuses and attacking opponents on streets all across America. The problem with rectitude is, as Blaise Pascal had so deftly explained centuries earlier, "Man is neither angel nor devil, and his tragedy is that he who tries too hard to play the first, too often ends up as the second." Although their day-to-day transgressions were a matter for the local police or the FBI, Antifa had crossed the line by attacking Unit 81. Payback was necessary.

He ran stealthily toward a window. It was partially covered by a miniature tree. Janusz parted the vegetation to peer inside. The room appeared unoccupied through the night vision goggles. He jiggled the pane of glass causing a small opening between the rail and the sill. If this place had motion detectors of any kind, chances are he would've been discovered by now.

Janusz slid the window to the right and climbed. Once inside, he unsheathed his combat knife before checking the bed for signs of life. It was empty, so he put the knife back in the holster. Janusz was only interested in Sean. The rest of his crew were the obstacles through which he had to tread. He wasn't looking forward to killing anyone, but he recognized the choice was not his. To minimize an accidental shooting, Janusz decided to use the knife and his fists while the SIG MPX rested against his back with a tactical sling.

Janusz gently turned the knob of the bedroom door, pulling it open slowly. There was a hallway beyond, he could see the glow of TV lights dancing through the dark. Hugging the nearest wall, he put one foot in front of the other as he made his way to the corner. His right eye protruded ever so slightly to scope out the scene.

A pair of heads, a man and a woman, facing away from him stared at the glowing box in front of them. The woman had blue hair. Neither of them were likely to be his target, but he had to make sure. Janusz crawled on the parquet floor using only his palms and the tip of his boots. His daily pushup routine was finally paying off. He was grateful the sound from the TV masked his movements.

Naked and Afraid, are you kidding me? Janusz thought as he tried to block out the TV show so he could focus on what would come next. He rested momentarily against the back of a loveseat. Janusz unsheathed the knife again, staring at the serrated edge before moving his eyes to the sharp tip of the blade. Could he plunge that thing into her throat? He was desperate for an alternative, but there was none. They were the ones who had started this war.

Janusz pushed the knife back into the holster before bringing the SIG MPX forward. He stood over their heads and pointed the weapon downward. It took a good five seconds before the occupants of the loveseat were aware of his presence. Index finger pressed against his lips, Janusz warned them to remain quiet.

After studying their faces, it was obvious they were not his target. He motioned for them to sit against a wall with their backs toward each other. The zip ties he had brought along were going to come in handy. Janusz reached into his pants pocket while keeping both eyes on the captives. The anger was visible on their faces. They would not hesitate to kill him if given the chance. Janusz bent down before placing the man's wrists inside the nylon loop. He pulled the chord as tight as possible.

The man grimaced and let out a low moan. At that moment, the blue haired companion made a run for it, crawling on hands and knees across the parquet like a rat that had escaped its cage. He lunged to grab her leg. She shoved his hand away with several quick kicks before he was finally able to hold on to her right foot. It was then that the bottom of her left foot connected with Janusz's nose.

He instinctively brought both hands toward his face, wiggling the nose to make sure it was not broken. As he did so, the woman circled back and jumped toward his crotch. He was certain she wanted to punch his groin, but she had her sights set on a bigger prize. The speed with which she unsheathed and removed his knife was a rude surprise. As soon as he tried to regain control of the situation, she scraped the blade against his arm, cutting cloth and skin similar to a hot knife through butter.

"Motherfucker," Janusz blurted out, regretting his earlier reticence to incapacitate her.

He had a sudden flashback to Stuttgart, Germany. During his first mission for the Unit, Ali had cut him on the exact same spot.

"What's going on out there?" a third voice demanded to know.

"In here, come quick," she yelled out as Janusz squeezed his bleeding wrist. It was no use. The wrist would have to wait.

"You're dead," she said while waving the knife in front of Janusz's face. They were still on the floor.

Mr. Zip Tie came toward them. "What are you waiting for, Fiona? Finish him!" he said.

Janusz jumped to his feet and, to his surprise, Fiona was waiting with the knife still in her hand. Rapid footsteps pounded through the hall. Fiona slashed the air repeatedly in a feeble attempt to cut Janusz again. On the fourth try, she lunged straight into his center mass. Janusz grabbed her knife wielding arm as he stepped aside to push her forward. He twisted the arm, forcing her to drop the knife before she caromed against the kitchen counter.

On the return, he kicked her on the side of the face. Fiona dropped like a sack of potatoes. Gunshots whizzed by his ear from behind. Janusz dropped to the floor and rolled over to avoid getting hit. He proceeded to crouch, and then punched the approaching target behind the knee.

The man crumpled to the floor, the pistol falling out of his hand. It was then that Janusz had a chance to examine him. He was fat, but he was not Sean. Out of nowhere, a kick landed on the side of Janusz's face. It was the dude with the zip tied wrists. Janusz tried to regain his breath as Mr. Zip Tie prepared to deliver another kick.

Janusz latched on to his calf, using his teeth similar to a rottweiler on a mailman. Mr. Zip Tie screamed at the top of his lungs before losing his balance and falling backwards. Janusz bit hard enough to puncture the skin and draw blood. He finally let go to deal with the fat fellow.

Fat man slithered toward the pistol. Janusz used his leg to kick it away. At this point, both men rose to their feet while facing each other. Fat man was a few inches taller and much heavier, mostly due to blubber. Fat man used a head fake before throwing a punch that hit nothing but air. Janusz was about to deliver a counter punch when Fiona jumped on his back while screaming. She wrapped her arms around Janusz's neck while biting his ear.

"*Ahhh,* you bitch!" Janusz shouted.

He was distracted long enough for fat man to land a punch straight into his gut. The blow angered him. Janusz ran backward as fast as he could while Fiona swayed from his neck. He slammed her against the nearest wall. The sound of shattering glass was probably the breaking of a framed picture.

Fiona peeled off and fell to the floor. But not before fat man punched him on the side of his face. Using an open palm, Janusz transferred his weight straight into the fat man's solar plex, right below the sternum. Fat man gasped for air, fell to his knees, and collapsed.

Just then, Fiona was getting on her feet again. Janusz was in no mood to deal with her. He delivered a powerful surgical kick to her jaw. Her head snapped back before crashing against the wall. Unconscious, she fell straight down to the floor. Fiona was out cold. On to the last leg of this trio. Mr. Zip Tie was nowhere to be found.

After wrapping the bloody wrist, Janusz frantically scanned the room for his last target. Then he spotted something. Blood drops led to the hallway. Like Dorothy in the *Wizard of Oz*, he followed the trail to see where it led. At the end of the hall, the man was squatting against the wall in a futile attempt to bring his tied wrists forward. As Janusz approached, Mr. Zip Tie shot a menacing glare at him.

"Let's make a deal," Janusz said.

"For what?" the injured man replied.

"I'll lock you up in this room," Janusz pointed to the closest bedroom, "and let you go later if you tell me where to find Sean."

Before Janusz could finish, a violent sound ripped through the entire house. *Tat, tat, tat, tat, tat...tat, tat...tat, tat, tat... tat, tat, tat, tat, tat, tat, tat, tat, tat, tat, tat, tat, tat, tat.* Janusz reflexively hit the floor, hugging the parquet to minimize exposed surfaces. *Tat, tat, tat...tat, tat, tat, tat, tat, tat, tat, tat, tat, tat, tat, tat, tat, tat.*

The ripping sound finally stopped long enough for him to scan his surroundings. It was not a pretty site. The walls were full of holes. Same went for the wooden doors to the bedrooms. A warm liquid gripped his hand. Janusz looked down. There was a pool of blood. Had he been shot? His eyes darted to where Mr. Zip Tie sat moments earlier. His body resembled ground beef. Multiple holes had ripped through the poor bastard. Someone had fired off some sort of heavy caliber machine gun. The trick was to get to the shooter before the next lead storm began.

Janusz crawled on his chest down the hall, hoping to figure out his next move before he reached the origin of the lead fusillade. Cursing the turn of events, he suddenly chuckled out loud similar to a mad man. A doorway in the hall opened to reveal a small laundry room. There was just enough light to see the metal fuse box on the wall. He slithered snake like. One hand over the other, he moved against the frosty tiles.

Janusz took a deep breath, stood up, opened the box, and turned every switch to the off position. The house was pitch black and his opponent had not yet made a countermove. Judging by the last round, the son of a bitch had probably run out of bullets. Janusz pulled the night vision goggles over his eyes. He then brought the SIG MPX forward. The hunt was on.

The shooter would likely have some sort of vision enhancement technology as well. Janusz wiped his palms against the side of his pants, drying the sweat before grabbing his weapon. Fearing exposure to another lead storm, he got down on his chest and crawled forward. The closer he got to the shooter, the more he wondered why his opponent had stopped firing. The house was eerily silent. Something was not right about all this.

Janusz looked back toward the opposite end of the hall. The room from which he had entered was open, Mr. Zip Tie still sprawled in the doorway. Janusz had an idea, it was the only way this could work. He slithered back and held his breath as he climbed over the dead body.

It was wet with blood that now covered his own clothes. He stood up and climbed out the window. He cautiously made his way around the perimeter. Several minutes later, Janusz returned to the room and jumped back in the house. He proceeded to a position outside the shooter's lair down the hall.

Janusz read the decreasing numbers on his watch. Ten seconds. He placed his head on the floor to count down... *five, four, three, two, one*... there was silence, what if he had forgot somethin— *Booooooooommmmmm!* The house shook violently as the sound of the explosion burst through his occluded ear. *Thank goodness for earplugs.*

Within seconds the violent rattle of the machine gun commenced. *Tat, tat, tat, tat, tat...tat, tat...tat, tat, tat...tat, tat, tat.* The sound was directed toward the back of the house. His idea had worked, but he had bought only a few seconds. As the machine gun rattled, Janusz burst through the door. The muzzle flash emanated from the middle of the room behind a heavy desk turned sideways into a bunker. The tracer rounds shot toward the opposite wall where his time delay explosive had opened a hole. The shooter's head popped up above the desk. It was now or never.

Janusz lunged toward the target, grabbing the bastard around the neck. The rattling of the machine gun came to an abrupt end. They struggled mercilessly on the floor before Janusz finally put him in a choke hold. As Janusz tightened his grip, he studied the weapon up close. It was an M-60 machine gun.

Several buckets of magazines were stacked nearby. The ammo had the markings of the US Army. His opponent pushed against the floor to shake loose. Janusz tightened his grip even more. Within seconds the shooter had passed out.

Janusz calmly walked back to the fuse box to restore power. He was pleasantly surprised the hail of bullets had not disturbed the flow of electricity. There was no mistaking the fact that the unconscious man tied to the chair in the living room was Sean, the head of DC Antifa. There were also three dead bodies.

Crazy Fiona and the fat guy had most likely risen to their feet as Sean's lead storm ripped through the house. It had been the wrong move at the wrong juncture. Janusz piled the dead bodies in the nearest bedroom, one on top of the other. All three were oozing blood. Given the distance to the nearest dwelling, God only knew when the authorities would discover this macabre scene.

Janusz had bigger concerns at the moment. He found a pitcher in the kitchen which he filled with cold water. He emptied the chilled liquid over Sean's head. The man came to within seconds.

"You put up quite a fight. As a matter of fact, you're the first person firing off an M-60 I've had to tackle," Janusz said.

"Who the fuck are you?"

"Why did you send people to kill me?"

"I asked first, who the fuck are you?"

Janusz studied the man before deciding to play along. "I'm Janusz, two of your buddies tried to kill me in Georgetown nine days ago. Your turn."

Janusz could see the wheels turning in his head.

"What ya do to Fiona?"

"Me?" Janusz pointed at himself. "I only knocked her out. You on the other hand killed her. Are you ready to talk?"

"Fuck off, I've got nothing to say to a capitalist pig."

"Suit yourself," Janusz said as he approached, "what you fail to comprehend is that I'm not a government employee."

"So what, fuck-face."

Wwwhhhaaaammmm, the impact of Janusz's open palm landing on Sean's right cheek exploded through the living room and the nearby kitchen. The chair and its occupant fell straight back onto the floor before Janusz brought them back up. From the expression on his face, Sean was not expecting the turn of events.

"Fuck-face, very funny. The *so what* is that I couldn't care less about your constitutional rights. You'll be begging to join the pile of corpses in the bedroom if you don't cooperate," Janusz said.

Sean moved his jaw around while gently swaying his head from side to side. "Like I said, fuck off, Mr. Fuck-Face."

Janusz had dealt with this type before. Tough guys who think they can withstand pain. Then the screws are turned tighter and tighter. At some point the excruciating sensation overwhelms the central nervous system. That's when the toughest guys volunteer to give up their own mothers to make the agony go away. Janusz wondered if that could be avoided by engaging the man in conversation. Sean fancied himself a revolutionary. Perhaps there was another way to go about this.

"You know, you really surprise me, Sean. Here I was, thinking you Antifa guys were opposed to fascism. Come to find out, you're just as bad as those you despise so much," Janusz said before pacing around Sean's chair in silence.

Janusz was fishing now, all he needed was one bite on the line.

"Antifa is a figment of your imagination. It's just an idea," Sean said.

"Oh, that's right. You're all anarchists hiding under the banner of anti-fascism."

Silence. He had to kick things into high gear. "Your name is Sean Sutherland, is it not?"

"Yeah, so what?"

"Nothing. I was struck by the irony that your initials are S.S."

"What's that supposed to mean?"

Now, pull in the catch.

"Your tactics are reminiscent of the Schutzstaffel. Don't you find it ironic that despite all the anti-fascist platitudes you anarchists are no better than the SS enforcers of the Nazi party? Willing to use any means to silence your opponents while—"

"Shut up, we're nothing like the Nazis." *Buurp*. "We're opposed to racism, bigotry, and oppression. We risk our lives every day to keep society safe from fascism," Sean said as the veins popped out of his forehead.

Janusz had him right where he wanted him.

"By sending a hit team to kill me? I'll admit that I've engaged in a few questionable acts over the years, but fascism and oppression were never part of my portfolio."

"You were a means to an end."

"What are you saying?"

"We're not after you. That job was a favor."

"For who?"

"A generous contributor. What's it to you? Our benefactor is the one—"

Sean caught on. He needed to be provoked.

"So, you're a whore. You provide a service?"

"Fuck you!" *Buurp.* "If a billionaire calls and says he'll give you as much money as you need to finance your dreams and, in return, you have to break a few eggs every now and then, what would *you* do? Don't you do the same thing for the US Government? Does that make you a bigger whore than me?"

"That all depends," Janusz said.

"On what?"

"What are you going to do with the huge arsenal of weapons in the parked vans outside?"

"That's for target practice. As a loyal protector of America the exploiter, you must have no objection to the exercise of my Second Amendment right to keep and bear arms?"

Janusz was getting nowhere. "What about Jason Osborne? How'd you get to him?"

"Don't know a Jason, and if I did, I wouldn't tell you. Like I said, the questions you're asking have nothing to do with me or my soldiers in what you derisively refer to as Antifa. Our sponsor writes checks, and I do a few jobs here and there. End of story."

"This fellow who you sent to kill me, he introduced himself as Rage and said his buddy was called Hazard. What's that all about?" Janusz said as Sean shook his head.

"What a turd-brain!" Sean said.

"You seem disappointed?"

"I suppose he told you my name is Destruction?"

"No, but I figured you'd have a similar stupid name. Do you Antifa guys get off on giving yourselves silly nicknames?"

"Has nothing to do with Antifa. That's something I demand of my recruits. You see, the names we are given at birth are symbols of oppression. They reflect the values of an oppressive patriarchal society obsessed with consumption. I give the members a new purpose in life. By joining the struggle to end oppression with me, they're reborn. To reflect this new identity, some are assigned new names while more worthy individuals earn the right to choose their own names."

"I see, kind of a like a cult. You're the David Koresh for the age of political correctness."

"What would you know about it, shit-brain? You've been a slave to capital your whole life, and you'll continue to be a slave until you die. I wouldn't expect you to understand."

"Looks like you're not a good instructor. I mean, I killed Hazard without much trouble, and Rage didn't do too well against the FBI."

"Serves him right. I'm curious how you escaped from Rage?"

"That's the best part of the story. Glad you asked," Janusz said as he pulled up a chair.

Janusz sat facing Sean, separated by only inches. "It wasn't that hard really. I should be dead if you want to know the truth. Rage had the pistol right up against my forehead. But lady luck was on my side, your man had forgotten about the M9's manual safety. So now, here I am chatting with you."

Sean's eyes were about to fall out of their sockets. His face turned beet red as he breathed more rapidly.

"Ffffucking, arse-wipe."

"Calm down, Sean. You're going to give yourself an ulcer."

"I don't give a fuck."

"Good, but you should know that your boy also left behind a bloody knife that I've stashed away as evidence. You and I will enjoy figuring all these things out tonight."

"I should've killed that fuck-face myself."

"Don't be so hard on him, Sean. You can't blame the student. He had a truly mediocre teacher if you ask me."

As soon as he finished speaking, Janusz's phone came to life. He pulled it out of his pants pocket to check the ID. It was Kim.

"Aaaaahhhhhhh," Sean cried out as he jumped out of his seat to tackle Janusz to the floor. Sean had a small knife in his hand with which he tried to stab Janusz. It was probably hidden in his sleeve, an oversight that had turned into a costly mistake. Janusz held onto the raging Antifa leader with all his might.

"You pig. I'm gonna cut your throat—" *buurp*, "and then I'm gonna take a piss down your windpipe. "

Janusz kicked him in the groin before using his legs to throw him off. Sean rolled on the ground and brought the knife forward for another charge. Janusz's muscle memory kicked in. He pulled the 9mm sidearm off his waist holster. He fired twice into Sean's chest with his right hand as his left deflected the blow from Sean's knife. His opponent collapsed.

The knife landed blade first on the parquet, suspended upright as if held by an invisible hand. This was the worst possible outcome. Janusz was not finished interrogating the suspect. He placed Sean's body on the floor before returning Kim's call. He told her to pick him up in front of the compound in thirty minutes. Janusz hung up and ran towards Sean's office.

He intended to gather as many documents and computer hard drives as he could. The evening chat did not turn out to be as enlightening as he had hoped, but perhaps he could put the pieces of the puzzle together using Sean's files.

31. GEORGETOWN UNIVERSITY, WASHINGTON D.C.

January 20; Inauguration Day

The obtuse reporter from the *Main Street Journal* wasted five minutes looking for another pen in his bag. This despite the fact she had offered him one of her own. What did he think? That if he took her pen, he could no longer write objectively?

This was the one part of her job Lesley hated the most, giving interviews to reporters. Few and far between was the journalist who understood the urgency of this juncture in history. The United States was under assault from racists and all they were worried about was the need to cite sources and the imperative to be objective. On top of everything else, Lesley wanted to keep abreast of the inauguration on her office computer.

Antifa cells from all over the country were descending on Washington to combat fascism. This national emergency called for one thing, and that was activism. It did not matter whether you were a journalist, a nurse, a corporate CEO, a movie director, a high school teacher, or a university professor. There was no choice but to take the war for social justice to the front lawn of the enemy. That's why, with Destruction's leadership, DC Antifa was going to bring down the entire system by tomorrow.

"Ah, here we go. I found one. Sorry about that, I'm very superstitious about my writing implements," Ron Sterling, the *objective* journalist, said.

"I understand."

"Let's continue," Ron said before launching into a piece titled *Q & A with Georgetown Professor Lesley Gantz*:

Ron Sterling: Some of your students, and I've spoken to a number of them, complain that they're afraid to voice their opinions in your class. They maintain your lectures are one sided and tend more toward advocacy instead of an objective analysis of different views. Is this really necessary Professor Gantz?

Professor Gantz: Absolutely. We're living in a critical period. After centuries of neglect, American universities are actively recruiting historically repressed groups. We're finally at the precipice of progress. So, yes, activism in the classroom is necessary to change this society for the better. That starts in universities and spreads outward.

RS: I think this is an important point. How is academia rising to the challenge of recruiting historically marginalized groups at this critical juncture, as you call it?

PG: In a number of ways. The first is to emphasize, through interviews such as this, that minorities can finally feel safe on campuses. The reason is that we no longer tolerate bigoted speech, misinformation, disinformation, jokes, hurtful comments, racist or misogynist comments on campus.

RS: Some people call this suppression of free speech.

PG: Let me be clear, no one has the right to spew hate speech. Fear of hate speech is one of the reasons minorities are not represented in higher education in proportion to their population. Our speech codes are a way to remedy that.

RS: But the United States Supreme Court says that even what you refer to as hate speech is protected.

PG: Well, they're wrong. On this campus and many others

around the country, we're not in a courtroom. We're in a space that needs to be safe for a diverse group of people and, in order to do that, we need rules to combat hate speech.

RS: Please, continue.

PG: The other way in which we're transitioning to a more welcoming environment for repressed minorities is by getting rid of entrance exams. Whether they be the SAT, the GRE, the MCAT, or the LSAT we're no longer going to require students from marginalized groups to take these onerous exams.

RS: Aren't you hurting them by lowering the bar? Shouldn't there be some sort of standard for higher education.

PG: Standards, yes. Racism, no.

RS: Please, elaborate.

PG: Over the years, many academics have determined that these tests are racist. They were created by white men with the intention of allowing only white men to enter academia. Furthermore, white people have the means to hire tutors to teach their children how to excel on these exams. Minorities, who almost always are poor, don't have the resources for tutors. Finally, the questions themselves are written in a way that gives an advantage to white test takers. For all these reasons, we're eliminating these racist exams in the name of social justice and diversity.

RS: Aren't you ignoring the results of Asians on these exams.

PG: Next question!

RS: Some of your students complain you're constantly advocating for an open borders policy. Is this true and, if so, why?

PG: Absolutely, Ron. The United States is a country of immigrants. Nobody complained when people came here by the thousands over a hundred years ago from England, Ireland, Germany, or Russia through Ellis Island. Why is it a problem when the immigrants are coming through our southern border in places such as San Ysidro, California or Laredo, Texas? I'll tell you why. Because our racist voters and politicians don't want more brown people in this country.

RS: But there are credible reports it's not just Latin American asylum seekers that come through these borders. Our sources indicate that drug smugglers use the same routes to bring large quantities of narcotics into the United States that ravage our communities. A few months ago, a team of Iranian terrorists crossed into the US from San Ysidro headed for the town of Pine Valley, CA. If not for the valiant actions of a concerned citizen, the entire city could've been exposed to the Marburg virus.

PG: This is pure propaganda dreamt up by the new administration of President Patrick to scare Americans and radicalize his base. As a respectable reporter, you should not repeat these lies.

RS: Any parting thoughts for our readers?

PG: Yes, they need to remember every relationship has an element of exploitation.

RS: Professor, I want to thank you for answering my questions.

PG: My pleasure, Ron.

After the interview, Lesley logged onto the cable news website to catch a glimpse of the new dictator taking the oath of office. As soon as she sat back in her chair, the phone on her desk lit up. She checked the ID. The dean was on the line. She had hoped his office would be empty today. It was not to be.

"It's Betty, calling on behalf of Dean Souter," the caller said.

"Yes, what can I do for you?"

"The dean wants to see you in his office, right away."

"The dean is in today? On Inauguration Day?"

"Yes, he's been working around the clock to clear a recent donation."

"How did he know I was here?"

"Because I saw someone leave your office on my way to the bathroom."

"Thank you, Betty. Please tell him I'm on my way."

Lesley used the mirror behind her office door to check her hair. She sprayed on some perfume and brightened her lipstick. Dean Souter had barely been on the job for six months and already he was acting the part of a big shot. At age forty-three, he was the youngest Dean in the history of Georgetown College, the primary undergraduate program at Georgetown University.

During his short tenure, Dean Souter had raised ten million dollars for the college. The money had gone straight to his head. Lesley approached Betty and was seated in an adjacent waiting area. Ten minutes later, Dean Souter arrived in a gray suit and black tie, along with his signature pompous grin. He proceeded to escort her inside his cavernous office. The room was adorned with books. A cheap amaranth dyed Persian rug covered the wooden floor.

The dean guided her to one of two oxblood chairs with nail head trims before seating himself on a brown leather sofa across from her. The wood paneled walls reminded her of the interior decorating style of the sixties. The display of books all around reflected the size of Souter's ego.

"You're a difficult person to track down, Lesley. I've been trying to reach you all week. So glad you decided to come to work today."

"Sorry, I've been bombarded with personal obligations lately."

"Nothing too serious I hope?"

"Not at all. It'll all be over soon," Lesley said while laughing on the inside.

"Good to hear. You've been with us approximately four years if I'm not mistaken?"

"It'll be five years this coming fall, to be more precise."

"Straight out of grad school? No tenure track experience at other universities?"

"That's right," Lesley said.

Dean Souter clenched his jaw and shifted uneasily on the leather sofa.

"Ordinarily, this calls for a celebration, but the circumstances are quite unusual," Dean Souter said.

She knew exactly what he wanted to say. Lesley did her best not to show premature signs of excitement before he finished his thought. It was the hardest thing she had ever done.

"We've received a large gift from a generous donor. I'm sure you're familiar with Octavio Souza, an incredible businessman who is also a conscientious supporter of higher education. Mr. Souza has turned over five million dollars to the college to create an endowed chair in his name."

"Oh, that's wonderful," she blurted out despite her best efforts.

"Yes, but that's where we have a slight problem," Dean Souter said, crossing one leg over the other with palpable trepidation.

"Oh?"

"For some reason, this is none of my business, Mr. Souza has stipulated that the chair is to be bestowed on you," Dean Souter said before pausing to glare awkwardly at Lesley.

She held his gaze for as long as possible before replying, "and it is a problem because?"

"I'm sure you're aware it's quite unusual for an associate professor with four years' experience to get an endowed chair at a prestigious institution such as Georgetown. Be that as it may, currently, there are two candidates we believe should get priority over you. They're both colleagues of yours in the history department. Ms. Tameka Washington is African American, twenty-two years teaching experience, Harvard

PhD, and has written five books about black history that are national bestsellers. Mr. Oscar Ramirez, Mexican-American, grew up in a gang-infested neighborhood in East Los Angeles. He has eighteen years teaching experience and is considered the leading expert on Chicano history in America. I was hoping to choose between the two of them for the next endowment that came to the department."

"I fail to see what I can do here. Like you said, the grantor has stipulated specific provisions as a condition of the gift." She was not about to make this easy for him.

"Well, *mmmhhhhh...*" he said, sputtering and starting up repeatedly before he was able to get the words out, "I was hoping you would request to have the position go to one of the two candidates just mentioned. I know how this sounds. I promise you will be next in line for an endowed chair in the history department, even if it's one of the other chairs that becomes vacant upon a retirement or death. If I'm no longer here, I'll make sure the next dean is aware of this arrangement."

"Obviously, Mr. Souza's staff conducted thorough research and found me to be the most qualified for this position. I don't understand why you want to take this away from me?"

"It's not that. These two candidates have been waiting patiently, over a decade at Georgetown for each of them, for such an honor. If I pick another white professor, well, you know how it is, we could be accused of racism in the current climate."

"I've been speaking out for social justice since I was a young girl in Connecticut. That wasn't a popular thing to do in Greenwich. All the kids on my block came from old money. They made fun of me every day, called me a guilt-ridden white liberal. It was the same at Andover Academy where I started our first African literature club—"

"What was the turnout like?"

"We had three people, including myself. The point is that I've paid a high price in terms of ridicule and shame to champion diversity and inclusion my whole life. Now, you're telling me I'm not worthy of this gift."

"That's not what I'm saying, Lesley. That's not it at all. It's just a matter of optics. The other two candidates grew up with myriad economic disadvantages. They both clawed their way out of the ghetto for Christ's sake. How would it appear to give an endowed chair to someone four years out of grad school, who grew up in Greenwich and went to boarding school in Andover?" Dean Souter said, raising his voice slightly.

She needed to increase the pressure. From great adversity came great triumph. She wasn't going to get what she deserved without breaking a few rules and taking some risks. Would innocent people get hurt? So what! Let the chips fall where they may.

Lesley slid over to the edge of her seat. Looking intently at the dean, she whispered, "I was hesitant to mention this earlier but seeing how this award could bring publicity to the university, you have a right to know."

"Please, speak freely."

"It's about Oscar and Tameka."

"Yes," the dean said eagerly, tightening his fist and tapping his foot rapidly on the Persian rug.

"I've been hearing all kinds of stories. Mostly rumors, mind you, which is why I paid no attention at first."

"Yes, of course."

"Anyway, the rumors were extremely salacious, all kinds of stories about sex in the office, in the library, and even—"

"Please, continue."

"Even in the dean's office. This was supposedly going on for quite a while. One afternoon I had a question about right wing disinformation claiming the Black Panthers and similar groups were on the payroll of the KGB in the late sixties. I needed some ammunition to counter the rebellious conservatives in my class who repeat this garbage. When I arrived outside Tameka's office, the door was slightly ajar. I knocked several times, but a strange singsong squeal was the only reply."

"A squeal?"

"Yes, it was sort of like *eeeehhhh...eeeehhhh...eeeehhhh... eeeehhhh...* Like that."

"I see."

"I must admit, at this point, despite my better judgment, curiosity caught the better of me. So, I finally mustered up the courage to push the door open."

"What happened next?" Dean Souter said. He was obviously enraptured by her story.

"I don't want to be crass, so I'll just say I saw Tameka Washington and Oscar Ramirez in flagrante on the floor of her office."

"Did they see you?"

"I doubt it. They were too busy, well...you know."

"But they're both married with children."

"Which is why I haven't mentioned it before. I didn't want to ruin anyone's career, especially these two. But seeing how this could cause a scandal for the university if it ever got out, I think you should know about it before you make your decision," Lesley said, trying her best to feign sadness.

"Have no fear, Lesley, you did the right thing. Rest assured your tip will remain anonymous. I'll investigate this matter personally and will announce my decision about the Octavio Souza Chair of American History shortly," Dean Souter said as he stood to shake her hand.

As she walked out of the dean's office, there was an extra spring in her step. It was a fantastic victory after weeks of uncertainty, engaging in activities she was never trained for. But do them she had. Lesley had earned the right to the endowed chair. Sure, she had to lie at the end to get it, but she deserved this prize for risking her life to attack Kim and her gang of fellow capitalists.

Lesley wanted to celebrate. She was no longer in the mood to observe Antifa destroy Washington. She switched her focus to a certain Vicuna coat that cost twenty-four thousand dollars. She had fantasized about that coat for months. Octavio's gift included an extra one hundred-thousand-dollar bonus to be deposited directly to her private bank account. The money was on its way. Tyson's Galleria in Virginia was the perfect venue to spend her well-earned windfall. Tomorrow was going to be a great day.

Lesley marveled at the Vicuna coat in her office mirror. She still couldn't believe how soft the damn thing was to touch. The lustrous camel colored sheen of the coat was truly a miracle of nature. Similar to its cousins, the Llama and the Alpaca, Vicuna is a South American mammal valued for its soft wool.

Found mainly in Peru and Bolivia, they were on the verge of extinction until conservation efforts brought their numbers back up. It's a good thing they had, otherwise Lesley would have been deprived of the experience. A coat so rare that only the wives of Wall Street billionaires and Russian oligarchs could afford to have one or more in their collection. Lesley rapidly pirouetted counterclockwise before immediately reversing her motion, as the tail of her twenty-four-thousand-dollar coat swayed in the mirror.

"Professor Gantz," the voice said before stopping in mid-sentence. "I'm sorry, I can return later. I saw your door was open so I thought I'd check in with you," the woman said.

"I'm off today like everyone else, but there's no need for you to leave. I was just trying on this coat to see if I should keep it," Lesley said. *The mortician won't be able to pry this coat off my rotting carcass,* she thought. "Are you here regarding one of my courses?"

"My name is Emma. I'm in your History 111 class, America in the twentieth century," the woman said.

She had a pretty face and was rather tall for a woman, with a voluptuous yet slender figure. Her hair was jet black and her eyes were soft brown. Her aura was rather mysterious. Although Lesley did not recall her, there was something distinctly familiar about this woman. She would make a perfect addition to MIS.

"Have we met before?"

"No, I usually sit in the back. Everybody tells me I resemble the girl next door."

"Take a seat. How can I help?"

"I'm having trouble wrapping my head around something you wrote in the lecture notes posted online. You mentioned America's founding was so inherently evil we may need to scrap the Constitution and start from scratch. What did you mean by that? A violent overthrow? A revolution perhaps?"

"Well, that's a topic for a long conversation. I may have to ask you to come back later. I'm celebrating an upcoming promotion and—"

"Congratulations, I'm very happy for you."

"Thank you. Like I said, you're welcome to return during normal hours, but I'll try to explain so you get a basic understanding. First thing I tell all my students is that every relationship has an element of exploitation. Second, the Founding Fathers were mostly slave holders, it's only natural they wrote the Constitution to protect white privilege. Despite years of efforts, we've still not been able to create equality of outcomes in America, and so—"

"That's interesting. I had mistakenly thought that you were trying to recruit students for the upcoming attack on the White House by Antifa."

Emma's words stung like hell. Lesley looked closer at her face.

"Don't I know you from somewhere?"

"Maybe. Think very hard," she said.

Out of nowhere, a punch landed on Lesley's face before Emma stood up and threw her on the floor.

"Recognize me now, your rotten whore?" she said before peeling away a layer of her face. Emma proceeded to remove her wig, revealing a head of flowing blonde hair.

"Wait a second, you're, you're… You should be dead. I-I-I—We killed you."

Lesley could not believe her eyes.

"You first," Kim said before jumping on top of Lesley. "By the way, the attack on the White House tomorrow has been canceled. I bet you didn't know about that?"

"Destruction will find a way," Lesley replied.

"Oh, I guess you're not aware. Janusz cleaned out Bakunin Farm. Your master and Fiona are having an orgy in Hell as we speak. But don't worry, you'll join them soon enough."

An excruciating pain shot through Lesley's ass.

"There we go," Kim said before dangling a syringe in front of her face.

Lesley's hands and legs went numb. Her tongue was next.

You fucking bitch, Lesley wanted to say, but couldn't before the darkness took over.

32. CAPITOL HILL, WASHINGTON D.C

January 21

He rapped four times. There was no reply. Janusz then pounded his fist against the wooden door until footsteps approached on the other side. There was a peephole, but he made no attempt to hide his face.

"Open up, Jason. We need to talk," Janusz said.

Janusz was dressed in a suit and tie holding a black leather briefcase. It was not unusual for a government official to get a late hour visit in this part of the city. Moments later, the chain on the other side came undone before the knob turned and the door opened.

"Janusz, wha-wha-what you doing here?" Jason said with a trembling voice.

He wore pinstripe pajamas. His hair was a mess. It was half past one in the morning, and the bastard had probably been asleep. Given what Janusz had to endure over the past several weeks, he had zero sympathy for Jason.

"Get a me a beer," Janusz said.

He waltzed into Jason's apartment like he owned the place. It was small, no more than nine hundred square feet. The door to the bedroom was barely open. The location made these tiny apartments very popular.

"Jesus, how much do you pay for this place? It's smaller than my home office."

"Forty-two hundred a month," Jason replied.

Jason was on the other side of the counter that separated the living room from the kitchen. Janusz tried to get under his skin.

Moments later, Jason walked in with the beer bottle, "Sorry, I forgot to open it."

"It's not necessary," Janusz said, twisting the top with his bare fingers. "Political correctness has turned our men into little girls. Take a seat," Janusz said, pointing to a brown couch against the wall.

Jason was apparently surprised to see a beer bottle opened in that way. The room was lit with several nightlights. Janusz walked over to the wall. Flipping a switch, he illuminated the living room. Jason threw his hands in front of his eyes like Dracula at daybreak. It took a moment for Jason to adjust to the imposed lighting regime.

"I was hoping to go back to sleep, but what the heck. I presume you found the people trying to take down the Unit?"

"Not exactly," Janusz said while taking a sip of beer. "Not exactly."

Jason fidgeted with his feet, moving back and forth on the couch. He was unable to make eye contact with Janusz.

"Don't worry, I'm not here to hurt you. If I was, you'd be dead by now."

Jason chuckled nervously, "Why would you want to hurt me?"

"Cut the crap, Jason. We both know what you did. What I want to know is, why?"

Jason looked around the room before throwing his gaze to the floor. He was silent for quite a while. Janusz gave him the chance to gather his thoughts while sipping on the beer. Janusz walked over to the window to rest against the ledge. Out of the corner of his eye, Jason bolted toward the door. The beer bottle dropped straight to the floor, splashing his suit pants as he ran to catch Jason.

The door swung open, and Jason dashed out. Janusz tackled him several feet down the hall, halfway to the elevator. They bounced off the wall before hitting the ground. Janusz stood and pulled Jason up by the collar. The man did not resist. Janusz pushed him forward toward the apartment. Once inside, he locked the door behind them.

"Okay, Jason. You threw me off track with the Russians and set me up for a hit by Antifa assassins. What the hell is going on?"

Janusz could not believe what came next. The grown man standing in front of him cried as though he were a child.

"I needed money. When Donald Patrick left the Senate, I couldn't find a job. Out of the blue one day, I get a call from this guy."

"What guy?"

"Said his name was Placido, you know, like the guy from the three tenors. Anyway, this Placido tells me a wealthy businessman on the West Coast is willing to hire me as a consultant."

"How much?"

"Is that important?"

Janusz grabbed his neck, digging in with his fingers. "How much?"

"Three million dollars. Does that make you happy? He said he'd pay me three million dollars, cash, for information about Unit 81 and its employees."

"Unit 81, those were his exact words?"

"Yes. I wondered how they knew, but I didn't press the issue."

"So, you decided to sell us out instead?"

"I didn't know they were trying to kill you guys. At least not at first. I thought they just wanted to blackmail you."

"What's your excuse after Stan and Tony were shot and Bill disappeared? Why didn't you get out then?"

"It was too late. Placido said if I didn't help, he would kill me and my entire family."

"What did he want?"

"Names, addresses, personality profiles."

"Jesus, Jason, how could you?"

"I just wanted to take the money and run. I was gonna move to South America and live in a small village for the rest of my life. I'm sorry, Janusz, I really am."

"Are you sorry for what you did or sorry you got caught?"

Jason was silent.

"I thought so," Janusz said. "What do they want?"

"How would I know?"

Janusz smacked Jason across the left cheek. The sound bounced off every wall.

"Please don't hit me. I asked Placido again and again. He told me to mind my own business if I wanted to collect my money."

"Stan, Tony, and Bill weren't enough? You had to sell out Kim? Worst of all, you're in bed with Antifa?"

"What Antifa? I never dealt with Antifa. It was some rich guy on the West Coast speaking through this Placido. I figured it's a tech billionaire gone mad."

"So, you didn't know about the attack on the White House that was scheduled for later today?"

"What attack?" Jason said incredulously.

"Forget it. It's not your problem."

Janusz took a moment to clear his mind. "Your mysterious benefactor is using Antifa to hide his tracks. The national media is so in love with anarchists they won't dig into the murder of my colleagues. In a weird way, it's good. The lack of coverage allows the Unit to remain hidden despite the fallout from this fiasco."

"Does this mean you're letting me go?"

"Not so fast. How did this Placido know about your ties to Unit 81?"

"He never said, and I knew better than to ask."

"Somebody must've known. A girlfriend perhaps? A colleague? Have you been posting on social media?"

"No, man. I haven't had a girlfriend in quite a while. Too much effort to have a relationship. I need a top secret clearance for my job on the SSCI, that's why I don't use social media."

"What about LinkedIn?"

"My profile is generic. Just says I'm a staffer on the Intelligence Committee. Never mentioned High Risk Capital or

Unit 81. It's possible one of the other staffers blabbed. Three others know about the existence of the Unit. I can give you their names. But that leaves open another door?"

"What door?"

"If any of the others talked, why would they come to me? I mean, whoever else Placido contacted could've given him the same information."

"Perhaps the others didn't know as much as you. Perhaps Placido's employer viewed you as a better conduit. Whatever the reason, you're going to help me get to the bottom of it."

"How?" Jason said.

Janusz looked at him with a wide grin.

33. GEORGETOWN, WASHINGTON D.C.

January 22

"Seventy-one, seventy-two, seventy-three, seventy-four, seventy-five," Janusz counted off on his way to the top. It was the first time he had a leg cramp from climbing the so called Exorcist Stairs in Georgetown.

Although illuminated by lamps on an adjacent brick wall, one had to admit the narrow stairwell was rather spooky at night. A perfect setting for a horror movie. The empty lot below felt a few degrees warmer. Up here, he was greeted by a howling wind that blew across Prospect Street. Combined with the bone-chilling temperature, it was enough to blur his vision with tears. Across the street was the sign for the rendezvous spot. The appropriately named restaurant, The Tombs, faced the Exorcist Stairs. The evening grew more surreal with each passing minute.

Did this Placido character know his way around Georgetown? Letting Placido pick the location for the meet was the only way to draw him out. Janusz fidgeted with the keys in his pants. His only regret was having to rely on a traitor. Without that son of a bitch Jason, the evening was doomed. He decided to take a walk around the block.

As he scanned the perimeter, a man in a trench coat appeared in front of The Tombs sign. Jason had finally arrived. Just then, another man walked by on the other side of the street. He was taller than Janusz, wore jeans along with a black coat. The man stood erect and walked with a confident stride. From the back, his shoulders were quite broad, forming a V as they sloped toward his waist. The man's hulking figure filled out every square inch of his coat. Janusz hid behind a pillar near the front entrance of the Car Barn Building. From behind the shadow, he observed the two men shaking hands.

The listening device in his ear came to life within seconds. Jason was wired.

"What's so important you had to drag me all the way from California?" the larger man said. "I hate the cold weather, and I hate Washington. Nobody does what their supposed to do around here."

"What's that supposed to mean?"

"Forget about it."

"I appreciate your coming out on such short notice, Placido. It's about our mutual friend, Janusz."

"Wait!" Placido said, grabbing Jason by the arm. Placido guided the shorter man to walk in front of him toward Prospect Street. "Let's take a stroll around the block."

There was an unusual period of silence as Janusz waited for sound. Fearing he was out of range, Janusz went after them. He stepped cautiously, taking great care not to make noise. It was a strange dance, jumping from shadow to shadow in the darkness behind parked cars. The sound in his ear was reassuring. The conversation had picked up again.

"I don't like talking out in the open. Force of habit," Placido said.

"Whatever you say. Our mutual friend called the other night. He was irate."

"Irate?"

"Angry. He was very angry. He thinks I set him up. He said he'll get me as soon as he finishes with Antifa."

"He mentioned Antifa?"

"Yeah. What does it mean?"

"I wonder what that *puta* knows?" Placido said.

"About what?"

"Don't worry yourself. However, you'd be wise to take a long vacation. Somewhere far from here."

"I would, but I need money first. Which is the other reason

why I wanted to meet in person. Where's my money?"

"We agreed to pay you once everyone on our list is dead. With Janusz still on the loose, our list is obviously still open."

"You got most of 'em. I'd say at least fifty percent of the top guys. I deserve at least fifty percent of my money."

"Relax, *amigo*, you'll get your money. We need to tie up a few loose ends. What else did he say?"

"Not so fast. I risked my life for you. I think I'm entitled to a few answers."

"Answers to what?"

"Why me? Why did you pick me to help you against Unit 81? There were other people in Washington who knew. Why didn't you go to them?"

Placido fell silent. Janusz waited for the conversation to pick up again.

"We had a source. Our source provided a name, and we came to you."

"Wait a minute, you're telling me someone gave my name to you? Someone knowledgeable about Unit 81?"

"In a manner of speaking. That's all I can give you."

"There's something else I don't understand. The Unit deals with foreign governments and terrorist organizations. You told me you represent an American businessman. What could you possibly want with Unit 81? And how is Antifa mixed up in all this?"

"It doesn't concern you."

"It does now that Janusz and his buddies are coming for me. I'm their number one target. I think I deserve to know why?"

Janusz was impressed with Jason's ability to act out the lines. He had put just enough emotion to make his concerns seem real. Perhaps they were.

"Keep your voice down, *puta*. People will hear you in one of these houses."

"I don't care."

"Well, I do. Antifa is not real. Janusz threw it out there to confuse you. My boss is trying to make America a better place. He wants to see this country keep the promise of the Constitution. As long as an illegal organization like Unit 81 is out there, this country is in danger. It's as simple as that," Placido said.

"You're not even American, are you?" Jason asked.

Janusz tried to make sense of it all. He was completely oblivious to his surroundings. Two men bumped into him on the sidewalk. Their preppy winter outfit was a dead giveaway for Georgetown students.

"Excuse you, buddy," they blurted out in unison.

Janusz ignored them. His heart sank when the earpiece was silent again. Across the street, he was no longer able to see Jason and Placido. Panic set in as Janusz considered the possibilities. He was forced to ditch caution and go in for a closer look. The farther he traveled, the more his heart raced. The men had vanished. On the corner of Prospect and 37th Street, he eyeballed every direction. Was it possible he had been double crossed? Perhaps the entire spectacle had been a show? Perhaps Jason had fucked him again?

"Looking for someone, *puta*?" a voice from behind called out.

Janusz turned rapidly to check his rear. The voice was located somewhere in between the streetlamps. It was impossible to see anything. Janusz slowly crept forward, cognizant of the fact there was more light on him than on the source of the sound.

"That's far enough, *amigo*," the voice said. It had to be Placido.

Janusz anchored his feet at an angle so as to keep an eye on a potential attack from behind. This was not where he wanted to be. He strived to get a better view of the voice hiding in the dark. Moments like these called for quick thinking, nothing one could prepare for. He placed a hand over the pistol in his coat pocket. The trick was not to panic. Escalating a volatile situation would mean shooting the wrong person.

"Your *cadela* insisted he wasn't working for you. I checked under his shirt. You know what I found?" Placido said.

"Jellybeans?" Janusz said. He inched closer to Placido's voice.

"I said don't move."

"Why not?" Janusz replied.

There was a shuffling of feet. Two figures crossed the street to the other side. Janusz followed them.

"Placido, I presume," Janusz said. "We've never been properly introduced. Where I come from that's considered extremely rude."

"You're quite a difficult man to kill, Mr. Janusz Soltani," Placido said.

"Have you considered the possibility you're just incompetent?" Janusz said.

Placido's hand moved up to grab Jason's forehead, pulling it back. Jason was clearly panicked.

"Don't, he's got a knife to my throat," Jason said.

"How do I know you two aren't working together?" Janusz said.

"Don't fuck with me. I'll kill him," Placido said.

"Right here? Come on, Placido, who do you take me for?"

Janusz slid forward inch by inch without further warning from Placido. When he got to within seven or eight feet, he anchored in place and studied the situation. Placido's size was quite impressive. It was more obvious now as he towered over Jason, holding a long hunting knife under the disgraced senate staffer's neck.

Should I draw the pistol?

"In Brazil, I was part of a special unit. It was special because we volunteered to do things no one else wanted to do," Placido said.

Jason's bare neck was visible. The edge of the blade pushed against the skin, moving the folds under the neck as if preparing the man for a close shave.

"You see we had a big problem with rats in Rio. But our rats did not crawl around on the floor. Our infestation problem was of the two-legged kind."

"Calm down. Let's talk about this," Janusz said.

"I'm afraid there's nothing to talk about, *amigo*," Placido said in a cold voice.

Janusz took a cautious step forward, maintaining eye contact to the extent possible.

"The *favelas* were full of troublesome kids who did nothing but rape, steal, and kill. I know because it happened to my mother. Since the government was impotent, we took matters into our own hands, using private security. I was head of one such group. Except I wasn't like the others. I didn't shoot kids from behind. I looked every one of them in the eyes, but that wasn't enough. I felt cutting off heads delivered a more powerful message. That was my specialty, *Senhor*. Cutting off the heads of troublesome kids."

Who the fuck was this weirdo? Was he bluffing? Why the hell was he telling this sadistic story?

"*Ahhhhhhh...kkkhhhhh...kkkhhhh.*" Jason choked. Blood gushed out as Placido cut slowly into his throat from ear to ear. Jason convulsed uncontrollably. The dark liquid flowed out of the opening like a river. For a second, Janusz thought his eyes were playing tricks on him. He wanted to help, but he was still processing the gruesome scene.

Placido gently placed the still shaking body of Jason on the sidewalk as if putting a baby in its crib. Placido then wiped both sides of the blade against Jason's pants. The amazing thing was that Placido did all this with the steady demeanor of a barber wiping his razor against a towel after a deluxe shave.

The Brazilian assassin looked at Janusz and smiled. He then sprinted off in the opposite direction. Janusz pulled himself together. He stood over Jason for a split second. There was nothing to be done. A wave of sorrow washed over him. How could he have just stood there as this butcher performed such a macabre spectacle? A part of him felt Jason deserved what he got. *No one deserves this!* The conflicting emotions had to be resolved another day. An electric current jolted every cell in his body.

"Placido, you're next, you motherfucker."

He ran faster than he had in years. There was someone approaching ahead. It wasn't Placido. The pedestrian stepped aside to let Janusz pass. He was finally able to see Placido as he reached 36th Street. The Brazilian assassin was headed for the Exorcist Stairs. Janusz pushed harder to close the distance. A man popped out the entrance to the stairwell. Placido plowed into him with such force the man bounced back against the railing and fell flat on his face. Janusz passed him several seconds later. The man was still unconscious.

Placido raced down the steps, using the metal railings to accelerate his stride. Janusz was left with no choice but to do the same. He had never slid down these railings. Janusz kept his focus on maintaining balance, trying to block out all distractions.

Teenagers often filmed themselves doing stunts like these. They posted the results for the entire world to see on social media. Most often, the end was catastrophic, especially if they used rollerblades or skateboards. Janusz once viewed a video of a boy who cracked his leg in half. The white of the bone protruded out of the skin as the boy went into shock while his friends continued to laugh. Janusz took the last step in stride, grateful to be in one piece. As soon as his feet landed on the bottom, he looked up. The next thing he remembered was going backwards. A powerful blow had knocked him to the ground. Placido lay in wait.

"Get up, *puta*. You're in such a hurry to catch me, here I am," Placido said.

Janusz tried desperately to regain his bearings. To his surprise, Placido waited patiently. Janusz grabbed the bottom rail and pulled himself up as if he were a boxer who had unexpectedly been knocked down.

"Were you ever in the military?" Janusz asked to stall.

"Yes. The Brazilian 1st Special Forces Battalion. I learned a lot from you Americans. It's ironic, isn't it?"

"What is?"

"Killing you with skills I learned from your military. Of course, I was also a national champion in Brazilian Jiu Jitsu, so maybe credit for killing you will be all mine."

Placido was getting under his skin. Defeating him would take a bit of luck tonight. Placido unzipped his coat before removing it. He casually placed it on the window ledge next to the stairs. Placido pulled up his sleeves, moving his fists similar to a bare-knuckle boxer. That's when it caught his eye. The huge gold Breitling. It was on his left wrist. Janusz could not take his eye off it. It was the one Tony had described in the hospital.

"You like this watch? A gift from my employer."

"Were you wearing it the day you shot up the SUV in Chantilly?"

"What?" Placido said as the wheels turned in his head. "Oh, yes, *certamente*." He laughed.

Janusz tightened every muscle before lifting his fists. The parking lot was lit with several lamp posts, one of which was directly over their heads. They circled each other like mixed martial arts warriors in an octagon. Janusz had never polished his Jiu Jitsu skills. That's why it was imperative to defeat this monster while standing up. Placido threw a punch that only hit air. He followed that up with two more that also missed. Both men were still getting warmed up.

"*Ahhh,*" Janusz yelled before grabbing his own lip. He had not detected the spinning roundhouse kick. Placido followed up with a heavy punch to the kidney. He caught Janusz on the side of the face with an elbow. Janusz let out a sigh in an effort to catch his breath. The reflection of light caught the corner of his eye. Placido had pulled out the knife he had used to butcher Jason. He swung it around to exhibit his skill.

Janusz kept his eye on the blade. "Whach ya gonna do with that? Stick it in your dead mother's pussy?" Janusz said.

Placido charged with blind rage. Now, it was Janusz who delivered the surprise. A rapid sidekick knocked the knife out of Placido's hand. The blade landed on the ground with a distinct *clickedy clang*. Janusz slammed his head straight into Placido's nose. The depraved Brazilian was clearly dazed as blood squirted out.

The follow up punch was even more unexpected. Placido stumbled back before turning one hundred eighty degrees to run toward the street. Janusz gave chase cognizant that he needed this man to find Octavio. Placido ran up M Street toward the Key Bridge. The Brazilian suddenly jumped from the sidewalk to cross the street. At that exact moment, two pairs of headlights approached rapidly. At this late hour, it had to be a drag race. Janusz anchored in place. The cars whizzed by as he waited for the impact. There was no noise. He looked up. Placido was still running and made it to the other side without a scratch. Janusz ran after him.

Placido dashed through a small park and onto the pedestrian path of the bridge. Janusz inched closer with every breath. His right hand shot up to grab the Brazilian assassin. Both men gasped for air as Placido miraculously gained a bolt of energy. Janusz's opponent was increasing the distance. An image of Tony flashed before his eyes. His mentor was in the hospital, riddled by the bullets of this man.

Janusz launched into the air. He landed with both hands wrapped around Placido's collar. Janusz pulled back with all his might. The distinct tearing of fabric indicated success. Placido fell backwards. Janusz jumped on top of him, repeatedly slamming his head against the railing that separated the bridge from the abyss. He pulled his arm all the way back.

"This is for Tony," Janusz said as he punched Placido once more.

"That *puta* didn't even put up a fight. Just looked at me as I aimed at his face. It was almost like shooting a baby."

Janusz could see nothing but red. His face grew hot as the blood boiled through his veins. He slammed Placido's head against the railing repeatedly to put an end to his sadistic laugh. Janusz grabbed his coat and pulled him up to his feet. Several cars passed from behind while honking their horns. Great, there were witnesses. He glared at Placido with murderous rage.

"What you going to do when we get arrested? I'll be out in less than a day. As you wait behind bars, I'll finish your friend in the hospital."

The railing behind them was barely six feet high. They stood in the middle of the bridge, about a hundred feet over the Potomac River. It was the only thing that made sense. Every muscle fiber came to life. Janusz bent down and grabbed the Brazilian assassin under his crotch. He then lifted him up over his head, turning him briefly sideways. Several items fell out of his pockets. Janusz could not tell what they were.

"Now what, you going to kill me? You'll spend the rest of your life behind bars," Placido said from above.

More car horns on the street. Janusz ran forward and pushed with all his might. Placido flew into the darkness.

"*Ahhhhhhhhh,*" Placido's fading scream was pure pleasure to his ears.

There was no sound of impact from below. It was one of the coldest nights in Washington he could remember. Even if Placido survived the plunge, he had no chance against the icy river. Janusz needed to disappear, but something kept him standing on that cold bridge. The object on the floor brought a smile to his face. He bent down to pick up Placido's cell phone.

34. TRUMP HOTEL, WASHINGTON D.C.

January 23

The SUV sped down Pennsylvania Avenue without much trouble. The plaza for the Navy Memorial was empty. Perhaps it was the cold weather, but DC seemed more somber than Octavio remembered. The wave of protests he had funded around the country were taking their toll. They drove right in between the monstrous buildings that housed the Department of Justice and the FBI, flanking both sides of the street.

To his left was another architecturally insulting building that housed the Internal Revenue Service. Octavio couldn't help but to laugh out loud as he contemplated how many billions of dollars he had shielded from their prying eyes. What a truly naive government it was that allowed him to do as he pleased in the name of social justice. The investments he had made in this town over the years, meeting with politicians at the Mayflower Hotel, donating to NGOs, and social activists in every corner of this city, had proven to be wise.

The driver turned left onto 11th Street. The valet waited to open his door. Behind them was the Trump Hotel, a monument to the ego of a loudmouth billionaire he hated with a passion. Trump had run for the American presidency on a number of occasions. He was always defeated thanks to the cooperation of Octavio's friends in the media. To be a loudmouth billionaire was one thing. To do so while singing the praises of American workers and economic protectionism was quite another.

The twenty-first century had no use for such policies. This

was the era of globalization par excellence. This was the era of Davos Man as Samuel Huntington had so eloquently put it. Octavio had spent a fortune destroying protectionist regimes around the world. Uncontrolled borders and limitless immigration decreased the power of labor while increasing corporate profits. Anyone who opposed those policies, even a flamboyant billionaire, had to be destroyed. To agitate the social justice warriors, Trump had to be cast as a racist and a fascist.

Octavio climbed the stairs toward the entrance where another door was held open. It was strange to visit the most famous property of his nemesis. He had been thinking about it during the entire trip from San Francisco. Why had Placido chosen this location of all places to meet? As head of his security detail, Placido must have had his reasons. Perhaps this was the last place where Octavio's enemies would search for him. The message was strange.

"I've scratched the top name off our list and need to show you something in person. Meet me at the Trump Hotel tomorrow. I've arranged a room for your stay," Placido had said in a cryptic text.

Octavio had instructed Placido to let DC Antifa handle the business of eliminating Unit 81. It was not like him to disobey orders. They had agreed long ago never to discuss such matters over the phone or email. So now, here he was. In a way it was sort of a celebration. Antifa had been unable to eliminate the biggest thorn in his side, Janusz Soltani. There was no moving forward until Janusz was dead.

Meanwhile, Destruction and his gang of Antifa misfits had disappeared. They had probably decided to take his money without finishing their end of the bargain. The attack against the White House had not taken place for some reason and Octavio had not been briefed about the new arrangements. He decided right there and then to get rid of Destruction. Placido would take care of the rest.

The lobby of the hotel was quite grand. If there was one

thing this New York real estate developer knew how to do well, it was to put on a grand spectacle. Intricate glass chandeliers hung from gold painted metal trusses that ran from one side of the space to the other. Velvet sofas and chairs in the lobby created multiple private settings for the guests. A grand bar graced one end of the floor, above which hung an oversized American flag.

"Can I show you to your room, Mr. Souza?" the attendant said.

Octavio followed him to the elevators. Several minutes later, Octavio entered his suite. As he scanned his surroundings, he found it difficult to admit he was pleased. The decor reminded him of his own summer beach house in the Hamptons. Everything was draped in a cream color with tasteful navy accents. The spacious living room was adorned with large windows.

The valance around the edge of the windows was also a rich navy color. He stepped forward to take a gander outside. From his sixth-floor suite, he had a clear view of the Washington Monument. The marble studded obelisk was a testament to American power. Octavio took a curious step toward the bedroom. It was elegantly decorated like the rest of the space. He was particularly impressed with the bed and dresser made of intricately carved wood. The dark wooden frames were gilded around the edges. The same went for the nightstands. The entire ensemble had a French imperial flavor.

Octavio sauntered back to the living room and settled into a white upholstered chaise. He threw his feet on the table and pulled out his phone. There had been no more messages from Placido. The meeting with his chief of security was not scheduled for another two hours. Octavio leaned back and closed his eyes.

Janusz grabbed the glass of scotch from the bar tender and

placed it on the marble top. He settled into his blue upholstered bar chair and took a giant sip. The age of his scotch no longer seemed relevant. His palate was not convinced the drink was worth fifty dollars. Two more sips and his glass was empty.

He could not remember ever wasting fifty dollars so quickly. The beautiful blonde at the reception desk informed him that his guest was settled in the room. Janusz could still not believe that he had somehow managed to coax Octavio to DC. Luck seemed to be on his side as Placido's body had not yet been discovered. Exceptionally pleased with himself, Janusz ordered a beer. Within minutes, the bartender placed a bowl of mixed nuts in front of him.

Janusz had visited the Trump Hotel often since it had opened. The food was fantastic and the service exceptional. But those were not the reasons he had chosen this venue for the meeting. As he sipped on his beer, Janusz recalled reading that Octavio harbored a deep animus toward Trump. Apparently, the New York billionaire had outbid the Brazilian private equity giant during an auction not too long ago. Their feud had started over a painting called *Salvator Mundi*, which depicted Jesus Christ.

As it turned out, both men were fanatic admirers of the Renaissance painter Leonardo da Vinci. The da Vinci painting of Christ had been put up for auction a few years back in New York. Octavio had been present at the auction house in Manhattan. For well over an hour, he had outbid everyone present in the room. Once most of the competition had withered away, an anonymous caller had dialed in. The two remaining bidders had pushed the price of the painting north of four hundred million dollars.

Octavio was universally recognized as a fearless negotiator. He had never been outbid at an auction. When they had reached four hundred and ninety-five million dollars, the caller had raised the stakes to five hundred million. To this day, Octavio is adamant he had countered at five hundred and five million. The manager of the auction house was also the cousin of Mr. Trump. He claimed there were no bids after five hundred million, and so he sold the painting to Trump.

Not accustomed to losing, Octavio raised a big stink. He had made it his life's mission to ruin everything Trump tried to do. When the New York developer had run as a candidate for president, Octavio poured hundreds of millions toward the opposition. It was fair to say Octavio's greatest passion was his hatred of Trump. How delicious it was that Janusz had chosen this location for Octavio's final act.

When Octavio opened his eyes, his room was completely dark. There was someone at the door. It took a moment to remember where he was. The Trump Hotel, a meeting with Placido. His eyes shuddered as someone turned on the lights.

"Hello, anyone home," the voice said.

Octavio remained silent as the footsteps rounded the corner and entered the living room.

"Octavio? Octavio Souza?"

"You're not Placido. How did you get inside my room?"

"Very sorry. I paid for this room so, technically, it's mine. Allow me to introduce myself. The name is Janusz Soltani," the man said.

Octavio glared as the lowlife took a seat in front of him, across from the white chaise. How could this be? Was he still dreaming? He was here to discuss the death of this man with Placido, and now Janusz sat right in front of him.

"Vel, what kind of a joke is this? Where's Placido?"

"Last I saw, he was flying into the Potomac River. I believe he's still there."

Octavio stood up. He had enough and was ready to leave. His legs wobbled as he grabbed on to a chair.

"What's your hurry? We have a lot to discuss," Janusz said.

Octavio recognized the man was much younger and also more agile. He sat back down and decided to listen.

"That's better. I've read a lot about you, Mr. Souza. It seems you've done quite well for yourself since coming to this country as a penniless boy. Why in the world would a man in your position want to destroy Unit 81 and kill its employees?"

"So, you really are Janusz Soltani?"

"I'm afraid so."

"What happened to Placido?"

Janusz reached into his pocket and pulled out a cell phone. Janusz placed the phone on top of the coffee table in between them. Octavio recognized the phone right away.

"Like I said, Placido has been in the Potomac River since last night. I don't think the authorities have recovered his body. Then again, you have more connections in this town than I do. So, perhaps you know something I don't."

If Janusz had indeed killed Placido, he was not someone to mess with.

Octavio tried to stall. "Let's get down to it, what do you want? Money?"

"You disappoint me, Octavio. I didn't go to all this trouble for money."

Octavio swallowed hard, "Do you want to kill me?"

"I could've done that when I first walked in. How about you start by telling me why?"

Octavio looked around the room. There was nothing he could use as a weapon. His shotguns were in San Francisco, and Placido was dead.

Octavio was not about to let this pest ruin everything, "I don't have to tell you a damn thing. I'm an honest businessman who gives billions every year to make America a better place. You're an intruder. All I have to do is make one call to the mayor and the entire DC Police Department will descend on this godforsaken hotel."

Janusz stood and walked around the table. He placed his hand around Octavio's neck and squeezed.

"Why...are...you...obsessed...with...Unit 81?" Janusz said.

Octavio put his hands up to indicate surrender.

"Influence…because of influence," Octavio said as he gasped for air.

Janusz let go of his neck. "Influence over what?"

"Influence over your Unit. Influence over Unit 81 or High Risk Capital or whatever else you call yourselves. You're not part of the US Government."

"That's true."

"I've bought lots of influence in the federal bureaucracy. Through the politicians, I have clout over every one of the executive enforcement agencies."

"But not Unit 81," Janusz said shaking his head.

"That's quite right. I also conduct lots of business around the world. The US Government agencies stay out of my way. I have zero influence over your organization. My sources told me Tony Volpe was not a man who could be bought. I don't like it when I have no influence."

"So, you decided to kill everyone in the organization, you son of a bitch," Janusz said as his face turned red.

"Vel, what would you have done if you were in my shoes?"

"I'd be grateful to the country that gave me opportunity. You came here with nothing. Now, you're a stinking billionaire. Instead of thanks, you use money to destroy anything that stands in your way."

Octavio had thrown the man off track. "Vel, I don't expect you to understand."

"I do understand. You're a greedy bastard who cares only about himself. Thank you for the enlightening conversation," Janusz said as he walked out.

"What're you going to do? Let's get down to it. No one will believe a word you say."

"I'm going home. Good night, Octavio."

The door slammed shut with a *bang*. A shiver ran down Octavio's spine as his hands and feet jerked uncontrollably. Octavio had looked death in the face and survived. Did this Janusz fellow think it was all over? No matter, he was going to call Janet over at *Impressionable Magazine* and have her spin this story in the proper fashion. Then he would ask his friends in DC Government to arrest Janusz for trespassing. Octavio walked over to the bar to fix himself a drink.

Janusz stepped toward the reception desk. The attractive blonde he had chatted up earlier was still there. He waited for her to hang up.

"You're back," she said with a smile.

"Could you do me a huge favor?" Janusz said.

"Of course."

Janusz placed the room key on her desk. "Could you give this to my friend when he gets here. He goes by the name of Smash."

"Certainly," she said coquettishly.

Janusz had found the cell number for Avery Soholt, aka Smash, among Destruction's notes. He sent the text on his way out of the hotel. "Octavio is in room 627. The keys are with the receptionist."

The cold wind outside was exceptionally delightful. With any luck, it would all be over in a matter of hours.

Octavio sat in front of the TV nursing his third drink. It had taken about an hour, and his nerves were more settled. He was ready to speak with Janet yet was too lazy to dial the number. A little more rest, and he would make the call. He almost dropped his glass after turning on the TV. The news coverage was about Jason Osborne, who Placido had flown out to meet the prior evening. Someone had slit Jason's throat.

The funny thing was that it had happened during the same interval Janusz took credit for killing Placido. The two events were somehow related. Sooner or later, the finger would be pointed at Octavio unless he used his connections to derail the investigation. He couldn't wait to board his Gulfstream at

Dulles Airport.

He placed the drink on a nearby table and pulled out his phone. There was noise by the front door. He wondered if that pest Janusz had returned. He got up to see who it was. Three men stood several feet away in front of him. They wore ill-fitting slacks and button-down shirts that were wrinkled. Something was very odd about these men. Perhaps it was their bleached hair and pierced noses. They looked like mendicants, and they reminded Octavio of Destruction.

"I think you're in the wrong room," Octavio said.

"I've seen your pictures before in *Impressionable Magazine*. I'm certain we're in the right place, Octavio," the one closest to him said.

He appeared to be the leader of this ragtag group. This was the second intrusion of the evening. If Placido was here, he would have dealt with these interlopers with the appropriate enthusiasm. That was the most important task now, finding someone to administer his security. Oh, what was the use? Placido was irreplaceable.

"Let's get down to it. What can I do for you?"

"Why did you betray Destruction to the FBI?"

"What're you talking about?"

"You declared war on our organization, you evil capitalist scum," the bleached blond leader said with steely eyes.

"Sit down and tell me what happened?"

"We've got nothing to talk about. I told Destruction not to trust a capitalist pig. He didn't listen."

"Where is Destruction? Are you with DC Antifa?"

"Don't play stupid. You set him up. You turned him over in return for tax breaks."

"Vel, that's ridiculous. Who told you this?" Octavio said.

If he had to guess, that un-flushed turd Janusz was probably involved. The men gathered around his chair. The hatred was plastered on their faces. Octavio tried to think of a way to appease them. What could he say?

"Listen to me. You've been lied to. I know—"

"You're quite right. We've been lied to by the likes of you."

"No, no. You don't understand. I've got money. I'll give you all the money you need to—"

"Don't just stand there, grab his hands and legs," the group leader said.

They all descended upon Octavio as someone taped his lips shut. Octavio tried to break free. It was impossible. From inside his pants, the group leader pulled out a short wooden baton. He raised his arm above his head and struck Octavio on the right kneecap. Octavio screamed at the top of his lungs, but his voice was muffled by the duct tape.

Within seconds, the man went to work on the left kneecap. Everything turned black as Octavio had the sudden urge to fall asleep. The stinging wetness of the cold water brought him back from unconsciousness. Octavio was on the floor, held down by two mendicants as a third held a knife over his face.

"You set us up, you capitalist pig! With me as leader, DC Antifa will emerge even stronger. You, on the other hand, will be another statistic of rising crime in the city. Say hello to Destruction when you see him," the lowlife said before plunging the kni—

35. ARLINGTON, VIRGINIA

January 24

They sat in his study exchanging war stories. Janusz and Kim were in no mood to celebrate while Tony was still on life support at the hospital. But the worst was over, so Janusz poured some wine and listened to Kim tell the story of what happened the day Lesley and Rage had visited her cabin in Pennsylvania. The pinkish hue had returned to her cheeks. This was not the pallid woman who had appeared in the backseat of his car the day after Rage was killed.

"What was it all about?" she said out of the blue.

"What are you talking about, Kim?"

"You know, Antifa's goons, Octavio, Placido, Lesley. What just happened to us, and where are we headed?"

"I still don't know where we're headed. That all depends on Tony. What happened is we avoided disaster by a fraction of a hair."

"Care to explain?"

"I'm still putting all the pieces together myself, but the files I found in Sean's office were frightening. Antifa is an umbrella organization for various anarchist cells around the country. The particular cell operating in our area, known as DC Antifa, wanted to overthrow our government in order to bring about its version of utopia. They were going to attack the White House using several of their soldiers, dressed as Secret Service Uniformed Division officers, to shoot into the crowd. This was supposed to create a national crisis."

"They had no chance in hell."

"Oh, but they did. They stole a large arsenal of weapons

from Fort Belvoir, which they had loaded into four large vans the night I dropped in for a surprise visit. They had also murdered Secret Service Captain Chambers, from whom they stole the uniforms. They were going to plant the murder weapon, a kitchen knife, on me."

"How do you know?"

"Because I have the knife. I'm going to provide the evidence to the FBI as soon as I get a chance. It'll allow them to tie the recent attacks in the area back to DC Antifa. The media has enjoyed spinning a narrative that racists and fascists were behind these events."

"Why was Octavio writing the checks?"

"Octavio used DC Antifa as his private army. He did not like the fact we operate outside the government, a government over which he exercised considerable control. So, he asked DC Antifa to get rid of us. Destruction, on the other hand, was using the money provided by Octavio to enrich himself and grow his status as a cult leader."

"And the media? Why are they covering for Antifa?"

"Could be a case of ideological sympathy."

"To think a professor was a part of this, it's just—"

"Don't judge her too harshly. As I said earlier, DC Antifa was a cult. Destruction exploited the vulnerabilities of his recruits to get what he wanted out of them, especially the women. He had created a small circle of sex slaves known as *Mulieres in Servitium* or MIS. This group, which means *women in service*, existed to satisfy Destruction's perverted sexual fantasies."

"Why did the women play along?" Kim said.

"Because there were hundreds of compromising pictures of the female members, including Professor Lesley Gantz. I have the photos to prove it. Destruction lured them with promises of a more meaningful life and kept them in line with evidence of debauchery."

"So, now what?"

"Now, we try to gather the troops and rebuild Unit 81. We'll have to see who's left and who wants to come back. We also need a succession strategy if something like this ever happens again."

"Who's going to run the show if Tony doesn't make it?"

"That's one of the things we have to figure out. Hold on," Janusz said as he paused to answer his phone.

It was a restricted number. He usually never answered those, but nothing about the past few months had been normal.

"Hello," Janusz said.

"Janusz Soltani?"

"Who are you?"

"*Khoob ghooshkon,*" the voice said in Farsi, *listen carefully*, "If you ever want to see Jennifer alive again, you've got twenty-four hours to drive to Shenandoah with two million dollars."

Janusz was not sure if it was a joke. He replied in Farsi as Kim observed with intense curiosity, "Very funny, but my wife's at work. How'd you get this number?"

"What's going on?" Kim said.

Janusz held his hand over the phone. "Kim, dial Jennifer's office. Number is on this card," he said in English before resuming his conversation with the Iranian.

"Your wife is with us you son of a whore, and I'm in no mood for jokes. We want our money. Twenty-four hours is all you get. Come alone."

"Shenandoah is a big place. Where am I supposed to go?" Janusz said.

"Come to the entrance on Skyline Drive from Front Royal tomorrow at noon. I'll call this number with further instructions."

"Do you comprehend how much two million dollars is? I don't have that kind of money in my house or in the bank. I need to make arrangements," Janusz said.

Could it be they were serious?

"Janusz, just spoke with the office. Jennifer is not there."

"What? She left for work hours ago," Janusz said in a daze.

"They said she never came to work."

Janusz spoke into the phone with steely determination, "You better pray to Allah nothing happens to her—"

"You're finally taking this seriously. That's a good thing. I'm giving you one week to get the money or she's finished," the man said before hanging up.

"Hey, hang on," Janusz yelled. The line was dead.

"What's going on?" Kim said.

"It's not over."

"What's not over?"

"I think the Iranian MOIS has Jennifer."

"Why?"

"They want their money back. The money I took with their help from Dr. Ahvazi in Moscow."

"Or maybe they want to kill you and are using Jennifer to lure you in."

"Oh, God," Janusz said, choking back tears.

"Calm down. We'll figure this out. Where do you want to start?"

Janusz was silent for several minutes as he weighed his options. Then it hit him.

"Germany, that's where we start."

"I'm confused," Kim replied.

"I'll tell you on the way to the airport."

36. IRAN AIR OFFICE, FRANKFURT, GERMANY

January 25

T he taxi dropped him off in front of the Frankfurt Central Train Station. From Kaiser Street it was mere steps to the Iran Air office. One could not argue with the logic of conducting their operations out of such a strategic location. Every intelligence agency in the world used civilian cover to mask its activities. So did the MOIS. The epicenter of their European operations, under the command of Morteza Karami, was in Germany. Over the years, Janusz had developed extensive contacts with the German Federal Office for the Protection of the Constitution (BfV). According to sources in the BfV the MOIS had numerous offices in the country. Their main recruitment center was the Iran Air Office in Frankfurt. Morteza had been the one that helped Janusz get the two million dollars from the Iranian Research Center for Emerging and Reemerging Infectious Diseases.

On top of that, Morteza had provided the location of General Kalantari in Moscow so Janusz could kill the QF chief. Along the way, Morteza must have had a change of heart. And now, he had crossed the line by kidnapping Jennifer and threatening to kill her. Janusz was prepared to annihilate every single MOIS agent in Germany by himself. The only problem was the Germans would not take too kindly to such actions.

The way to go about this was to cut the head off the snake. Morteza was probably taking these actions on his own behalf. It was unlikely he would have told his superiors in Tehran about the deal he had made with Janusz. Therefore, MOIS headquarters was unlikely to have ordered the kidnapping of Jennifer. Whatever prompted this act of desperation, Morteza and his subordinates must logically be the only ones involved. The BfV source had informed Janusz that Morteza served out of the Iranian Embassy in Berlin, although most MOIS operations were run out of the Iran Air office in Frankfurt.

It was a perfect arrangement as far as Janusz was concerned. He could dig around for information in Frankfurt before he decapitated the snake in Berlin. Janusz wore a heavy disguise to evade the multiple cameras that surveilled the inside of the facility. Security services around the world utilized facial recognition software. The MOIS was no different, and they could possibly match his face against images from a previous assignment in Iran.

Janusz casually walked toward the front door. A rather large Boeing 747 mockup was perched in the display window facing the street. He took a moment to admire it from the outside. It was the perfect gift for a young child who loves planes. Inside, a row of tellers sat behind a wooden partition. On the wall behind the tellers was a gigantic map of the world that displayed the various destinations to which the airline ferried its customers. The hub city was the Iranian capital of Tehran.

"*Salam,* I'd like to purchase a ticket to Tehran, please," *Janusz* said in Farsi to the lady behind the counter. She wore a name tag labeled: Mona.

"Have you flown with us before?" Mona said as Janusz passed her a blue American passport.

"No. I was born in Iran but raised in America. This is my first trip home since I was a child."

Mona had her head down, carefully leafing through the passport. "Mr. Mehrdad Javani?"

"Yes. Please, call me MJ."

"Are you going to visit family?"

"My family are all in America now. I just want to visit the land of my ancestors."

"Did you know you need to obtain a visa if you hold an American passport?" Mona said with suspicious eyes.

"No, I didn't."

"A visa can take a while for those without an Iranian passport. What do you do back home, Mr. Javani?"

"I'm an aerospace engineer at Boeing," Janusz said.

He tried not to notice that Mona's eyes were about to fall out of their sockets.

"Is that a problem?" Janusz said.

"Of course not. We have an excellent relationship with the embassy in Berlin. I'm sure they can expedite your application. Would you excuse me for a second?" Mona said, stepping away from her chair.

She soon disappeared behind the corner. If this gamble failed, it meant imminent death for his poor wife back in Virginia. Fifteen minutes later, Mona reemerged. She stood next to a tall thin man with a stubbly face. The pair walked over as Janusz prepared for the worst.

"MJ, I want to introduce you to our head of acquisitions in Europe, Soleiman."

Janusz stood to shake his hand. "What about my tickets? You also mentioned I need a visa."

"Mona will take care of all that for you. It's an easy fix. I want to show you around our office and tell you a bit about our fleet of planes," Soleiman said.

In anticipation of this moment, Janusz had studied the basics of aerospace engineering and learned all he could about Boeing and Airbus passenger planes. Janusz followed the tall Iranian around the ground floor as Soleiman described the activities of the Iran Air Office in Frankfurt. It was obvious he was being courted.

"If you leave your passport with us, Mona will procure your visa from our embassy in Berlin. I'll also see to it that you get first class tickets from Frankfurt to Tehran, compliments of the Iranian Government. Before you go, I'm wondering if you'd like to join me for dinner tomorrow night?"

"On one condition," Janusz said.

"What is it?"

"My wife is accompanying me on this trip. May I bring her along?"

Soleiman appeared uncomfortable with the proposition. That was the entire point. Devout Muslim men hired by the Iranian security services were usually not comfortable around women. As a beautiful blonde, Kim was sure to serve as a distraction all night.

"I'll ask Mona to prepare her papers as well," Soleiman said.

"That won't be necessary. She's not travelling to Tehran, which is why I want her to accompany me before the trip."

"I'm looking forward to meeting her."

I wonder if he suspects something, Janusz asked himself.

37. CABIN HIDEOUT, SHENANDOAH NATIONAL PARK

January 25

T he deer meandered confidently on the porch in search of food. It climbed the stairs with familiar ease. Stopping to taste the flowers in the planters, the furry animal moved right up to her window to gaze at Jennifer. Did this delightful critter recognize her plight? Did it empathize with her obvious pain? Perhaps it had come to rescue her, but what was the use? It had no arms with which to pry open the window and unbind her hands.

As soon as it was done staring at Jennifer, the deer continued its exploration of the perimeter. It was momentarily occupied by the sight of the porch swing before running off in haste. The opening of a door had startled the helpless creature. Jennifer would have reacted in the same fashion to these men if she had seen them coming. Except in her own case, there had been no warning. As soon as she had settled in her car seat, she sensed the frigid muzzle of the pistol against the back of her neck. The harsh accented voice warned her against turning her head. They then covered her eyes before transferring her to another vehicle. Hours later they arrived at this secluded cabin somewhere deep in the woods of God only knows where. They had taken her Movado and cell phone. She had lost track of time.

Sitting in an intricately carved wooden chair, Jennifer stared out the window with her hands cuffed behind her back. Even if she was able to miraculously unchain herself, she would not get far before her captors hunted her down mercilessly. There were at least three of them, maybe four, as far as she could tell. Jennifer had not seen their faces as they always came from behind before placing a straw sack over her head whenever she needed to use the restroom.

Every few hours she would yell "bathroom," before one of them knocked on the door. Her captor would then open the door and reply with "head down," before immersing her head in darkness. After uncuffing her hands, they waited nervously outside the door, rapping loudly and screaming if she took longer than they thought she should. The food arrangement was no better. She was served two meals a day, one in the morning and one in the evening. It might not have been that bad if they at least untied her hands to eat. Instead, one of the captors would drop some food on the wooden desk inside her room. The food was always served on a paper plate.

She was forced to eat leaning forward, using only her mouth. They wanted to dehumanize her by treating her as if she were a dog. They spoke Farsi among themselves, of that she was certain, having listened to Janusz speak with his father. This sort of brutality was standard practice in Iranian prisons. The fact pattern led to only one conclusion. These Iranians were hunting Janusz and using her as bait.

There was no doubt her husband would leave no stone unturned to rescue her. The only problem was that he had no clue where to search. The more she thought about it, her only chance for survival was to wait for the right moment to escape. But how? There was a wide clearing from the cabin to the tree line leaving her with no cover. A wooden fence surrounded the perimeter. An open shed, stacked full of firewood, was close. She could also see a barn outside her window but its doors appeared to be locked. Jennifer assumed her captors had rifles. Even if she got a head start, they could pick her off with ease unless she was able to sneak out under cover of darkness.

The creaking floors in the hallway caught her attention. The knob turned, and the door was opened. A sudden draft rushed in. The silence was broken by the sound of his breathing. He stood behind her. She dared not turn her head. A sharp pain shot through her skull as her hair was pulled from behind. She would not give him the pleasure of whimpering. Without warning, a hand smacked the back of her head.

"Your husband vill die. Ve don't vant to kill him right away. Ve take turns raping you vile he vatch. Then ve kill you."

Jennifer looked out the window with steely determination. "Is that supposed to scare me? Wow, I'm really terrified dontcha know—"

The slap on her face landed before she could finish her sentence. It was the sensation of a thousand bee stings.

"Who told you to espeek, American whore? I'm in charge here. You talk ven I give you permission to talk."

It was a good sign. Despite his bravado, the man standing behind her had revealed a weakness. He resented American women, and he had some sort of inferiority complex. Now, she knew how to burrow under his skin.

"Do you tink your husband vill come for you or, vill he run to save himself like scared American?"

She remained silent long enough to make it clear she was not intimidated. "You can be sure he'll come no matter vat, I mean, what," Jennifer said with a chuckle.

"You make fun of me?"

"Of course not."

"Good. That's very good."

"There is only one question?" Jennifer said.

"Vat is it?"

"Will you be ready when he comes to kill you?"

The barrel that emerged out of the corner of her eye seemed strangely familiar. He turned the rifle toward her face. She could see a finger over the trigger. The rifle suddenly disappeared from view. Seconds later, a jabbing pain worked its way down her shoulder. She screamed at the top of her lungs. He must have stabbed her, but it could not be. The sound of the impact was indicative of a blunt instrument. Her entire left shoulder was on fire. What had this deranged lunatic done?

"You estupid bitch. You have no manners."

It took a tremendous reserve of will to keep quiet. The pain in her shoulder radiated in all directions. It even reached her head, where it transformed into a massive migraine. It was as if someone beat the back of her skull with a bat. A vise-like force was pushing against her temples from both sides in an effort to crush her cranium in the middle. She would do anything for an extra strength tablet of aspirin.

The room went dark as the straw sack was pulled over her head once more. Her cuffs were untied from the back before the powerful arms pulled her off the chair. She was dragged across the floor and thrown onto a bed. Her hands were cuffed from behind once more. She instinctively crossed her legs while preparing for the worst. Rape was a common torture against female political prisoners in Iran. She was not surprised when her shoes and socks were ripped off.

"I vill do vat your parents did not do. I vill teach you respect."

Her imagination ran wild. Would he chop off her feet? A dreadful noise reverberated through the room. Something cut through the air, something sharp.

There was a slight breeze against her skin, and then, "*Oooooohhhhhhhhaaaaaaaa,*" she screamed.

The bottom of both feet were on fire. She was certain he had cut her with a knife. There it was again. The horrible ripping of the air.

"*Oooooohhhhhhhhaaaaaaaa!*"

The sting was twice as powerful. Try as she might, she could no longer keep herself from crying. Jennifer burst into tears as she waited for the next round. It was a discernable rhythmic pattern. A strike, a brief pause to let her imagination run wild, and then another strike. It was the most horrendous pain she had ever experienced. It was so bad she forgot the headache. Her burning feet was all that mattered. She finally figured it out after the third strike.

Bastinado, or foot whipping, had been practiced everywhere from China to the Middle East, and even Europe, until the twentieth century. It had been universally embraced as an effective torture because the bottom of the feet are sensitive due to the tight clustering of nerve endings. Now, she understood why.

She rolled up into a ball subsequent to what she estimated to be the fifth strike. It was eerily quiet in the room. She had not heard the door close, but she was certain he had left. What would he do when he returned? As she fought off incessant thoughts about her demise, she slowly fell asleep.

When Jennifer came to, she was back on a chair. Her feet had been propped up on a pillow and her hands were cuffed once more. Behind her neck, the frigid tip of the muzzle grazed her skin.

"Thanks to Allah, I'm a nice man."

Not wanting to further antagonize her captor, she kept quiet.

"You talk again, I shoot you in the head."

Jennifer looked down, wondering if Janusz would be able to rescue her before the worst came to pass.

38. KEKIK RESTAURANT, FRANKFURT, GERMANY

January 26

T he neighborhood was dark and eerily quiet, but Janusz was not worried. Historically, the MOIS invited its enemies to Greek restaurants when they wanted to murder them. That Janusz and Kim were meeting Soleiman in a Turkish restaurant was a good sign. They crossed the rail tracks on the narrow road as the sound of their shoes bounced off the adjacent buildings. Janusz wore black Italian loafers while Kim sported a pair of stilettos for the occasion.

Several cars were parked on the sidewalk in front of the brick building where the restaurant was located. Kekik was rumored to be the best Turkish restaurant in Frankfurt. The narrow street created the perfect conditions for a wind tunnel. A biting gust pushed them toward the parked cars as it entered Janusz's bones. He was not the only one affected. Kim picked up her pace to keep from shivering. Janusz stepped forward and opened the front door of Kekik.

Numerous pictures from Turkey hung on the walls. Soleiman was waiting at a table that seated four. He raised his hand as if he were a long-lost relative at the airport. An image of Jennifer held hostage by Soleiman's colleagues was enough to wipe every ounce of empathy from Janusz's heart.

"Soleiman, this is my wife, Emily," Janusz said as he approached.

Soleiman stood to shake Kim's hand. Since shaking hands with a woman was frowned upon by devout Shia men, this was a good sign. It meant Soleiman was practical. With the introductions out of the way, they all sat down and ordered dinner. Janusz and Soleiman spoke in Farsi while Kim observed. Moments later, Janusz and Kim ordered black tea to warm up. It was brought out scalding hot in ornate tiny glasses. Tea was the perfect antidote to the chill that had permeated Janusz's entire body.

Soleiman ordered the Turkish coffee, complemented with the Turkish Delights candy. Soleiman had several more rounds of coffee after the first, apparently immune from the heart pounding effect of caffeine. It was imperative to observe local custom during such delicate meetings. Jumping right into business without engaging in chit-chat was considered rude. Once they were warm on the inside, they ordered dinner.

Janusz waited calmly for Soleiman to make the first move. When they were halfway through their lamb and rice meal, Soleiman made his pitch. It began innocently enough with a conversation about airplanes. It quickly descended into an avalanche of questions to determine Janusz's position with Boeing.

"Are you aware we're hurting for spare parts?" Soleiman said.

"Yes, I know. The American Government has always been unfair towards Iran. I wish there was something I could do to help," Janusz said.

At that moment, Kim tossed her hair. Her luscious scent was distracting even for Janusz. He was certain the Iranian was experiencing a similar predicament. Soleiman had tried hard not to be obvious. But Janusz had caught him sneaking a peek at her every so often from the corner of his eye. How could he not? Even the waiter had lingered a little longer than necessary at their table.

Kim had played every dirty trick in the book so far. From tossing her beautiful golden locks, to lotioning her hands, dabbing perfume on her neck, and applying lipstick to her inviting lips as Janusz talked to Soleiman.

"Perhaps there is," Soleiman said while smiling at Kim more overtly.

"Obviously, you're in no position to help with the sanctions, and you can't help us get an entire plane. There are literally thousands of parts on these complex machines, any one of which could make a huge difference for our aging fleet."

"Spit it out," Janusz said.

"We need an inside man to help us attain parts from Boeing's Spares Distribution Center at the Seattle Tacoma International Airport. Do you have access to this facility?"

"I most certainly do. I work nearby at the Renton Factory on Lake Washington. I go back and forth to the SDC facility constantly. The guards all know me."

"I knew there was a reason you walked into our office. Allah works in mysterious ways."

"It's still going to be difficult for me to clear your purchases."

"I understand. We just need you to sneak out a few key components. We may be able to reverse engineer them ourselves if you can bring us some samples. As a matter of fact, if you have access to the design software for the components, that would be even better."

"That may be difficult," Janusz said.

"We're willing to pay a handsome price. I'm talking about millions of dollars for your assistance."

"I'll have to think about it."

"Of course. I don't expect an answer at the moment. Did I mention your flight to Tehran will be compliments of the Iranian Government, along with anything else you need when you get there?"

"That's very generous. You don't really work for Iran Air, do you?" Janusz said.

Soleiman smiled and looked at Kim once more. When his eyes were satisfied, they turned to Janusz. "I'm with the Ministry of Intelligence. On behalf of the Iranian Government, I want you to know you're in a position to do a great deal of good for your people. As you probably know, our fleet of Boeing planes are old. We constantly have to beg and steal spare parts around the world. If you could give us the software to design the parts for ourselves, you would be helping to save countless lives that are currently at risk of dying in a plane crash."

Bingo! Janusz had his man. He sat back in his chair to pretend it was the most difficult proposition he had ever considered. He huffed and puffed and tapped his fingers on the table before answering. Meanwhile, Soleiman stared at Kim more blatantly now. She knew how to play this game better than anyone. Her coquettish smiles and eye rolls had gotten Soleiman all worked up.

"There is one thing I don't understand," Janusz said.

Soleiman was so absorbed with Kim that he did not turn his head. Janusz cleared his throat to grab his attention.

"I'm sorry, did you say something?"

"I said I find it hard to understand why you're coming to me with this particular problem. I assumed you would have numerous contacts in America who could help with this predicament," Janusz said as he raised his glass to take a sip of tea.

"There was someone. An American billionaire who controlled a variety of companies. He was in the process of transferring the Boeing technology to us."

Janusz paused to take another sip of his tea. He made a loud slurping noise the way Iranians do when they drink their tea. He was certain Kim was annoyed by his efforts to appear authentic.

"As luck would have it, he was killed by bandits in his hotel recently. Washington DC has become a dangerous place these days."

The glass of tea dropped right through his fingers. It shattered into a million pieces on the ground as the hot liquid splashed against his pants. Soleiman immediately turned his head.

"Honey, what happened?" Kim said in English with palpable concern.

"Oh, it's nothing, just a headache," Janusz replied to Kim before turning to speak in Farsi to Soleiman, "I'm sorry about that. A jolt of pain ran through my head."

The manager came forward to express his concern. The mess was cleaned, and a glass of hot tea was sent to replace the one that was annihilated.

"You mean Octavio Souza, the billionaire killed in Trump Hotel three days ago?" Janusz said just to be sure.

"It doesn't matter who, it was just an unexpected surprise for us. We'll find a way around it. We always do," Soleiman said guardedly.

The epiphany opened the floodgates in Janusz's head. How had he missed it before? Octavio had no reason to care about the Unit. The entire explanation Octavio provided at the Trump Hotel was a misdirection. The billionaire was lying to conceal his business ties to Iran.

"I'll be honored to help any way that I can. I'd like to review the items you need if you have a list. I'll know right away which ones I'll be able to procure for you."

"Are you staying somewhere close by?" Soleiman said.

Janusz pulled a napkin from the table and wrote the address of his hotel. "I'm in room 714. Why don't you stop by tomorrow morning? I'll also give you my passport to arrange the visa for the trip. I forgot to leave it with Mona yesterday."

Soleiman stood to shake his hand. "Looking forward to it."

39. HILTON HOTEL, FRANKFURT, GERMANY

January 27

J anusz stood by a window overlooking downtown Frankfurt. Considered the financial capital of continental Europe, Frankfurt was also home to the European Central Bank. Decimated by allied bombing during WWII, the city was rebuilt with glass skyscrapers. The modern buildings transformed the architectural face of this metropolis, named after Frankish tribes, to something that resembled New York more so than Europe.

The Iranian intelligence services took advantage of Frankfurt's location, a hub for business between East and West, to expand their influence in Europe. A knock focused Janusz's attention toward the task at hand. He calmly walked over to open the door. Soleiman stood outside with a wide grin. Janusz welcomed him into the spacious hotel room.

Suddenly, Kim popped out wearing a short black skirt along with a white blouse with several of the top buttons left undone. Her bare feet had been freshly pedicured with a bright vermillion polish.

"*Salam Agha,* Soleiman," Kim said in a lubricious voice, *hello*.

Soleiman dutifully bowed with his hand on his chest and said, "*Rooz khosh,* Emily *Khanoum,*" before straightening to eyeball her, *good day lady* Emily.

Janusz slapped the MOIS officer on his back to hand him a refreshing drink. It was something he knew the Iranian would not refuse.

"What's this?" Soleiman said with a curious expression.

"*Sharbat-e Sekanjabin*. Emily made it just for you," Janusz said, holding the glass of *sweetened vinegar mint syrup*. The drink was an Iranian classic, and it would've been considered rude to decline such an offer, especially one made by a non-Iranian woman. Janusz held a second drink in his other hand with which he proposed a toast.

"*Be Salamati*," Janusz said as both men guzzled the mellifluous concoction, *to health*.

Soleiman handed the empty glass back to Janusz before pulling an envelope from his coat pocket. "This is the list of parts we need from Boeing. Anything you can do is greatly appreciated," Soleiman said, holding the envelope forward. His hand was clearly shaking.

"What's the matter, Soleiman? You're starting to sweat," Janusz said.

"My vision is blurry. I need to sit down."

Soleiman stumbled forward trying to hang onto Janusz. Within seconds, Soleiman collapsed to the floor.

He eyed the colony through the glass. There must have been thousands of them piled on top of one another. They had earned the nickname *fire ants* as a result of their tendency to bite their enemies, everything from small insects all the way up the food chain to large mammals. Janusz had purchased the colony at a specialty farm outside Frankfurt.

The flaxen haired man was from one of the German communities in Brazil. The man traveled deep into the Amazon every year to gather the most bellicose specimens for collectors back in Europe. Wealthy patrons paid a fortune to display them in the tropical forest exhibit of their estate. The difference between these ants and their nearest relatives was that the fire ants injected a toxic venom called *Solenopsin* from their abdomen. The compound was known to cause cardiorespiratory failure in victims.

Ordinarily, the ants were found in earthen mounds where they fed on plants and seeds. Janusz had paid top dollar to have this colony piled on top of one another in a large glass jar. According to the Brazilian vendor, there were approximately one thousand of the deadly insects in the container. The ants did not appear happy.

Janusz placed the jar on the ground to see how Kim was coming along. Deep in the woods of Hainich National Park, they had moved as far as possible from the nearest trail. Soleiman stood before them, tied to a large tree facing forward. His pants had been unzipped, and his genitals were exposed. Soleiman was still unconscious from the effects of the sedative Janusz had included in his drink. Based on estimates of Soleiman's height and weight, Janusz expected the Iranian to wake up at any moment.

Kim slowly opened the oversized jar of local forest honey for which they had paid a handsome price. She dipped a finger inside and brought it up to her lips as she slowly sucked it clean. Janusz tried not to laugh as he knew what was coming next.

Soleiman was now moving his head in a state of hypnagogia. Janusz gave the signal for her to prepare the victim for the grisly offering. She dipped her entire hand in the jar, pulling out a gob of the gooey substance which she proceeded to rub all over Soleiman's balls before moving on to his penis. From the shaft, she gradually went up to the bulbous glans. She proceeded to use her index finger, creating a thick layer of honey at the tip of the penis, which had become quite engorged.

Soleiman awoke with a fully erect penis staring into Kim's dazzling blue eyes. His face lit up with animal lust. He most likely imagined himself to be the hero of an erotic wet dream. Kim smiled at him as she scooped up another handful of honey, which she proceeded to rub on the Iranian's loaded penis.

"That's enough. You should back away before you get a little something extra on your clothes," Janusz said.

His sonorous voice snapped Soleiman out of his fantasy. The Iranian turned his head in all directions. He tried to move. It was no use. He was tied to a tree by a heavy thick rope around his shoulders, waist, and legs. At this point, Soleiman finally looked down toward his waist. Astonished by the sight of his pulsating manhood, Soleiman blushed as the woman stared directly at him. Her laughter snapped him back to reality.

"What have you done to me, you blasphemous heathens?" Soleiman said in Farsi.

"Dear Soleiman, it's rather rude to curse at a beautiful woman who is rubbing your penis with honey!" Janusz said.

"*Madar Jendeh*. What is the meaning of this?" Soleiman shouted at Janusz, *son of a whore*.

"You'd been staring at my wife all of last night and this morning. I thought you would enjoy this," Janusz said.

"Who do you work for?"

Janusz looked at him with amusement. "Israel...Russia... Great Britain...or maybe the USA. What difference does it make to you at the moment?"

"*Aaaaahhhhhh*," Soleiman screamed in anger.

"Okay, have it your way. Let's skip the foreplay and get right down to business."

"These actions are illegal. I'm an Iranian diplomat, and you're in violation of the Geneva Conventions."

Janusz laughed out loud. "In case you haven't noticed, we're not in Geneva. Even if we were, those rules don't apply to agents of terrorist regimes, in my opinion."

Janusz stepped forward and opened the ant-filled jar. He wore a heavy leather glove to protect his hand. As if on command, several of the ants quickly slipped out before he had the chance to close the lid once more.

"What are you going to do with those?" Soleiman said.

His face was ashen, and a faint tremor overcame his arms

and legs. Janusz noticed his penis was no longer erect.

"Ants are very interesting creatures, my dear Soleiman. Did you know there is an American scientist who has dedicated his entire career to the study of ants? His name is Edward Wilson, and what he's discovered about these tiny insects would shock you. I once enjoyed a documentary where a colony of ants devoured a large mammal in ten minutes. They cut its body into pieces, carrying off the arms and legs before tackling the trunk," Janusz said.

On the ground, he counted three fire ants that had escaped from the jar. Kim had laid out a trail of honey that led straight to Soleiman. Janusz stepped on the first two ants and let only one of them continue his march toward the helpless Soleiman.

"This is purely for demonstration purposes. I want you to get an appreciation of what these tiny monsters are capable of. We can talk some more in a minute," Janusz said.

Kim proceeded to roll up the fabric covering Soleiman's left leg all the way up to the knee. She dabbed a small amount of honey on the hairy skin covering his tibia. Soleiman tried in vain to resist, he was tied too tightly to the tree.

"It's coming straight at me. You fucking pimp. Kill it before it gets to me," Soleiman screamed.

"*Shhh*, settle down. This is the best part. You'll be amazed how ferocious these miniature predators are," Janusz said.

The little red legs picked up their pace as the ant closed the distance with its prey. The South American insect proceeded to climb over the loafers as it inched closer to bare skin. Janusz was mere inches away from the action. The ant climbed over the socks and found itself in a thicket of leg hair. Edward Wilson was right. The little devils had remarkable olfactory sensors. The ferocious red insect was obviously hungry. It attacked the honey drenched skin similar to a wild hyena on a gazelle.

"Aaaaaaahhhhhhh, *Ya'Allah*, please, help!" Soleiman begged.

"Keep it down, Soleiman. You're going to ruin the MOIS's

reputation for bravery. More importantly, you're embarrassing yourself in front of this beautiful blonde," Janusz said, pointing at Kim. He used his thumb to crush the red insect against Soleiman's leg, "It's just an ant bite. Now that the fun and games are out of the way, you and I have something to discuss."

Soleiman let out a deep sigh. Sweat ran down his forehead.

"What was the nature of MOIS's relationship with Octavio Souza? Why was Octavio cooperating with you?" Janusz said while shaking the ant-filled jar in front of Soleiman's face.

The Iranian turned his head away before speaking, "Business. It was all business."

"What kind of business?"

"You name it. Octavio's holding company owns Souza Plastics, already the largest pharma conglomerate in the world. Everything from plastics to pharmaceutical products require the crude oil feedstock that we supply. Octavio was making a play to buy his competitors."

"How did you, Morteza, and the European branch get involved in this?"

"Because Octavio was also bidding for BASF. We had a source inside the company that opened the door for the MOIS."

Janusz could not believe his ears. The German giant BASF, headquartered in Ludwigshafen, was the largest petrochemical company on the planet. Octavio would have become the biggest player in both the petrochemical and pharmaceutical markets if not for Janusz.

"You were going to help him undercut his competitors?"

"We had an arrangement. In return for crude oil at half of market price, he would do whatever we asked of him in America. None of the other companies could compete with an organization that gets its feedstock at half price."

"But you would lose billions of dollars in the transactions."

"I'm sure you also know Octavio owned portions of Boeing, Lockheed, Intel, Microsoft. You name it. Our business with Octavio was just the tip of the iceberg. He got rich, and we got access to the latest American technology. It's not a bad deal if you think about it," Soleiman said.

"What about the Unit?"

"What unit?"

"Unit 81. Did you use Octavio to go after Unit 81, a private intelligence firm in America?"

"It was all Morteza, I had nothing to do with that. Morteza had a personal vendetta against an American named Janusz. He took heat for two million dollars that had been stolen from one of our research institutes. He blamed the American and wanted revenge. Tehran had not authorized the operation."

Exactly as Janusz had speculated.

"Why Octavio of all people?"

"Do I have to explain everything to you. The man had connections with American media, politicians, think tanks, you name it. He even owned a top staffer on the Senate Intelligence Committee. We fed Octavio the information, and he executed on the ground. It allowed our hand to remain hidden the way we like it."

"And who gave you the information on the Unit?"

Soleiman turned his face and became silent. "I have nothing else to say to you."

Janusz loosened the lid, bringing the jar close to his still exposed penis.

"Put that away. It was this dirty whore Morteza had been using. She was fucking Morteza, the man who had her husband killed."

"Was she a new recruit?"

"No, she was an established source. Morteza had recruited her years earlier. We used her to keep track of the scientists in our research lab at Akanlu. She was fucking half the men in MOIS."

Janusz lost all empathy for the woman at that moment. He wanted to be sure before taking action. "I need a name," Janusz said, holding the jar to Soleiman's face.

"What do I care, the bitch was never interested in me. Marjan, that's her name. Are you happy now? Untie me so I can get to Frankfurt. I think I'll ask for a transfer back home," Soleiman said.

Marjan was the wife of an Iranian scientist who had risked his life to warn the world about a dangerous biological weapons program in his home country. Following the death of her husband, Dr. Roozbeh Navabi, the Unit had tried to protect her. Marjan had been extracted to America and provided a job with the Unit. She had also been granted access to Unit 81's operations against the Iranian regime under the mistaken belief that she, too, was being hunted.

It was sobering to hear that Marjan had revealed everything she had learned under the Unit's protection to her handlers in the MOIS. The mistake had cost lives. It was a betrayal of the worst kind.

"What about the woman prisoner? Where are you keeping her?"

"What woman prisoner?"

"The one you have locked up in Virginia."

"I told you, I don't care about that. She's a part of Morteza's personal agenda."

"Then you should promptly tell me where she is."

"In a town called Luray, near Shenandoah National Park," Soleiman said, giving Janusz the exact geo-coordinates for the location.

"How big is the team holding her?"

"Four men."

"When are they going to shoot her?"

"As soon as they get their money and kill her husband. Or they get the green light from Morteza, whichever comes first."

"How does that work?"

"Morteza calls them every twelve hours with updates. Morning call is at six local, and same goes for the evening call. If they don't hear from him exactly at the appointed hour, they'll kill her and abort the mission."

"Before I let you go, I need access to the agent identification file?"

"What file?"

"The file that has the code names of your agents, their real names, addresses, and payment records."

"Are you crazy? I'm not giving that to you. Octavio is dead, and Morteza is responsible because he acted on his own behalf. You want to use that information against Morteza, be my guest. But I'm not giving you anything more. Now, untie me at once."

"Too bad," Janusz said before turning to Kim in English, "we need more honey, if you don't mind."

Kim nodded in acknowledgement. She grabbed Soleiman's penis once more, gently rubbing his flesh between her palms.

"You American dogs. You'll pay for this."

"I've heard it all before, Soleiman. Save your indignation for the ants," Janusz said.

Once his penis was fully engorged, Kim dipped her silky-smooth hands in the honey jar. She scooped out several tablespoons worth of honey before hovering her hands over Soleiman's exposed erection. Kim gently tipped her right palm, aiming the honey toward the shaft of Soleiman's member. The Iranian suddenly shifted his waist a second before impact. The stream of honey hit his pants, and then his shoes.

"Ooops, see what you made me do?" Kim said in English.

After scooping out another handful, Kim grabbed Soleiman's erection and rubbed the honey all over it. He no longer protested. Soleiman waited for Kim to finish before spitting in her face. Startled, Kim dropped the jar of honey on the floor and used her clean hand to wipe her face.

"We're through playing games, Soleiman," Janusz said, twisting the lid off his jar of pain. He thrust a long metal tongue inside. The red fire ants grabbed on to this ticket to freedom with great joy. Janusz placed the jar on the floor so he could close the lid. He then held the ant covered metal rod over Soleiman's honey-covered erection. There must have been at least twenty of them, none too eager to jump off. Janusz used a pen in his pocket to flick them off one by one onto the hapless

Iranian. Soleiman squirmed as he frantically tried to break free.

"Hold still. You're making them nervous. You're about to be the first man in history to get a blowjob from angry fire ants," Janusz said with a straight face.

Soleiman continued to thrash about against the rope. It was no use, Janusz had gone to great lengths to make sure he could not get away. Janusz counted off. There were exactly five ants on Soleiman's honey covered flesh. The rest he threw on the ground. Several of them scattered in different directions. A couple followed the trail of honey to Soleiman's shoe and up his leg.

The ants on the penis experienced difficulty getting a grip at first. They were mired in honey and appeared doomed. Janusz had just about given up when Soleiman screamed at the top of his lungs. Two of the ants had grabbed onto flesh and were digging in to keep from slipping.

"Aaaaahhhhhh, get them off. Please, get them off."

"Agent files? Where are they?"

"I'm not telling you."

"That's a shame."

The ants on Soleiman dug into their positions. They were furiously biting skin as they eagerly ate the honey. For some strange reason, Soleiman remained erect as the tiny devils moved back and forth around his shaft. Janusz could see their pulsating abdomen as they injected their victim with deadly venom. Two of the ants that had worked their way up Soleiman's pants were approaching their objective. Soleiman's zipper had been left open to let his testicles hang out. The ants landed on the honey drenched ball sac. It did not take them long to latch onto an area of exposed skin.

"*Whoooooooaaaaaaaaaaaa,*   I...can't   take...the...pain. There's...a...safe house in Frankfurt, I'll give...you the... address," Soleiman said in between his screams, "the files are on a disk in the safe."

"I'm going to need the combination to the safe."

"You...you...got it," Soleiman said as he yelled out the alpha numeric sequence to the inner sanctum of the MOIS's clandestine operation in Europe.

"Janusz, he's shaking. He can't breathe. I should get the ants off," Kim said.

"Not yet," Janusz said reluctantly as he remembered his imprisoned wife back in Virginia.

"I need the number for Morteza's personal cell phone," Janusz said as he slapped the convulsing man to focus his attention.

"Can you hear me? Morteza's cell—"

"Yes, you son of a whore, the number is—" Soleiman said.

Janusz entered the number into his own phone.

"Okay, untie him," Janusz said.

Kim moved quickly. She picked each fire ant off with her fingers, making sure to crush them in her palm before grabbing the next one. While she was busy with the ants, Janusz used a knife to cut the rope. He moved systematically from top to bottom moving as fast as he could to free the Iranian. Soleiman had stopped screaming now and was barely breathing. Kim guided him down to the floor where he lay unconscious.

"Janusz, he has red bumps on his penis from the bites."

"That's probably because he was allergic to the venom."

"I think he stopped breathing."

"Let me see," Janusz said.

He checked for a pulse, but there was none. Janusz performed CPR to no avail.

"What happened?"

"Anaphylactic shock. There's nothing we can do."

"Can we get him to a hospital?"

"Even if we could do that without implicating ourselves, it would still be too late. Just remember, they tried to kill you, and they'll do the same to Jennifer if we don't stop them. We need to leave this place," Janusz said as he motioned for Kim to join him.

40. OST PARK, FRANKFURT, GERMANY

January 28

T he wind slapped his face. He popped the collar of his coat before pulling the newsboy cap tighter over his head as he walked toward the rendezvous point. Morteza wanted more than anything to lay on a bed and take a nap. But that would be impossible.

He had driven his team overnight to arrive by early morning in Frankfurt. Morteza had to see for himself, not believing someone would dare steal the agent identification file disc from their safehouse. When they arrived at the apartment, the safe was still open. There was a note inside, signed by *director of X Committee*. The same man had called his cell phone the prior evening to inform him of the intrusion.

Until now, the X Committee had been a farce, a made-up label used to smear opponents of the Iranian regime. The MOIS had never given the group a second thought. But now, he had to reconsider. Perhaps the X Committee had been a real thing all along. Rumor had it that the X Committee was made up of disgruntled reformists inside the regime that wanted to sabotage Ayatollah Mashhadi's agenda.

Supposedly, members of the committee had burrowed deep inside the MOIS. If this group was real, how many individuals were members? What did they want? Most vexing of all, where the hell was that imbecile Soleiman? It was quite unusual for the head of the Frankfurt station to disappear at exactly the same moment the X Committee had entered the picture. Perhaps Soleiman *was* the director of the X Committee. If that was the case, every single MOIS operation in Europe was now in jeopardy. The timing of this fiasco could not be any worse. Morteza was about to exact revenge on the American cretin, Janusz.

Several kids swayed on the swings as their parents observed nearby. Were these their parents? Who the hell knew in this corrupt country. The Germans, just like their American allies, were a culture mired in degeneracy. Co-habitation, bastard children, homosexuality, trans-gender sex changes, legalized drugs, prostitution, pornography, bestiality, along with an assortment of other vices were now the norm in Germany. The *fesad*, or *corruption*, had penetrated every stratum of Western society. This was the Achilles Heel of the enemy. Generations of Germans, and other Westerners, with no morality, no meaning in their lives. Instead of wasting resources on monitoring the opposition, his government needed a two-pronged approach.

On the one hand, they needed to open up their borders with Afghanistan to let the opium and heroin bound for Europe pass through. The greater the number of addicts, the fewer opportunities Western governments would have to meddle in Iranian affairs. More to the point, the Iranian regime needed to convert as many Europeans as possible to Shia Islam. So many of these lost souls were in search of meaning. How sad that the buffoons who ran the government in Tehran were too busy fighting proxy wars to notice. Victory for Shia Iran would come through the heart of Europe, not the deserts of the Middle East.

Morteza was unable to concentrate. He was more worried about his unfinished business in America. Morteza was using a hostage to lure Janusz. He had gone to great lengths to track down Janusz's wife. There was no way Morteza was going to let the blasphemous American get away with what he had done. He still could not believe it had happened.

In the middle of his power struggle against the QF, Janusz had convinced Morteza it was a good idea to get rid of General Kalantari, the QF chief. They might have gotten away with it if not for the two million dollars. The money belonged to the QF. They had loaned it to the Iranian Research Center for Emerging and Reemerging Infectious Diseases for purposes of completing the Marburg program. Operation Devil's Vengeance having turned into a complete failure, the QF wanted its money back.

Call records showed that Morteza was the last person Dr. Ahvazi had talked to before withdrawing the money and taking it with him to Moscow. From there, Dr. Ahvazi and the money had both disappeared. The morons who ran the QF did not care who was responsible. They just wanted their money back, and Morteza was the man they blamed. Before he could deal with Janusz, Morteza had to contain the problem created by the X Committee. Fortunately, the X Committee director had agreed to wear a hat for this meeting.

The team leader peered inside the scope in search of his target. Kids played on the swings through the crosshairs. His magazine contained exactly five rounds, but he only needed one of them. Pulling back on the bolt, he loaded a .308 Winchester round into the chamber. The expert sniper was hidden behind a tree over four hundred meters from the play area. The conditions were made worse by the wind. He was using a thick branch to stabilize his rifle instead of the bipod.

As a sniper, you never get to choose your environment. You have to make the best of things no matter where you are. That's what separates a true marksman from the impersonators. The orders had been clear. Shoot the man with the cap as soon as you have an open shot. The only thing that was not clear was whether the target would wear what he was supposed to.

The DSR-1 bolt action sniper rifle was truly a thing of beauty. It was produced right here in Germany for situations just like this one. What worried the team leader was the power of his ammunition along with his own deadly accuracy. If for some reason he shot at the wrong target there would be no second chance. The unlucky victim would not even make it to the hospital.

Sure, they would eventually get the man they were looking for. But what about the victim who had been killed by mistake? The media would portray his colleagues and himself as the bad guys. They always did. Careers were on the line. The team leader could not afford to worry about that now. His aim was only as good as his ability to focus. No matter what happened, he would have to live with his own conscience. Especially if his bullet struck one of those children.

The frigid wind numbed his nose. Thoughts of everything that could go wrong bombarded his imagination. What if someone found him and his teammates hiding in the trees? What if an off-duty policeman decided to intervene? What if a bird landed on his head at the last second, causing him to miss the target? The possibilities for failure were endless.

He gently moved his index finger toward the trigger guard. The finger was itching to wrap itself around the trigger. He had practiced this scenario repeatedly at the academy. But nothing could prepare a marksman for his first real world test. His cheeks grew colder with every passing second. His pharynx struggled to push the saliva down toward his esophagus. Finally, a voice crackled in his ear. One of the spotters had identified the target.

He pulled a stick of gum from his jacket, removing the aluminum wrapper. The movement of his jaws against the gum helped to calm his nerves. He placed a finger on the earpiece. The target was moving toward the play area. Peering through the scope, he got his first glimpse of good fortune. The target was wearing the cap like he was supposed to.

An alarm went off in his head as soon as he spotted it.

At first, he thought it was his imagination, but there was no mistaking it. From in between the swinging children, he spotted the hat strolling through the playground. He had specifically instructed the X Committee director to find a seat in a secluded area away from the crowds. Was this an intentional act or an oversight?

Morteza warned his team to be vigilant. The fallout from an accidental shooting was more than he could handle at the moment. He carefully studied the figure as it moved in between the children. Morteza's men were dispersed throughout the park. They could use several angles from which to eliminate the X Committee director, but he was not willing to convey the orders without making certain that this cretin was carrying the code book with him.

If they killed this man prematurely, they would never know. Morteza walked faster for a better view. He pulled a miniature set of binoculars out of his coat pocket. He looked briefly through the lens, being careful not to gawk too long. It was generally not a good idea for a solitary grown man to observe small children with binoculars in a park. Morteza had learned this lesson during the surveillance course at Imam Bagher University. Such behavior was sure to arouse suspicion that the man was a child molester waiting for the right moment to snatch his victim.

An odd sensation washed over him as the hairs on the back of his neck stood straight. Butterflies churned in his stomach as his palms grew moist. The eeriness infected every cell in his body. Someone was eyeballing Morteza besides his own team. Perhaps it was just paranoia. He stopped in his tracks and turned in all directions. The enemy could be behind every tree.

Morteza checked in with his men. They had not spotted anything out of the ordinary, but he did not believe them. The self-proclaimed X Committee director was now seated on a swing several meters from a group of children. The collar of his coat was popped up while his hat was pulled down to mask his face. A swing next to the imbecile was empty. If Morteza was going to approach, it would have to be now or never.

Morteza carried a hand-sized pistol inside his coat, but that would not do. His left pants pocket contained a switchblade, but that too was out of the question at the moment. In his right pocket was an ordinary looking pen. He could reasonably pull it out to take notes. The tip of this particular pen was a small needle laced with a poison. All Morteza had to do was scratch the X Committee director with the pen and it would be all over.

When he was five meters away, Morteza's target nodded in acknowledgement. The face was still unrecognizable. Morteza sat down on the empty swing. Something was not right. Morteza could not place his finger on it.

The team leader adjusted the sight on his scope with twelve clicks on the elevation knob and seven clicks on the windage knob. The biggest worry was movement. His target sat still while children swayed around him. The sniper rested his itchy index finger above the trigger guard and waited. Perhaps one of his teammates had a better shot.

With his left eye, the expert marksman checked the time. The local kindergarten would release its students any minute now. That meant more children between his team and the target. If they did not act soon, they would lose this chance. His index finger was twitching. It took all his might to keep it in a safe place.

Out of nowhere, a child ran into his field of view. The smiling blond boy with the tiny legs was eager to get on a swing. The boy stood anxiously on the side waiting for his turn. The only problem was the boy blocked a portion of his target. At that exact moment, two men wearing sanitation uniforms stepped onto the sand. They used long wooden sticks with a sharp bayonet at the end to pick up the trash in the play area. The sanitation men moved among the swings, forcing everyone to pause temporarily.

The target, the nearby children, and several adults on the swings were pushed out of the area. The chief had not spoken a word into his earpiece for an unusually long while. The commotion by the swings had likely confused the other members of the team. The team leader adjusted the sight on his scope once more as the target moved out into the open field. He spoke into the microphone, requesting permission to take the shot. The only response was static.

It happened unexpectedly. The first bit of good news this afternoon came as a pleasant surprise. The wind had died down and the target was approximately three hundred and fifty meters away. Under these conditions, he could make his .308 Winchester round land on a fly with deadly accuracy. He had no idea what his target was supposed to look like, but the cap in his crosshairs matched the description provided by the chief earlier in the day.

The marksman's index finger pushed the selector from safety to fire. For a fleeting moment, he had a vision about his own wife and children. As a matter of fact, his country and all the children in it would not be safe if men like this were not eliminated. That was the reason he had signed up for the service.

His muscles tightened as he spit out the gum. His heart was beating faster, but that was a good thing. He was completely focused on the task at hand. A trickle of sweat ran down the back of his shirt. His index finger wrapped around the trigger. On the periphery of the scope, he saw several others moving toward the target. Who the hell were they?

Another individual stood less than a meter from the target. It was now or never. A voice crackled through the earpiece. The static was so loud he could barely understand the command. What great timing for the communication gear to give out. Unlike his rifle, the radio equipment was not German. He had warned the chief about trying to save money on field equipment. As always, the stubborn man had not listened, but that was irrelevant now. His orders from this morning had been clear.

He pressed his face into the rifle and tightened his grip. He did not remember any other commands emanating from the earpiece. His index finger did the rest. A cloud of red mist was visible through the scope. There had been no recoil. Chunks of meat were strewn all around. The closest bystander was covered in blood but uninjured. His first real world test had been a resounding success. He had eliminated the target with one shot.

41. INTERSTATE 66, GAINESVILLE, VIRGINIA

January 28

Fuck! He banged the dashboard with his fist. The congestion on Virginia's I-66 was as bad as ever. There was no decent music on the radio and, even worse, there was no quicker option to get to his destination. Given everything he had just been through, he was not about to let the traffic defeat him.

Janusz stared out the window at the idiot who was weaving in between lanes as if that would help to move any faster in a parking lot. Janusz waited for news from Germany. As he rested his head, the cell phone finally rang.

"Jesus, Kim, I thought you were finished."

"It's done. Morteza's dead."

"Are you injured?"

"Not physically. I may need plenty of therapy and rest to get over it."

"Get over what?"

"I've got chunks of Morteza's flesh all over my clothes and in my hair. The GSG-9 sniper blew his head right off."

"I'm sorry you had to go through that."

"I'll be all right. You just focus your energy on saving Jennifer. Don't let this be for nothing," Kim said before hanging up.

Janusz breathed out heavily while closing his eyes. From the moment they had called to let him know his wife was a hostage, the odds were stacked against him. This was the first bit of significant good news. After stealing the MOIS's agent identification file disc, which sat next to him in the car, he had requested a meeting with Morteza in a Frankfurt area park as a condition of returning the valuable information. Morteza had asked Janusz to wear a hat to help identify him. That was when Janusz got the idea.

He immediately reciprocated by asking Morteza to wear a newsboy cap to their meeting in the park. Janusz used his contacts in BfV to inform the GSG-9, Germany's elite police anti-terrorism unit, that MOIS was about to assassinate an Iranian dissident in a park. It was nothing new. The MOIS had assassinated three members of the Iranian Kurdish opposition at Mykonos Restaurant in Berlin back in 1992. It had been an embarrassment to the Germans that such barbarity could happen in their national capital. He knew they were determined not to let such things happen again.

As expected, the Germans had sent the GSG-9 to neutralize the MOIS before they could act. The only thing Janusz regretted was using Kim as bait. Since Morteza did not know who he was meeting with, Janusz had asked Kim to wear a heavy coat and a hat, anything but a newsboy. The GSG-9 had been told to ignore all hats in the park except the newsboy cap.

Meanwhile, Janusz had flown back to reach Jennifer in Virginia before Morteza's next phone call. The BfV owned Gulfstream took seven hours to cross the Atlantic. It had taken him another hour to reach the traffic chokehold in Gainesville. He had four hours left before the MOIS would execute his wife. This parking lot was not going to make his job any easier.

Jennifer sat on the corduroy couch in the living room. As usual, her hands were cuffed from behind. Her captors had left a tray of food on the coffee table for her to eat out of. Despite the gnawing emptiness of her stomach, she refused to give into their games.

On a small tray was a plate of mixed rice and vegetables. She thought she detected chunks of chicken strewn into the mix, but she could not be sure. Her only hint that there were bits of poultry, much needed protein, in her trough was the smell. The aroma of the chicken made the churning acid in her stomach even more active.

How the bastards wanted to walk into this room and see her feeding out of the trough. Inevitably, one of the sadistic agents of the Iranian regime would come over after she had finished her meal to wipe her face. How they loved to wear down her resistance with such symbolic acts of degradation. She spent most of her waking hours wondering how she would exact revenge against these depraved monsters. Over the years, she had always wondered how ordinary people were inspired to kill.

Most soldiers throughout history had been drawn from the ranks of society. Many had been schoolteachers, nurses, pharmacists, or farmers. Yet, at some point, something had snapped in all these people allowing them to commit heinous acts of barbarity. Having endured what she assumed to be four days in captivity, mercilessly beaten for no reason, Jennifer understood how some people crossed the line between civility and atrocity.

She spent every waking moment imagining what she would do if she was able to break free from her tormentors. How she would enjoy taking an ordinary knife from the kitchen to stab them in the eye. Jennifer thought about picking up a baseball bat and bashing them in the head until their skulls broke open like piñatas. Best of all, she imagined herself using a pair of scissors to cut their scrotums at the base, instantly transforming them into eunuchs. Sure, it would be bloody and painful, but these men deserved every horrible scenario she could conjure.

A crackling fire burned with intensity in the fireplace. Her captors kept this room warm using chopped wood that had been piled outside by whoever it was renting out this cabin. Above the fireplace, a large flat screen TV was left running for her entertainment. Perhaps they thought they were being kind by letting her view the TV. But she had no interest in either the TV or the food.

By now, she was so angry at Janusz she imagined herself cutting off his balls for getting her into this mess. A door opened in the hallway. One of the captors stepped out and walked toward her. As he stood in front of the fireplace, she finally saw his face. They never liked to show their visage, and she was worried about the change in protocol.

His face exhibited a dark intensity. He sported a thick trimmed beard that complemented his dark eyebrows. His skin was tanned and his eyes full of hate. He was of average height, with broad shoulders and a powerful build.

It was difficult to observe him for too long, but not because he was ugly. The man harbored such deep animus in his eyes, she had not seen anything like it before. It sent shivers through her body.

"You didn't eat," he said with a growl. It was the same man who had beaten her. She recognized that voice anywhere.

"I'm not hungry."

It was obvious he did not appreciate her answer. He peered out the window before walking back to one of the bedrooms. On the other side of the closed door, two men argued in Farsi. Several minutes later, her tormentor returned more flustered than before. Whoever this man was, he was definitely not in charge.

"You think this is joke? You must eat!" he said.

The man slammed his fist on the coffee table in front of her. As he stood over her, she noticed a bulge under his shirt pocket. She was certain the outline was that of a key.

"If you want me to eat, then untie my hands. I refuse to eat like an animal."

"You eat how I tell you to eat. If you don't listen, I beat you again."

She was ready to seal the deal, *"kos-e nanat,"* Jennifer repeated a curse she had learned from Janusz, *your mother's pussy*. It was the worst thing you could say to a man in Iranian culture. Her captor stepped forward with determination. She did not see it coming.

The sonorous slap bounced around the room. The iron flavor of hemoglobin washed over her taste buds. She threw her head down for several seconds and gathered the blood-stained saliva for her next act. She immediately looked up, spitting everything right into his shirt and pants. He was obviously not expecting her boldness. He bent over to grab the plate of food.

"Eat!" he said as he shoved her face forward.

She held her jaws shut, refusing to surrender.

"Okay, I teach you," he said before walking into the kitchen.

It was the opening she had been waiting for. She used her right foot to bring the tray over the edge of the table. Her tormentor loudly dug around the utensils in the kitchen. She extended her foot under the tray. He urgently returned holding a large metal spoon in his hand.

"Now, you eat," he said with a sinister laugh.

She waited for him to get closer. When he was two feet away, she snapped her leg. Her right foot sent the tray, along with the plate, flying into the air. Chunks of rice, vegetables, and possibly chicken were embedded into the corduroy couch as well as on her pants. The rest of the food was on the floor and on her captor's shoes. He just stood there, as helpless as a deer about to get run over by a car. He dropped the spoon before cursing in Farsi. She tried hard not to laugh as the bearded Iranian bent over to pick up the food. He got down on his hands and knees as he scraped bits of rice off the wooden floor. She prayed her gambit would pay off.

Seconds later, it happened. She held her breath, hoping he had not noticed. The key finally fell out of his shirt pocket right next to her leg. The Iranian kept picking up the sticky pieces of rice. No matter what happened now, she was entitled to this victory. As soon as he pushed off against the floor to stand, she placed her left foot over the key. Her heart fluttered with joy.

"I'm not finished with you," he said as he walked over to the kitchen with hands full of food.

She nodded compliantly as he walked off. Jennifer dropped to the floor to pick up the key with her cuffed hands before he returned.

◆ ◆ ◆

The dry underbrush crackled under his boots as he quickened his ascent. The car was parked several miles downhill by the side of the road. Carrying a bag full of specialty gear on a frigid afternoon following a seven-hour transatlantic flight was more challenging than Janusz had imagined. He thought about Jennifer for inspiration.

Due to the heavy ice and traffic, the ninety-mile drive from the airport had taken longer than expected. He was forced to march faster through the woods to make it. Once the sun went down, he navigated the forest using night vision goggles.

Where the hell is this place? Janusz checked the geo-coordinates once more. According to the GPS he was close. He gazed at the timepiece. Jennifer only had twenty-five minutes. Janusz removed the goggles in a panic. Something crashed onto the forest floor from behind. He made a swift turn with the sidearm in his hand. *Thud...thud.* There it was again. The next round hit him squarely on the shoulder. They were just icicles falling off the trees. As he cleared the ice off his clothes, a light caught his eye. A cabin was on the other side of the tree line. *Bingo, there it is.*

Janusz moved into position to observe the compound using night vision binoculars. The perimeter was surrounded by a wooden fence. Within the fence was a wide snow covered clearing which surrounded the cabin on three sides. The fourth side was heavily wooded. There were two structures on the compound in addition to the main cabin. One was a shed filled with firewood. The second was a barn with all its doors and windows shut.

Janusz removed the TruPulse laser range finder from his bag. The devise was perfect for taking measurements in wooded areas. The shed was barely fifty feet from the cabin while the barn was closer to a hundred feet. Beyond the clearing, the compound was surrounded by a dense patch of trees, which could mask his movements. He tried to picture the best approach. Suddenly, he couldn't take his eyes off his wrist. Fifteen minutes until six. Janusz wished that he had been the one who pulled the trigger on Morteza instead of the GSG-9 sniper.

From deep inside the darkness, he observed a faint glow. Janusz brought the night vision binoculars to his face. A man stood about ten feet away from the cabin, smoking next to a tree. As best as he could determine, the cigarette had just been lit. That gave him at least five minutes to separate this wayward fawn from the rest of the herd. He had a sniper rifle with a night vision scope in his bag, but that would not do. Even with the suppressor, these woods were too quiet and too dense. Any noise out of the ordinary would lead to Jennifer's prompt execution.

He packed all his gear in preparation for the approach. Janusz darted in between the trees as stealthily as possible. Similar to a pilot moving toward an airport gate at night, he was guided by the faint glow. The forest floor was littered with obstructions. The best part was the hidden pothole under a pile of leaves. Janusz almost twisted his ankle. He slowed down the closer he got, not wanting to make any noise. The cigarette smoker would be done any second now. He was so close he could smell the smoke.

Janusz tightened the goggles around his face. His target was tall but thin. There was no rifle or pistol visible on his body or anywhere nearby. No more than two trees and seven feet separated the two men.

Kkkhhhhhhhh, the sound of static roared through the target's hand set.

"*Kojaee?*" someone asked through the walkie talkie, *where are you.*

"I'm smoking," Janusz's target replied.

"Get back in here. I want you to answer when the boss calls."

"On my way," the target said as he snuffed out the cigarette under his foot.

Janusz wrapped an arm around his face and pulled him straight back into the tree. His skull impacted so hard it bounced off like a basketball. From the other side, Janusz plunged the combat knife straight into the motherfucker's larynx. The Iranian immediately shivered like an epileptic in the midst of seizure.

Janusz pressed harder against his neck pushing him down toward the ground. He twisted the blade to cut off any remnants of life. The warm liquid had drenched the dead man's clothes as it soaked into Janusz's sleeves. He latched the walkie-talkie on to his own belt after turning it off. He pulled the dead body away from the tree, depositing it next to the house. *What now...what now? Think...think.* On the side of the house, away from the porch, a rectangular metal box was the answer to his prayer. He opened the lid. It was the outdoor breaker.

The sounds of arguing continued outside her room. They had never screamed at each other in this way. Jennifer was angry with herself for giving in to her stomach. She had become so hungry that when her captor had thrown her in the bedroom with another plate of food, she could no longer resist. She threw her whole face in the food with reckless abandon. Like a greedy little pig, she cleaned the entire plate using only her maw.

When her tormentor entered the room, he let out a hearty laugh before cleaning her face with a wet towel. He then placed her on the floor, hands cuffed behind her back as usual. But now, she had a key in between her fingers. What if this wasn't the right key? What if the gorilla who had lost it recognized his mistake? He would eventually come back for Jennifer. She would surely receive a beating. Perhaps that's what they were screaming about outside her room, the key. Jennifer wanted to cry, but that would not solve her problem. She would soon be dead if she didn't think of a way out of this mess.

Jennifer shut her eyes for a brief second. When she opened them again, her room was completely dark. There was silence in the hallway. At first, she assumed the bulb in the old lamp on top of the desk had died. Underneath the doorway, there was no light outside her room either. *It has to be him.* She was so excited, she almost dropped the key in the blackness. She fumbled with her hands to get them into the perfect angle.

Jennifer closed her eyes again, picturing the key entering the hole. She used her thumb and index finger to explore the edge of the cuffs. It did not take long for her to find the opening. The wooden floor outside her room let out a soft *creak*. Someone walked towards the front door. She shoved the key forward, taking care to remain steady. On the second try, she knew it was a perfect fit. She turned the lock as quickly as possible. Someone pulled on the door knob to her room. There was a jiggling of keys outside. Jennifer pulled her left hand free, then immediately her right. She crawled on all fours as fast as she could.

She pressed herself against the wall right next to the door seconds before it flew open. It was eerily silent as no one stepped inside. Someone was breathing outside her door. She did her best not to move a muscle. He could probably reach around to grab her. Except he had no idea where she was.

A beam from a flashlight lit up the far end of the room. The man stepped forward. The elevation of the beam was a good approximation for the location of his groin. As soon as he entered the doorway, her leg flew up. The man let out a heavy gasp, dropping the flashlight. She jumped on his back, wrapping her right arm around his neck while shoving the middle finger of her left hand into his eye.

"*Aaaaaaakkkkkkhhhhhhh, khahar Kos-e,*" he yelled, *Your sister's pussy.*

He carried her across the room, gyrating like a bucking bronco at a rodeo. The inside of the room was now visible from the glow of the flashlight on the floor. He turned to slam her against the desk. The desk lamp crashed to the floor as a sharp pain ran up her leg. She hung on for dear life. He lurched forward once more before slamming her even harder against the nearest wall. The jolt rocked her head as nausea radiated out of her stomach.

Her head was so light she could no longer hold on. He turned to throw her on the bed. She tried to hang on to something, anything. Her left arm finally lost its grip, but not before her right pulled something out from the back of his pants.

He shuffled his feet quietly, stopping before the first set of windows. Janusz tightened his grip on the SIG MPX with an attached suppressor. Ever so cautiously, he extended his neck toward the glass to peer inside. Through the green light of his goggles, the silhouette of a man walked slowly toward the front door. If he shot at this target, there were two more in the house. One of them could be standing over Jennifer with a gun pointed at her head.

He placed a hand over the combat knife attached to his hip. If he waited just a bit longer, the silhouette might come outside. At that point, Janusz could give him the same treatment he provided to his buddy with the cigarette. The sharp sounds of a commotion emanated from inside the house. The silhouette froze in his tracks. *Pow...pow.* Two distinct gun shots went off. *Oh, fuck...Jennifer.*

Janusz snapped. He aimed squarely at the silhouette... *Pow...pow...pow.* He pulled the trigger in quick succession. The figure inside dropped instantly. *At least two more if Jennifer is still alive—*

Janusz shuffled rapidly toward the front door and shot one round into the knob. The door flew open with one swift kick as he ran toward the figure he had just shot. He checked for a pulse. There was none. Janusz grabbed the dead man's rifle, placing it on a nearby dining table after removing the magazine. Something was not right. A strange silence saturated the house.

There had to be at least two more people in here. With the SIG MPX ready to fire, he crossed the living room. His left leg caught against something, launching him forward. He bumped into a couch before regaining his balance. Resuming his previous stance, Janusz pressed ahead. It was never a comforting thought to move inside a house where the enemy was lying in wait. He placed one foot in front of the other. Ready...come what may!

At the end of the hall, the door to the bathroom had been left open. To his left was another room where the door was ajar. He had to enter. Janusz pushed forward, placing his left hand against the wood while holding the weapon with his right. With a slight shove the door was wide open. *One...two... three...* Janusz jumped through the doorway covering every corner.

A still body lay in a pool of dark liquid. It was definitely not Jennifer unless she had grown a beard since he saw her last. The room appeared empty otherwise. *This has to be her handiwork.*

"Pssst, Jennifer," he whispered ever so softly.

A small head popped up from the other side of the bed. "Janusz?"

A soothing wave of relief passed through his body. She was

alive. He ran around the bed toward her. She held a pistol.

"Put that thing down, for Christ's sake," he said before bending over.

Janusz lowered his SIG MPX before grabbing his wife and pressing his lips against hers.

"I think there may be a few more of them," Jennifer said.

"Just one."

Claaaaaannnnng! Something smashed violently through glass from one of the other rooms.

"That must be him," Janusz said.

"How do you know?"

"Because I killed the others. Now, I'll finish this. Stay here," Janusz said before running out the door.

Once outside the house, he used the thermal scope to search for his target. It didn't take long to find the heat signature of the trail. Janusz followed the trail into the woods. The temperature had dipped dramatically since sundown. The crackling of leaves came from somewhere close. The heated prints of his opponent had vanished. The rustling in the forest was louder now.

Janusz deposited the thermal scope in his coat pocket before lowering the night vision goggles over his eyes. Wherever the sound came from, it was close. In between two trees was a tall pile of leaves. He approached guardedly, with his index finger over the trigger.

Yeeeaouuuuuhhhhh. Something darted out of the leaf pile in front of him. *Pow...pow.* Janusz paused briefly before shooting again. *Pow...pow...pow.* A tail was visible in between the trees.

"Whew, it's just a squirrel," Janusz said.

A crushing pain shot down from the back of his head all the way down to his legs. The SIG MPX flew out of his hands as his knees buckled to the floor. The second impact was more powerful than the first. He fell face forward toward the ground. Still disoriented, Janusz turned onto his back.

Staring up into the forest, a silhouette stood over him, holding some sort of large caliber rifle. He searched frantically for his own sidearm to no avail. His heart pounded through his chest. Janusz was cognizant of his own heavy breaths. The figure above him aimed his weapon. How could this be? There was no point reaching for anything. Janusz said a prayer and closed his eyes. *This is how it ends, all alone in the woods on my back. Pow...pow.* Two shots echoed through the forest. There was no pain. Something crashed to the ground several inches away from him. Janusz opened his eyes and patted his chest. Footsteps over dried leaves grew closer.

"Janusz? Janusz? Are you hurt?"

Jennifer stood over him. Lying face down on the ground was the Iranian.

"I thought I told you to stay put."

"And who would save your sorry ass if I did?"

"How the hell were you able to see in the dark?"

"My tormentors left a night vision goggle on the coat rack by the front door," she said, extending her hand for him to grab.

"For once, I'm glad you didn't listen to me."

"What now?" Jennifer asked.

"We bury the bodies and go home. I think we're finally out of the woods," Janusz said.

42. UNIT 81 HEADQUARTERS, HERNDON, VA

January 31

They sat around the sixth-floor conference table in shock. There were only three of them in the room, and one was not even an employee. Janusz remembered the countless meetings around this very table with his mentor. It was hard to believe Tony was no longer alive.

Following a month in a coma, Tony's heart had just stopped. Janusz was hoping to tell his mentor the Unit had finally prevailed over its enemies. Instead, the hospital staff had delivered the awful news. The Unit's headquarters was almost empty these days, with the exception of the armed security in the lobby. The new badging system prevented unauthorized personnel from entering the building. Unit 81 had to be rebuilt from the ground up, that is *if* their colleagues were willing to return.

The events of the past few months had changed everything. No one had ever expected members of the Unit to be hunted down in their own country. Janusz observed Jennifer and Kim across the table. It was one of those strange moments when one is certain that nothing will ever be the same.

"Such a fucking shame Tony did not live long enough to see this day," Janusz said.

"He knew we'd find a way. He wouldn't want us to sit around feeling sorry for ourselves or for him," Kim replied as her chin quivered ever so slightly.

"So, what now? Where do we go from here?" Jennifer said.

"We need to start calling everyone and find out who is alive and who is dead. Then we find out who wants to come back and who's had enough. I suspect many of our friends may not want to return," Janusz said.

"You'll need new leadership as well," Jennifer said.

"She's right. All the senior leaders, with the exception of Tom Stone, are either dead, or they all quit. We don't even know where Tom is at the moment," Kim replied.

Janusz agreed. The MOIS, Jason, Octavio, and DC Antifa had taken quite a toll on the Unit. They had to build from the ground up, with more resiliency.

"Whatever you decide to do, Janusz, you'll have to do it with me in the picture," Jennifer said.

"I have a radical idea," Kim said.

"Please, enlighten us," Janusz replied.

"Let's start at the top and work our way down. I nominate Jennifer as CEO and director of operations."

"Are you kidding me? She's got no prior experience with the Unit," Janusz shot back.

"So what? She had plenty of experience with the CIA. She also worked with the intelligence community as a Booz Allen consultant. We need new blood around here."

"Absolutely not, she's my wife—"

"What's the matter, you afraid I'll get hurt?" Jennifer asked.

"That's not the point," Janusz said.

"That is the point, you don't want her in harm's way. But without her, you'd be dead," Kim said.

Janusz took a moment to consider the proposition. Kim was right, and Jennifer could bring a fresh perspective to the organization.

"On one condition. No matter what happens, you won't stand in the way of my going out to the field unless I'm ready to call it quits," Janusz said looking at his wife.

"Done!" Jennifer shot back.

"What about the others?" Kim said.

"They're not here, so they don't get a vote," Janusz replied.

"We can pick who gets to do what once we know who else will return," Jennifer said.

"Next order of business," Kim said. "Can someone tell me what the fuck happened? I mean, how on earth did a foreign-born billionaire, Antifa, and the Iranian Government all end up working together?"

There was a momentary silence as they all looked awkwardly at each other.

Janusz was the first to speak, "The answer to your question requires familiarity with psychology and philosophy. Where do you want me to begin?"

"Wherever you like," Kim replied.

"Recall how DC Antifa was first and foremost a cult?" Janusz asked.

"Of course," Kim said.

"Let's start with the widest category, encompassing the largest number of people. Most activists, social justice warriors, and Antifa foot soldiers exhibit the characteristics of cult members. By that, I mean they've been conditioned to view contrary opinions as bigoted or racist. This allows them to dismiss anything they don't agree with using character assassinations instead of rational analysis."

"What about the so-called intellectuals, academics, and journalists?" Kim said.

"They, too, operate inside a cult, except they are at the leadership level. Their function is to provide justification for why things are the way they are. For a variety of reasons, a set of alien ideas captured the American intellectual class in the sixties. These ideas were imported from Europe, and they symbolized a break with the Enlightenment and its emphasis on empiricism and reason.

"I'm talking about the destructive legacy of the Frankfurt School, the most famous being Critical Theory. The Frankfurt School also gave America the likes of Herbert Marcuse, Theodor Adorno, Max Horkheimer, and Erich Fromm. Marcuse wrote, for example, about how the masses don't know anything and why society should be run by intellectuals. The theorists of the Frankfurt School believed the United States was morally corrupt with nothing to offer humanity."

"Ah yes, the archetype of the elitist snob," Jennifer observed.

"Another European school of thought was post-modernism. There were many early theorists, the most prominent being the French Algerian, Jacques Derrida. His claim to fame was *Deconstruction*, or the notion that there is no objective truth. The aim was to destroy the philosophical foundation of modernity by questioning its reliance on objectivity. These concepts slowly seeped into American academia, media, Hollywood, and politics.

"The point being that so called progressive ideas of social justice are un-American. They fall outside the principles upon which this republic was founded, and they seek to rebuild America and the Western world on a foundation of nihilism," Janusz said.

"Sounds like truth itself is the enemy of Frankfurt School Critical Theory and post-modernism. Truth and the ability to think critically," Kim observed.

"Yes, but that's not all," Janusz said.

"I wasn't finished. I was going to add that the only way to destroy truth and critical thinking is by taking away the universal right of humans to use their judgment. That's probably why the purveyors of Critical Theory and post-modernism are so vehemently opposed to making judgment. They immediately label people who judge as racists and bigots in order to create an automatic reluctance to use this essential human faculty."

"Now, you're starting to see the big picture. This is why we're going to have an uphill battle when we rebuild Unit 81. We can no longer count on the same sense of loyalty to the founding principles enshrined in the Constitution from various levels of the US Government. We have to choose our allies carefully, so we don't get betrayed by another Jason Osborne," Janusz said.

"If these ideas are truly un-American, why do they have such wide appeal among our fellow citizens?" Jennifer asked.

"Because nihilist activists aggressively sought positions of influence in academia, media, and Hollywood so they can indoctrinate the masses. Kim asked me about the media last week. Many in the media are themselves activists, or they've been trained to see the world through the post-modernist lens in journalism school.

"Even worse, in order to gain sympathy among the population, the proponents of the Frankfurt School and post-modernism actively infiltrated the civil rights, gay rights, and women's rights movements. They understood that by combining their anti-American ideas with the struggle of minorities for more rights, they could gain wider appeal among ordinary Americans. Better yet, anyone who opposed Critical Theory and post-modernism could now be labeled as a racist, misogynist, homophobe, or a bigot, allowing them to be canceled without debate," Janusz said.

"What aboot the wealthy elites? By that I mean Wall Street financiers, executives of multi-national corporations, you know, people like Octavio Souza. Why are they supporting these ideas that will ultimately hurt them more than anyone else?" Jennifer said.

Janusz took a sip of water before answering, "Samuel Huntington described this phenomenon as the rise of Davos Man. He meant that American businesses and investors have more money invested outside the US than at home. As a result, their interests are now international. In order to increase profits, they must be sensitive to the needs of authorities in China for instance. In our case, Octavio had massive financial incentive to work closely with the Iranian Government. Patriotism and national loyalty are seen as antiquated concepts.

"It stands to reason people such as Octavio would support open borders, unrestrained immigration, and divisive identity politics. Since they don't want to get arrested during a protest, they do the next best thing. They write the checks for academics who espouse those principles while sponsoring foot soldiers in Antifa that intimidate anyone who opposes their beliefs."

"So, it's all aboot greed?" Jennifer wanted to know.

"Greed and self-interest. Remember that most mainstream journalists in America are under the spell of Critical Theory and post-modernism packaged under the umbrella of diversity. What better way to win the sympathy of reporters than to support their causes? Open borders and mass migration dilute the power of wage labor. Defunding the police is meaningless for those living in gated communities with private security. Public schools overcrowded by illegal students don't affect the children of people who send their kids to private schools. Higher tax rates don't threaten people with assets sitting offshore or invested in a foundation or some other non-profit enterprise.

"The bulk of billionaire's income is from dividends, which are taxed at a lower rate than salary. The cost of the policies advocated by the so called woke billionaires fall squarely on the professional class. The wealthiest Americans are mostly hypocrites, just like Octavio," Janusz said.

"There is something I still don't understand. Why do people like Rage, Fiona, and Lesley join Antifa in the first place?" Kim said.

"It goes back to what I said earlier about cults. One of the things that cults do is to exploit human vulnerabilities. The head of DC Antifa, Destruction, was a corrupt sociopath who craved sex and power. He used anarchist ideology to exploit those searching for meaning in their lives. Rage had huge student debts. His parents told me he was worried about finding a job and buying a house when he graduated. Fiona had been taught she was oppressed by the patriarchy.

"As for Lesley, she was an academic who identified with the plight of the oppressed. Feigned virtue is the most popular religion among American academics. Like any good cult, DC

Antifa told these people that they could no longer achieve their goals through the political system. In order to change society, and find meaning in their lives, they were encouraged to take the fight to the *enemy* through Antifa," Janusz said.

"But why didn't anyone stop them?" Kim followed up.

"Stop who?" Janusz said.

"The activist academics. Why didn't anyone stop them before they took over our colleges?"

"Because America is a true democracy. No one was going to purge them from the universities. Besides, nobody grasped that Critical Theory and post-modernism, disguised as liberalism, were a threat to the long-term stability of the United States."

"I don't mean to change topics, but our focus should be on rebuilding this organization to combat external enemies. We don't have the luxury to pontificate on long-term cultural degeneracy and the culture war?" Jennifer said.

"Sorry, Jennifer, I got distracted," Janusz said.

"Before we wrap up, I want Janusz to explain what can be done to combat the trends we just discussed," Kim said.

"I'll make it short. It'll have to start at the universities. Activist professors and departments need to be starved of funding. Trustees have to ensure that activist professors with an agenda are not hired. The university exists to teach critical thinking. That means encouraging debates on the merits of differing ideas and points of view regardless of their origin."

"What aboot the arts?"

"Yes, we need philanthropists to encourage patriotic Americans to enter the entertainment sector in larger numbers. We need writers, directors, producers, composers, and playwrights to extoll the virtues of our Founding Fathers and the Enlightenment ideals for which they stood. If we can make headway in academia and the entertainment industry, I think the rest will fall into place," Janusz said.

Jennifer handed over a stack of papers to shift the conversation, "I've broken the roster of our employees into three groups. Each of us will contact a list of names to encourage their return to the Unit. Kim, I want you to start with the names on this list. Janusz, find Tom and see if he still wants to be a part of this organization. I'll give you the rest of your list when you're done with Tom. If there are no further questions, I move to adjourn this meeting."

Janusz was happy to see his wife embrace her new job with enthusiasm. The Unit needed a passionate leader more than ever. With the so-called social justice warriors permeating every branch of the American Government, Unit 81 would have to work more closely with trusted allies. He needed to meet with the President of the United States, Donald Patrick.

On his way out the building, Janusz made a stop on the first floor to grab his wallet. Inside his office, the wall mounted TV was still playing. Janusz had forgotten how to work the remote. He pressed a button, which only served to turn the channel to cable news. As he fiddled around for the off button, the name Janet Smears struck a nerve. Janusz froze in place with the remote stuck in his hand.

It was the same woman who wrote a piece in *Impressionable Magazine* blaming his chase from Georgetown into Arlington on white supremacy. The more he thought about it, the more familiar her name sounded. Yes, Janet Smears had been mentioned in the files he had extracted from Destruction's hideout in Bakunin Farm. Janusz turned up the volume:

We've just learned that human smugglers on the US side of the San Ysidro crossing took Ms. Smears hostage late last night. The intrepid woman was conducting field research for a series about the benefits of mass migration. According to her colleagues, the smugglers believe Ms. Smears was at the border to expose their activities in the hopes of stemming the tide of illegal crossings.

The smugglers granted the owners of the profitable magazine just ten days to hand over a five-million-dollar ransom. If the money is not delivered, they threatened to decapitate the fearless correspondent. We know from past experience that the outlaws working the border are more than capable of fulfilling such sinister promises. There is widespread speculation that the ransom is just a distraction and that Ms. Smears may have been murdered already. This is the latest example of the sacrifices American journalists make to bring you the truth.

Janusz finally found the off button before tossing the remote on his desk. He grabbed his wallet, then walked out to lock the door. Unfortunately for Janet, poetic justice was often a real bitch.

43. EPILOGUE
Wittenberg Platz, Berlin, Germany

March 19

The yellow train deposited the crowd on the underground platform as if it were a queen bee laying eggs in her nest. The mass of humanity moved in unison up toward Tauentzien Street, the heart of Berlin's shopping district. Her target stirred somewhere in between the pulsating swarm.

Kim wasn't worried. She knew where the target was headed. Kim had placed a transmitter inside the traitor's bag moments earlier. At the top of the stairs, three large sets of engraved doors opened out into Wittenberg Platz. Rays of sunshine penetrated the stairwell, illuminating the myriad heads in the crowd with an angelic aura. As they stepped outside, the blinding light symbolized a rebirth.

It was imperative to cut the umbilical cord with a past that was nearly dead. The commuters scattered through the plaza in every direction. Kim anchored in place, staring dead ahead at the hoisted clock on top of the decorated metal pole. It was exactly twelve noon. She marveled at the punctuality of the U3 U-Bahn trains. It had taken less than half an hour to get here from the gated house on the leafy Peter-Lenne Street behind the Iranian Embassy.

Kim glanced at the screen in the palm of her hand to get an update on the target. The traitorous woman was going to buy some goodies for the upcoming Iranian New Year. It was a bit too generous to dispose of this woman without her awareness she would be killed. Kim walked over the grassy median of the busy, shop-lined street. A long row of Mercedes taxis was parked in front of her. Across the street was the front entrance of Europe's second largest department store. The cars came to an abrupt stop as she crossed.

Kaufhaus des Westens, or KaDeWe, was a shopping behemoth only slightly smaller than Harrod's in London. Inside was a paradise for shopaholics. Kim's favorite section was the food court on the sixth floor. Kim pushed through the crowd in the lobby.

Janusz had offered to take this mission, but Kim had refused. There was something about this miserable turncoat that hit a raw nerve. All around, the elegant German ladies wore the latest fashion. They had much to teach Americans about style. Perhaps it was the way they carried themselves. Poise was the word she was looking for.

The escalator went past the third floor as Kim continued her ascent. The irony of this, perhaps it was the icing on the cake, was that her target had a sweet tooth. Kim didn't really need the tracking device to know where Marjan was headed. Stepping through the crowd, Kim opened her purse to grab the trendy white gloves. Once her hands were covered, Kim promptly removed the bottle of perfume, clutching it in her palm. It seemed as though everyone was in line for some of the best treats in Berlin. So, too, was Marjan.

The Iranian woman was probably going to present these confections to her masters in the embassy. The woman who had sold out the Unit to the MOIS wore tight jeans over trendy black lace shoes. Marjan's tight short sleeve top provided lots of exposed skin for the nerve agent to do its job.

There had been no debate about the best method for success. The North Koreans had proven the efficacy of using nerve agents in this way by successfully assassinating their supreme leader's half-brother. The hapless North Korean victim waited to board a flight in Kuala Lumpur International Airport. His eyes had burned before he vomited red liquid.

The only problem was that VX was too powerful. It had worked too fast, allowing the perpetrators of the attack to be identified. The Unit was using a more sophisticated sample of the V-series of agents.

Kim turned side-to-side as if expecting someone. This particular nerve agent would take at least a day to do the job. The result would be a cerebral hemorrhage that resembled a stroke. Kim casually walked past the customers in line, taking care to avoid eye contact with the crowd. After spotting the shoes, Kim paused to observe. Marjan stared at the delicacies behind the glass. The Iranian woman was completely oblivious to her surroundings. Kim removed the top of the perfume bottle. She pointed the nozzle toward Marjan's bare left arm. Kim pressed down twice, catapulting the deadly droplets into the air. Marjan winced as her arm grew wet.

"Oh, I'm sorry. I was pointing the wrong way. I didn't mean to spray you," Kim said in perfect German.

"*Kein problem*," Marjan replied, smearing the deadly liquid with her palm, *no problem.*

Kim smiled at Marjan before walking away into the crowd. A strange joy filled her heart as she remembered her favorite Berlin eatery was around the corner. She was in the perfect mood for the filet mignon, oozing blood, with red wine.

THE END

GLOSSARY OF TERMS AND NAMES

Antifa: Antifascist Action is a far-left militant movement with origins in Germany. In the United States, Antifa is an umbrella organization for a collection of anarchist groups that emerged in the 1980s under the banner of Anti-Racist Action. Today, these anarchist groups, operating out of different cities, coordinate their activities as part of the Torch Network. Antifa trains its recruits to use violence against opponents.

Bakunin Farm: DC Antifa facility in Beltsville Maryland where Destruction indoctrinated the recruits and taught them how to use guns in preparation for the attack on the White House.

BfV: German domestic intelligence agency, known as the Federal Office for the Protection of the Constitution. The BfV has a function similar to the FBI in the US.

Bill Turner: Head of Operations at Unit 81.

Captain Chambers: Secret Service Uniformed Division officer in charge of physical security for the White House.

Christopher Lasch: An American historian and university professor. Lasch wrote a book titled The Revolt of the Elites where he explained how America's elites have turned their back on their own country.

Critical Theory: Developed by the philosophers of the Frankfurt School to attack reason and rationality as oppressive and racist. Critical Race Theory, Political Correctness, and Wokeness have their origins in Critical Theory.

Davos Man: A term coined by the late Samuel Huntington to refer to global elites whose primary loyalty is to international institutions that help to increase their power and wealth.

Destruction: Leader of DC Antifa. His birth name is Sean Sutherland.

Donald Patrick: Former Chairman of the Senate Select Committee on Intelligence (SSCI) who has been elected President of the United States in The Billionaire's Conspiracy.

Fiona: Georgetown college student who is recruited by DC Antifa for the battle against the US Government.

Freedom Coalition: A network of wealthy donors who coordinate their contributions to approved organizations supporting their agenda. Each member is encouraged to donate ten million dollars a year by Octavio

Souza.

GRU: The acronym for the Russian military intelligence service. The GRU is subordinate to the Russian Ministry of Defense under the General Staff.

GSG-9: An elite German anti-terrorism and hostage rescue unit of the German Federal Police.

Hazard: A member of DC Antifa and Destruction's right-hand man. Hazard's birth name is Neil Bakke.

Herbert Marcuse: One of the most influential members of the Frankfurt School and the father of the New Left. Marcuse helped spread the concepts of cultural Marxism and political correctness in American universities and eventually all of American society.

Intersectionality: A concept derived from Critical Theory. Intersectionality is the idea that there is an intersection of multiple type of oppression for some individuals in American society.

Iran Air: The Iranian national airline.

Islamic Revolutionary Guard Corps (IRGC): A branch of the Iranian military founded after the Iranian Revolution to safeguard the new Islamic regime.

Janet Smears: Reporter with Impressionable Magazine.

Janusz Soltani: Operative working for Unit 81.

Jason Osborne: SSCI senior staffer/intelligence analyst who liaises with Unit 81.

Jennifer Soltani: Janusz Soltani's wife.

John Brown: American abolitionist who was executed in 1859 for his role in the raid on the federal armory in Harper's Ferry, West Virginia. The raid caused seven deaths. Today, armed anarchist groups around the US call themselves John Brown Brigades in his honor.

Justice for All: Octavio Souza's Foundation used to gain favors with the media and liberal elites through donations to causes they endorse.

Kalugin: Russian GRU officer Janusz approaches in order to find out who is hunting members of Unit 81.

Kim: Kimberly Jennings is Janusz Soltani's female partner in Unit 81.

Lesley Gantz: Georgetown Professor who is a member of DC Antifa and head of DC Antifa's inner sanctum for women, MIS.

Marjan: MOIS asset who is secretly providing information about Unit 81 to the Iranians.

MIS: Acronym for Mulieres in Servitium or Women in Service. This group is comprised of the top women in DC Antifa.

MOIS: The Iranian Ministry of Intelligence. The MOIS is a cabinet ministry under the office of the Iranian President. Similar to other governmental institutions in Iran, MOIS is de facto under the control of the Iranian supreme leader.

Morteza Karami: Head of MOIS operations in Europe stationed in Berlin, Germany.

Nihilism: A belief system that denies objective truth and morality while rejecting the notion that life has any meaning.

Noel Ignatiev: A Harvard trained academic, Noel Ignatiev introduced such concepts as "white privilege" and called for the abolition of "whiteness."

Octavio Souza: Brazilian immigrant billionaire who uses his wealth to change American society through various means.

Placido: Octavio's personal assistant and chief of security.

Postmodernism: A school of thought founded by philosophers such as Jacques Derrida and Michel Foucault. Post-modernism is opposed to Enlightenment rationality and the concept of truth. Postmodernists declare that truth is relative.

Rage: Georgetown student recruited by Destruction into DC Antifa. Rage's birth name is Jake Van Dorn. Rage is pessimistic about his future due to the amount of his student loans.

Redneck Revolt: A far-left militia group that supports direct action tactics and the use of firearms to achieve its political goals. Most members are anarchists and anti-capitalists who hold rallies with guns.

Repressive Tolerance: A 1965 essay written by Herbert Marcuse in which Marcuse explains why tolerance against opponents of the political left is unnecessary. This essay is the origin of university speech codes and intolerance among the academic left in America.

Smash: A rebellious member of DC Antifa chosen by Destruction to infiltrate the Secret Service on the night of the attack against the White House.

Soleiman: MOIS officer working under cover of Iran Air in Frankfurt, Germany. Soleiman tries to recruit Janusz to procure Boeing spare parts for Iran.

Souza Enterprises: A private equity firm and holding company controlled by Octavio Souza to run his empire.

Spetsnaz: Acronym for Russian special forces units.

SSCI: Senate Select Committee on Intelligence. The SSCI is responsible for oversight of the US intelligence community for the American people.

Stan Roth: Tony Volpe's deputy at Unit 81.

SVR: Russian external intelligence agency analogous to the American CIA.

The Frankfurt School: A school of thought associated with cultural Marxism. Members of the Frankfurt School took refuge in American universities in the 1930s. From there, they promulgated critiques of western culture and civilization. The Frankfurt School's opposition to the Western Enlightenment, rationality, and the concept of objective truth was expressed through their development of Critical Theory analysis.

Tom Stone: Head of research and intelligence at Unit 81.

Tony Volpe: CEO of HRC and director of Unit 81.

Universal Basic Income: A policy proposal where all citizens in a given country receive a pre-determined amount of financial payment, at regular intervals, regardless of need.

Unit 81/High Risk Capital: Unit 81 is a private intelligence agency set up in 1981 in the aftermath of the US congressional investigations that curtailed the powers of the CIA. High Risk Capital is a private equity firm that serves as the cover for Unit 81. HRC is located in Herndon, VA.

BOOKS IN THIS SERIES

Janusz Soltani Series

The Buraq Project

Operation Devil's Vengeance

The Billionaire's Conspiracy

IF YOU ENJOYED THIS
STORY, PLEASE PROVIDE
A REVIEW ON AMAZON